One Step Behind

One Step Behind

BRIANNA LABUSKES

This book is a work of fiction. Names, characters, places, and incidents are the product of the author's imagination or are used fictitiously. Any resemblance to actual events, locales, or persons, living or dead, is coincidental.

Copyright © 2016 by Brianna Labuskes. All rights reserved, including the right to reproduce, distribute, or transmit in any form or by any means. For information regarding subsidiary rights, please contact the Publisher.

Entangled Publishing, LLC
2614 South Timberline Road
Suite 109
Fort Collins, CO 80525
Visit our website at www.entangledpublishing.com.

Select Historical is an imprint of Entangled Publishing, LLC.

Edited by Candace Havens
Cover design by Erin Dameron-Hill
Cover art by Period Images

ISBN 978-1-68281-301-0

Manufactured in the United States of America

First Edition September 2016

*To my family: Bernie, Deb, Dana, Brant, Raegan and Grace.
For your love and unconditional support.*

Chapter One

London, 1812

Gemma Lancaster held her breath and stood perfectly still as if that would make her invisible. It wasn't a good strategy. She knew this. But the only other option was gathering enough courage to pry one of her eyelids open to see who had come into the room.

It took her a few seconds, but when she did she regretted it immediately. Of all people, it had to be him.

"Bloody Hell," Lucas Stone, Earl of Winchester, muttered into the quiet of the darkened library.

A similar, though slightly more lady-like, sentiment was about to slip from her own lips but it died at the sound of laughter right outside the door. More company. Brilliant. Exactly what she needed.

This time, though, Gemma kept her wits about her and dashed toward the heavy curtains that flanked a large window behind the desk. Her triumph was doused by alarm when she turned to find Lord Winchester a half-step behind her.

"Find your own spot!" she whispered, swatting ineffectively at his shoulders.

"Too late," he said as he pulled the thick velvet curtain around them. Gemma sucked in air as every inch of her body pressed up against his, but she had to admit he was right when the door swung open mere seconds later. At least it wasn't the owner of the room who had discovered her. She was not quite sure that an excuse of getting lost on her way to the ladies' withdrawing room would have sufficed if it had been their host, Lord Howard, who had pulled back the curtain.

She closed her eyes and tried not to think about the strong, muscled legs now imprisoning her own as indecipherable whispers and groans filled the air around them. From the sounds coming from the other side of the curtain, an amorous couple had entered the library for an intimate interlude. Gemma hoped they would not be long, and she tried to shift her body so that less of her was against so much of him.

"If you wish to make this less embarrassing for both of us, you will want to stop squirming," the earl murmured, his warm breath tickling her ear. She immediately froze as warmth rushed to her face.

Gemma cursed the fates that had landed her in her current predicament. Of course it was Lord Winchester who now pressed her back into the wall. Of course it was the devilishly handsome gentleman whom she had not been able to shake for the past two weeks, ever since they'd met at the Dorchester ball. Of course it was the one person of the *ton* who saw past the disguise of dowdy gowns, spectacles, and boring conversation she had cultivated so carefully. To the rest of the glittering butterflies that flitted through society, she was a mousey nobody. But with those piercing eyes, he seemed to see beyond the facade.

She was not sure what had captured his attention. She was not the type to attract suitors under the best of circumstances.

Her unfashionable, unruly red hair alone was enough to deter any eligible gentleman. She had also long ago given up the hope that she was a late bloomer, and she was coming to—not terms with, perhaps, but maybe acceptance of—her boyish figure. She was well aware that she was never going to be the type of woman to turn heads when she walked into a ballroom.

No, she did not know why she had piqued the interest of one of the *ton*'s most eligible gentlemen, but she did know she was growing to resent the very sight of him. When he was watching her, it was difficult to sneak off without notice, which was a crucial element of her plan and instrumental to its success.

She had so carefully planned every detail. When the darkness of grief had threatened like an angry thundercloud, she had researched. When she'd become discouraged by the lack of clues, she'd made lists. When her rational side insisted she was mad for pursuing vengeance, whispering that it could only bring ruin, she'd mapped out the finances she would need to be successful. She had planned every detail. But she hadn't planned on him.

None of that mattered now, though. What mattered was not being discovered in this compromising position, and finding out exactly why he had intruded upon her hiding space.

Why couldn't he be like the other dandies who frequented the balls and society affairs? Why did he have to be a constant distraction from her plan? So much so that she now stood hidden, literally between a wall and a hard place. She now had firsthand knowledge that he did not need the padding the other young bucks used to build up their frame.

He was all muscle, a fact of which she was uncomfortably aware with his arms wrapped like steel bands around her. His black-as-night hair was overgrown, but she could tell it was not for fashion's sake. A lock of it fell over into his sharp green eyes, and she itched to push it back behind his ear. It was not just his looks that drew her, though. It was something more than that. Something she had not quite been able to put her finger on since she'd first seen him that night of Lord Dorchester's ball.

A grunt followed a loud thud, bringing Gemma back to her current predicament. She imagined that the unseen pair had knocked the heavy crystal decanter she'd seen earlier onto the thick Persian rug.

"Is that it?" An outraged female's voice sounded in a sharp staccato against the sudden silence. "Really, Reginald, I could have had a better go at it with my coachman. I cannot believe I wasted my time with this. You are no better than a rutting schoolboy."

"But Sylvie…"

"No." There was a rustle of skirts then the muffled tread of footsteps. "We're through here."

Gemma listened for the man to leave, but he was still uttering oaths about his departed partner.

After what seemed like an eternity, but which was probably only a minute or two, the man collected himself enough to storm out of the library, a rush of noise from the ballroom tumbling into the room before growing dim again.

Gemma waited a beat in the renewed hush and then placed her hands on Lord Winchester and gave him her best shove. He didn't budge, just squinted down at her fingers, which were now resting on his chest, then back at her. Heat radiated into her fingertips, and she struggled not to blush again, having done so more in the past ten minutes than in all her life previously. But since he did seem to be remaining cautious rather than deliberately torturing her, she picked a spot above his shoulder and stared at it as his scent drifted over her.

Sandalwood.

"I believe they are gone for good," he said, finally stepping out from their hiding place. He glanced around, as though confirming his statement, before turning back to her. He clasped his hands behind his back and towered over her. He was trying to intimidate her, she was certain. Well, he clearly did not realize with whom he was dealing.

"Now," he said, the epitome of an arrogant, demanding lord. "Explain yourself."

What? She'd been here first. If anyone had any explaining to do, it was he. After all, he'd disrupted *her* search of the library.

...

"Excuse me?" uttered the little creature in front of Lucas. She was the picture of disgruntlement, her eyes blazing and cheeks flushed. She all but stomped her foot on the ground.

Lucas ignored the question, not quite sure what to make of the evening, only knowing that when he'd opened the door to the library and seen her there, part of him hadn't been surprised. He'd known Gemma Lancaster had secrets.

A sudden thought struck him, however, and for a reason he could not quite name, it did not settle easily in his mind. "Should we be expecting other company?" he asked, watching her face in the semi-darkness. "Were you meeting someone here?"

A tiny gasp escaped her rosy lips. If possible, she looked even more outraged than she had a moment ago. Her reaction answered at least one question: she was not using the library as a quiet place for a lovers' tryst.

He admitted to himself why it mattered when the memory of her small, soft body snug up against him made his tighten. He had fought the overwhelming urge to bury his face in her hair when her subtle scent had perfumed the air around them. It was nothing like those expensive fragrances many of the ladies chose to douse themselves in. She smelled of soap and fresh air. Looking down at her animated face now, he wanted to pull her to him and kiss the vexation from her pursed lips.

Lilting notes from the ballroom permeated through the heavy door, and he remembered why he was in a dark library with Gemma Lancaster.

Not the time for fantasies. No matter how tempting.

"Never mind." He turned abruptly from her. She might be annoyed with his manners, or lack thereof, but she would be a trifle more than that if they were discovered together. And so would he. He would not endure the kind of forced marriage that had destroyed his parents. He went back to scanning Howard's library. It was well used, not one of the more fashionable, decorative libraries favored by the dandies of the *ton*. Dark, leather-bound books filled every space on the mahogany shelves.

He pulled up an image of Lord Howard in his mind and tried to picture him as the blackmailer he sought. It didn't fit. Howard was a stocky, balding man in his early fifties. He mostly concerned himself with his books and his hounds. Lucas couldn't remember a conversation with the man that hadn't revolved around the latest agricultural techniques. Still, appearances could be deceiving, he thought with an amused glance at Gemma. He switched his attention from the books to the paintings. There were three in the limited blank spaces on the walls.

Two strides brought him to the first, an innocuous landscape of Cornwall. He tipped the frame gently. Just a wall, nothing behind it. He repeated the move on the second one. Nothing. That left the hounds behind Howard's desk.

Of course.

He eyed the gold frame as he walked closer. Heavy, but

not impossible. He gripped the edges and lifted it to the ground.

"Ah, lovely," he whispered as he stared at the safe tucked into the wall. He was in luck; he knew the type. The designer was a good friend from Eton and a fellow gentleman in the service of his country. They had practiced many a night on just this type of safe.

"Are you a thief?" Miss Lancaster's crisp voice broke his concentration. He'd forgotten she was there for a moment. He had always been able to focus in even the most distracting circumstances. He turned to look at her. Distracting, indeed.

He found it interesting that her tone had not been accusatory, merely curious. She did not even appear overanxious as she observed him. There were plenty of ladies of his acquaintance who would be clutching for their smelling salts after the events of the evening thus far.

"What would you do if I answered in the affirmative?" He was partly deflecting and partly curious. If she had known him well, he would be insulted at her question, but considering he was about to break into the library safe of a lord of the realm, he didn't have much ground to stand on. However, she was unmarried and skulking about in a darkened room with a gentleman. She didn't have the higher ground, either.

"Well…" She bit her lip. Squaring her shoulders, she said, "Could you look for an item for me? I don't want to steal it…I just need to know."

"Ah," he said, a few missing pieces clicking into place. Maybe that's why she was always slipping out of ballrooms and musicales. He had noticed but had not wanted to dwell on the reason for it. "You are expecting to find a particular item, then?"

"Perhaps. It's a pocket watch. Gold, inscribed. Are you able to get into the safe?" She slipped closer to him, peering over his shoulder at the formidable door.

He threw her a curt nod. "How were you planning on perusing the contents if I had not come along and been so obliging?"

"I have my ways."

No, she was not near fainting. He wanted to pursue the line of inquiry, but first he had to get them out of here as quickly as possible. He turned his attention back to the lovely puzzle in front of him and stroked the door with one hand as he removed the tools from his coat pockets with the other.

"A thief who comes prepared," Gemma commented.

"Of course. You never know when you'll need to come to a lady's aid and break into a safe," he said without looking at her. "Ah, that's it," he murmured as he slipped his tools into the lock. He continued his soft coaxing until he felt a pull of satisfaction as the final tumbler gave way, and the safe relinquished her secrets.

"Well, it clearly is not your first time. Impressive, my lord," she said as he popped open the door.

"I've heard that before," he said, amused at her quiet intake of breath.

But that humor was quickly doused by disappointment: save for a few baubles and a stack of pound notes, the safe was empty. Not unexpected, but frustrating nonetheless.

"Oh." Her face fell for a brief moment when he turned with outstretched hands to show her what he'd discovered. Lucas braced himself for tears, but she simply nodded once and composed herself. Curiosity, tinged with a bit of admiration he couldn't deny, tugged at him.

Later.

He would get answers from her before the night was out, but for now it was time to remove them both from the library. He replaced the items and the painting in their rightful places. After a cursory search of the desk, he felt satisfied that he could mark Howard off his list. He took Gemma's arm, ignoring her dissent, and guided her to the door that would lead her back to the ballroom.

Speaking over her protests, he said, "Here is what we will do. You'll make your way back to the ballroom, and after a few moments issue your excuses. You came with your aunt, yes?" He didn't need it confirmed. He'd noticed them when they had made their appearance, the vivacious Rosalind, Lady Andrews, and her dowdy niece of a cousin twice removed. He was never quite able to lock down the exact connection when he asked, but he always noted when they arrived. "You have a headache, so you'll take her carriage home and send it back for her."

He didn't wait for her answer, just nudged her out the door, closed it in her face, and then walked to the exit that would take him outside to the terrace. He would skirt the house and be waiting in Lady Andrews's carriage, with the coachman none the wiser. He was rusty when it came to this stealth game, but some skills he would never lose.

...

"Rude, insufferable man," Gemma muttered at the door in her face. She glared as though she could see the earl in all of his arrogance standing just beyond the wood.

She could not blame him entirely for her foul mood, but it felt better to focus on the anger instead of the disappointment. This whole night had been one unpredictable mess after another. At least she could cross one more off her dwindling list of suspects. She had not had much hope, anyway, but no lead was too obscure to rule out at this point. Because they were all obscure.

As she made her way toward the noise of people and music, she thought of all that Rosalind had told her about Lord Winchester. Standoffish. Rarely in town for the Season.

Intelligent. Arrogant. She scoffed. She could tell all of that within a minute of meeting the man, and nothing in their conversations since had changed her mind. Rich as Midas came to mind. Which made her pause and reevaluate her lord-thief assumption. But many in the town were not what they appeared, she had come to realize. In her snooping, she'd found many a seemingly well-to-do family on the edge of financial ruin. He'd put the jewels back, though, without much of a glance. She did not think she'd been the reason for him not taking them—he was the type to do what he wanted, regardless of her opinion.

She reached the edges of the crowd and scanned the gathering. It was a crush, and she imagined Lady Howard was preening over the turnout. Her aunt, though, was no fading wallflower, and Gemma spotted her bright chartreuse gown and followed the unladylike—but completely delightful and infectious—laugh. Rosalind was not the type to mask her enjoyment with ennui, as was so fashionable. And thus, she was always the life of the party.

Gemma made what she hoped was a delicate gesture to get Rosalind's attention, though she probably failed miserably. Uncle Artie had taught her many things, but the artful ways of society had not been one of them.

She stood off to the side while Rosalind disengaged herself from her many male admirers.

"Did you find anything, dear?" Rosalind asked without any preamble.

"No," Gemma told her, glancing around to make sure they were not overheard. She lowered her voice to a whisper and said, "But the night has taken a startling turn."

Rosalind took Gemma's hand, immediately worried. "Are you all right?" she asked. "Did something happen in your search?"

"Yes," Gemma said, knowing she did not have time to

explain and that it would kill her aunt not to know. It would be a minor miracle if she could persuade Rosalind not to trail her out to the street. "I will tell you everything as soon as possible, but for now I must take the carriage to the house. I will send it back for you. All is well, I just need to leave with some urgency."

Rosalind gave her a hard look, and Gemma wondered if she should have told the headache lie.

"Someone might notice…and talk," Rosalind warned. Her aunt was constantly torn between shielding Gemma's reputation and helping with her investigation. It could have been worse. She could have been stuck with a stickler for all of society's absurd, restrictive rules for ladies.

"I doubt anyone will even realize I'm not here," Gemma said. In fact, that was part of their scheme: to make sure as few people as possible paid attention to her. It was why she dressed in unflattering, colorless gowns, wore fake spectacles, and tried not to say more than one or two words to anyone attempting conversation with her. No one ever paid her a bit of mind.

Except Lord Winchester.

"Just be careful, dear heart." Rosalind squeezed her hand once before turning back to her crowd of admirers. "I am positively parched," her aunt told them, and they all but fell over themselves to secure the honor of procuring her a refreshment.

"Thank you," Gemma whispered to her aunt's back, and she faded into the crowd. No one gave her a second glance.

She breathed a sigh of relief when Rosalind's carriage pulled up to the steps.

Would Lord Winchester be inside?

Unexpected nerves fluttered along her insides, and she stumbled as she reached the driver. Did she really want to keep tempting fate by being alone in dark places with him?

Not only was her reputation at stake, but his ability to see past her disguise simultaneously intrigued and frightened her. It also put her mission in jeopardy, and she refused to fail Nigel in this. Accepting John's proffered hand, she climbed into the monstrosity Rosalind insisted on taking about town. The thing was more suited for old country roads, but Rosalind would have her way.

The shadows didn't shift until the door closed behind her. She didn't care to admit it, but she almost let out a small shriek as Lucas's sharply contoured face emerged in the moonlight. He reached across and tugged the curtains shut, blocking out prying eyes.

"My lord, you are quite skilled in clandestine affairs. I didn't even notice you in the dark there, and I knew to look for you," she said, her hand still covering her racing heart. Lucas lounged in the corner of the seat, one leg propped on the opposite bench, much too close to her skirts. His sleek dark hair and green eyes gave him the appearance of a panther holding deceptively still during a hunt.

Does that make me his prey?

"That is the point, my dear," he said, his voice low enough that she had to lean forward to hear him. She remembered the coachman not too far away from them. The driver was discreet, as was fitting for how well Rosalind paid him, but even the most careful person could slip at times. She had to remember to keep her wits about her.

"Now," Lucas said, "I believe you are about to tell me just exactly what you were doing in Lord Howard's library tonight."

She narrowed her eyes. She'd followed his plan out of curiosity, and out of the hope that perhaps he would be a help to her. But she'd had about all she could take of his autocratic demands. She smiled at him sweetly.

"Why…hunting a murderer, sir. What was it that *you* were doing?"

Chapter Two

He was in a carriage with a madwoman.

"You believe you are tracking down a murderer?" he repeated, measuring each word. She had never seemed out of her mind. The few conversations they'd had before that evening had been innocuous, perhaps even purposely dull. But he'd seen sparks of sharpness and wit behind those deep blue eyes.

"You don't believe me," she said, her voice steady. "Well, I don't need you to, my lord. I just need you to stay out of my way." She tipped her chin up, a move he'd seen from countless young gentlemen in the ring at Jackson's who had more bravado than technique. It was as if she were preparing to spar with him for a few rounds. He supposed that was, after all, what they were about to do.

She was such a fierce little thing, all vibrating annoyance. It surprised him that she thought they could go their separate ways now, as if nothing had occurred. That was as likely as him forgetting his own name. "Ah, see, now that's where we'll have a problem," he informed her.

"I don't see why. We were both engaged in questionable activities tonight, but you more so than I. 'Tis you who broke into the safe, and you still haven't answered my question as to why. I say we should forget this night happened and stay out of each other's way in the future."

The little minx. "Are you threatening me?"

"Do you know, I believe I am," she replied, with a self-satisfied expression that made him want to lean forward and nibble at her lips.

"That is unwise, Miss Lancaster," he said instead, injecting steel into his voice. Her eyes widened at his tone, then narrowed. Her face was so expressive. How had she ever tricked anyone into thinking her a dull, uninteresting relation? The answer was surprisingly easy, though. He'd learned long ago that people saw what they wanted to see. And if they were helped in the right direction, it was easy to manipulate preconceived notions. She had done it artfully.

"And it is unwise for you to underestimate me, my lord."

She wasn't pretty. Not in the conventional manner so prized by society. Her lips were too big, her nose too sharp. Freckles dusted her cheeks and nose. Her face reminded him of a fox, an image enhanced by the sunset-streaked mass of curls bundled atop her head. Though she certainly had some curves beneath the hideous, pea soup colored dress she wore—he could attest to it personally—she was far from voluptuous. But something about her pulled at him.

"Let's start over. Whom did this murderer of yours take from you?" He had a notion that was where her particular brand of logic would lead. If she was hunting a killer, as she claimed, then it followed that the victim had been important to her.

The anger seeped out of her. She slumped back against her seat and looked away from him, toward the heavy curtains, possibly wishing she could look out at the black of the night. The clatter of horse hooves on the cobblestone was the only sound in the darkened carriage for a moment. He had touched a raw nerve and intruded on something deeply personal.

Had her lover died?

Jealousy burned in his gut, but annoyance quickly overtook it. What was wrong with him? He had never been so possessive of a woman so quickly.

"His name was Nigel Shaw." She turned back to him and finally said, "He…was my cousin." She stumbled over the past tense, but otherwise she looked composed.

Cousin.

Not lover.

Cousin.

The knot in his chest relaxed.

"Ah," he said. "I think you should start at the beginning."

• • •

"That's what I have been trying to do," Gemma said, secretly thankful the man seemed to only utter things that annoyed her. It allowed her to fight off the wave of grief that had threatened to consume her a moment earlier. She would have been mortified if she had cried in front of him.

Since the horrible morning she had read the letter from her cousin's man of affairs telling her that Nigel had been shot dead by a burglar at a house party, she had focused all her energies on finding his murderer. As long as she was moving forward, she could channel her emotions into something productive. She could imagine no greater hell than sitting in their empty manor house doing nothing while Nigel's killer walked free. The idea haunted her before she had set out to catch the villain. The Misses Blythe and Reverend Connors may have had heart palpitations when she'd announced she intended to visit her aunt in London after only a few weeks of mourning, but they could all be consigned to the inferno for all she cared. She was honoring her cousin in the only way she knew how: through action.

She shook off the gloom of the past and focused her attention on the problem at hand.

"My parents died when I was very young, in a carriage accident. I was passed around to various relations until my Uncle Artie took me in many months later." Her heart swelled at the memory of the big bear of a man. He had taken in a bedraggled, unwanted child when many of her other relatives had been unable to cope with a terrified, nearly comatose girl. He had been kind and patient and helped her recover from her tragic loss. He and Nigel both had. "Nigel's mother had died in childbirth several years earlier, so it was just the two of them, and Uncle Artie raised us as siblings. Nigel was my best friend."

"I'm sorry," Lucas said when she paused, and he sounded genuine. Her eyes had adjusted to the darkness so she could make out his face, even though its contours were bathed in shadows. No longer sprawled on the seat, he sat up straight, hands clasped on his muscular thighs.

"Nigel attended a house party about two months ago," she continued. "They found him the second morning, shot to death in the library. The local inspector said it was a burglar, but only one thing was taken: Nigel's pocket watch."

"Ah," Lucas's voice sharpened as he snapped to even more directed attention. "Only the pocket watch?"

"Yes," she answered, wondering if he would reach the same conclusion she had. "Nothing else in the study. Nigel also wore an expensive family ring, which was left on him, and he was carrying several banknotes of considerable value."

"So he was the intended victim," Lucas deducted.

"Precisely!" She tapped him on his knee, excited that

they were of one thought. Her cheeks heated when she realized what she had done, and she withdrew her hand from his person. He stared at the spot she'd touched before giving his head a small shake and clearing his throat.

"Why would he be targeted?" Lucas mused, and she sensed it was posed more to himself than to her. She had been mulling the same question over in her head for the past two months. She had not gotten far. Or rather, she had gone down the pathways of farfetched notions only to find disappointment.

"I do not know, my lord," she said, her frustration evident in her tone. She was searching for a murderer without knowing the cause of the attack, and she was, quite frankly, getting nowhere with it. "Nigel did not gamble, he was not a rakehell. He did not conduct affairs with married ladies…"

"Hmmm." Lucas hummed at the last, a low sound of doubt, which was both expected and aggravating. Did he think her naive for believing the best of Nigel? She was aware that many so-called gentlemen had liaisons with the wives of their peers; that they risked their fortunes at the card tables every night; that they bet each other on who could ruin the most innocents in a Season. But what the earl did not understand was that Nigel would have told her of the adventures. It was not that her cousin had been indelicate, but that they had been the closest of confidantes.

If he had been involved in some sort of sinful or scandalous endeavor he would not have been able to avoid confessing to her. It had always been that way. When Nigel had snuck an extra pudding from the cook on his ninth birthday he had immediately rushed to her rooms, sticky sugar on his fingers, and blurted out the truth. When, at sixteen, he'd pulled Martha, one of the maids at their manor, behind the bushes for a stolen kiss, he'd hunted Gemma down to give her all the details. No confession was too small or large for it not to be shared between the two of them. The earl, of course, knew none of that, and he did not seem inclined to believe her.

"He was not perfect, but I do not believe it was some secret vice that got him killed." She sighed as his expression remained doubtful. It would be fruitless to argue the point. At least now he would have to admit it would be better to go their separate ways. A tug of regret pulled at her. He still hadn't told her why he'd been searching Lord Howard's library, but having him there had made her feel not so…alone. It had felt so good to confide in someone besides her aunt. If nothing else, he'd sparked her interest. "I am not going to spend energy convincing you of anything."

"What were you doing in Lord Howard's library tonight?" He shifted directions, without acknowledging her consternation. The change in questioning caught her off guard.

"I told you I'm…"

"Yes, yes, 'hunting a murderer,'" he said with a dismissive wave of his hand. She bristled at the gesture. "'Why Lord Howard's library?' would perhaps be a better, more precise question."

It was a thin line, this. How much more should—or could—she divulge before she ended up revealing everything? She had spent much of the time answering his questions and not learning anything in return. The encounter thus far had only resulted in his doubting her claims.

"I think the better question is why were *you* in Lord Howard's library, my lord?" she asked instead of answering him. It was time to take control of the situation, as Uncle Artie would say. She would not be bullied by an arrogant man, earl or no. She savored the irritation that tightened his jaw before she realized the carriage was slowing. "Oh, we're almost home!"

She was more dismayed than she should be that their

time was cut short. It was only because she had not learned anything from him. It was just as well she would be able to rid herself of the earl. No amount of curiosity was worth the aggravation he would bring her. Although she had not come very far in her investigation as of yet on her own, having Lord Winchester as a partner would only lead to disaster.

"Damn." His curt tone told her he was not happy with their arrival at Lady Andrews's home, either. "My apologies."

She waved it away. "Uncle Artie cursed like a sailor. Women are not so delicate as all that, you know." She bit her lip as a thought struck her. "You will not hamper my mission, my lord, will you?" If he concluded that she was putting herself in danger, he could take it upon himself to attempt to stop her, thus destroying all that she was working for. While he might not seem the type of man to interfere—especially when he was up to something himself—she could not rest until she extracted his word that he would not thwart her efforts. She had met plenty of gentlemen in the past few weeks who would think they were doing what was best for her. The patriarchal condescension ran strong amongst the noblemen of the *ton*.

He considered her for a moment before sidestepping her question. "We are not done with each other yet, Gemma. You will not rid yourself of me quite that easily."

Gemma's stomach dipped at the soft promise and his use of her Christian name. For the sake of her emotional stability, it would be less than wise to become attached to this man in any fashion. He was much too mysterious—and much too attractive—for her to be fully safe around him.

"I will call on you and your aunt tomorrow to discuss this matter further," he said.

She felt a spark of excitement at the prospect of seeing him again that she wished she could dismiss. Perhaps she should be angry, frightened even, at what he might have planned. But, no, she was acting like she was just out of the schoolroom and not a spinster of twenty-five.

So silly.

He would be horrified at her train of thoughts. That alone steadied her.

"I expect some answers as well, my lord," she told him.

The carriage finally creaked to a stop. She knew John was clambering from his perch to assist her down from the vehicle, and she realized this was Lucas's moment to escape unnoticed. She shifted to block him as much as possible as he reached for the opposite door. Right before he slipped out of the carriage and into the fog of the night, she felt his lips graze her ear. "We are in this together now, my dear."

She did not react to the whispered vow as her door opened at the same time the one behind her *snicked* closed. The chilled air of the spring night felt refreshing against her flushed cheeks as the coachman helped her down to the street. Yes, Lord Winchester definitely spelled trouble.

Chapter Three

Gemma was surprised to see Roz seated at the table when she walked into the breakfast room. Her aunt was of the opinion that only a madwoman came downstairs before ten a.m. Yet there she sat, with her tea and eggs, reading the post. Gemma chuckled and moved to the sideboard while calling out a greeting.

"Finally, Gemma! Really, a soul would think you were planning to laze the day away in your room." Rosalind tossed the invitations she'd been perusing to the side.

Gemma clucked her tongue, amused at her aunt's melodramatic tendencies. However, she was impressed by the restraint Roz had shown. If the roles had been reversed, she probably wouldn't have been able to stop herself from bursting into Rosalind's bedroom at the crack of dawn. Or even the night before.

"Rest assured, I haven't much to tell, yet. The situation is continuing to develop," Gemma said as she began to tear into her sausage.

"Dear heart, you fled in the middle of a ball after an illicit search of the host's study," Roz summed up, clearly aghast at her niece's apparent nonchalance. "I need details."

"Well, when you put it that way…" Gemma bit back a mischievous smile. She couldn't help but tease Roz a bit, even though she knew her aunt was dying a slow death.

"That uncle of yours made you too sassy for your own good, child," Roz shot back.

"Yes, no one else in this family is cheeky," Gemma said, letting the grin slip out. Roz harrumphed and picked up her tea, attempting to be the picture of indifference. "Now don't hurt yourself!" Gemma laughed before taking pity on her. "I was hoping to find Nigel's pocket watch in Lord Howard's study."

"I still do not know if that's the best way to go about this," her aunt said, singing the same song she had been since Gemma had started the investigation. "Nor will I believe that bore had anything to do with your poor cousin's demise."

"After last night, I believe you are right. We should press on, I think," Gemma said. Despair clawed at her, but she pushed it away. Her lack of success in finding Nigel's killer bothered her, but she would not stop until she found the justice she sought. Roz supported her, but worried about her. They only had so much time before the trail went cold. As much as Lucas intrigued her, she couldn't waste her time trying to convince him to help her. "But I was in the midst of my search when the door swung open."

"No!" Her aunt gasped and clutched at her heart, horrified and enthralled at once.

"I was quite startled, obviously," Gemma told her. "It was, in fact, Lord Winchester. I, unfortunately, was not quite as quick to react as I would have liked and he caught me gaping at him in the middle of the room." Roz leaned forward in her seat. "Oh, dear."

"Indeed. It's not over yet, though. Before we could even

begin to question each other, we heard someone right outside the door. We made it behind a curtain in time to avoid that disaster. Though, why he had to pick the same hiding spot…" she trailed off still slightly peeved. Roz just stared at her, apparently at a loss for words. "So, there we are, trapped against each other while a couple carries out an assignation in Lord Howard's library…"

"Did you hear who it was?"

"Just a Sylvie and Reginald."

"Oh my!"

"Which didn't last long, thank heavens."

"Hmmm." Her aunt hummed, and Gemma knew she was filing the information away in case it came in handy at a later date.

"Once they left, the earl broke into the safe without so much as blinking," she continued. "There were only a few baubles in there, so we can cross Howard off the list."

"Well, I can't say that I'm surprised at that, at least," Roz noted.

"Mmmm. Then Lord Winchester tells me to leave the ball and get the carriage, in which he will be waiting for me, so that we can discuss what has transpired. And he somehow got in there without John noticing."

"Did you tell him about the murder?" her aunt asked.

"I did," Gemma said, "but I think he believes Nigel was the victim of a cuckolded lord and not some other scheme. I'm not sure he'll be very much help to us. He seemed quite doubtful of me the whole time."

"That would be the obvious explanation, dear heart. You can't blame the man for arriving at it," Roz said gently. "Did you find out what he was doing searching the safe?"

"No, but I intend to today," Gemma said, determined not to let Lucas avoid her questioning again. "I know you told me a little about him when we were first introduced, but is there anything else you've heard from the gossipmongers? I need to be prepared."

"You sound like you're headed into battle, dear heart," Roz said.

"I feel like I am," Gemma assured her.

"Well, his mother died some years back, and his father about two years ago. They seemed like fine people, if somewhat reclusive," Roz rattled off.

"You knew them?" Gemma asked.

"Here and there we would see each other at balls," Roz said. "He was some years older than I, so we did not run in the same circles. He seemed to be a tough man, though I remember some stories of his wild younger years. Nothing to warrant a scandal, of course, but some curricle races in Brighton, a few flirtations with ineligible women, the usual mischief-making of the wild young set, you know."

"And the mother?" Gemma did not want to be as intrigued as she was by the information.

"Beautiful, in a classical way. But it was not a love match," Roz answered, leaning in. "It was a typical *ton* marriage—his eye was on her inheritance, and hers was on his title."

Gemma murmured something sympathetic. That was so often the case when it came to high-society engagements.

They shared a look before Roz continued. "She disappeared to their country house, with the two children…"

"He has only one sibling, then?" Gemma cut in.

"Yes, a sister. Beatrice. Lovely girl, though the *on dit* is that she has a bit too much personality for her own good," Roz said, leaning in with a wink.

Gemma tried to call up an image of the girl. A pretty face and a halo of blond curls were all she could recall.

"I should think I would remember a young lady with too much personality," she said, and a pang of sympathy plucked at the back of Gemma's throat. The same thing could so easily be said about her. Uncle Artie hadn't exactly considered potential in-laws when he'd been teaching her how to fence or pick a lock. "I am quite thankful I am not husband hunting."

"My dear, if you had wanted, we could have made you into a diamond of the first water. You would have scads of proposals by now," Roz said.

Unbidden, an image of Lord Winchester slipped into her mind. She pushed it away. "I don't need suitors, Roz. I need answers."

"Mmmm." Roz was watching her with a gleam in her eye. "Maybe once this little mission of yours is over…"

Gemma held up a hand. "Stop. I'll be more than happy to return to my solitude in Northumberland," she said, and for a moment she wondered which one of them she was trying to convince.

Roz just peered at her over her teacup and Gemma hastened to turn the subject back to their investigation. "In any case, Lord Winchester is calling on us today to further discuss the situation. He really has some skills that could be of help, but he is just so arrogant. I fear he will want to dictate how I should behave and tell me it's too dangerous. I believe that it will be a fruitless visit this morning, but perhaps it won't be a complete waste of time."

"No," her aunt murmured. "I don't think it will be."

. . .

"You do realize, dear brother, that I have a right to know what's going on." Beatrice's voice was deceptively calm as she sipped tea at the breakfast table.

Lucas wasn't fooled. He knew that tone from years of growing up with his hellion of a sister. She locked eyes with him over her cup. He glanced at the clock on the sideboard, not wanting to delay his meeting with Gemma much longer.

He decided to not enter a battle with Beatrice. He could have told her that she had lost all her rights when she'd been so foolish last year. And if not then, definitely when she'd decided to commit those foolish deeds to paper. But he held his tongue. It was not worth the wasted time or energy, and she was sure to win in the end anyway. She was nothing if not stubborn.

"As I said before, *dear s*ister," he said. "There is nothing to tell at the moment. Howard's safe turned up nothing. We will simply have to carry on with the list and hope to get lucky."

She pouted prettily at him. "I have been telling you all along I want to help," she said. "And you will not let me. It is not fair to place the entire burden on your shoulders when this is all my fault."

At least she was admitting to that.

He tried to place himself in her shoes. He was too used to thinking of her as the five-year-old who needed his constant protection from neglectful parents. It had always been the two of them against the world. The other boys had teased him for letting her tag along when she had been so much younger than them. But from the minute she had been born, she'd owned his heart.

She was not a child anymore, though. Perhaps being a part of the investigation would allow her to feel a semblance of control over her own fate. At the moment, it must feel like her world was spinning wildly.

He studied her across the table and thought about his options. "I am going to bring George Harrington in to help me with the case," he finally told her.

"Lucas, no!" She straightened in her chair. "What will you tell him? I cannot have your man of affairs knowing such things about me."

"I will not tell him the details," Lucas assured her. "Just enough for him to be able to research a few things for us. He is quite brilliant, from what I have witnessed of his work on other tasks I have asked of him. And discreet."

"If he is so brilliant, he will figure out what we are investigating, and I will never be able to look him in the eyes again," Beatrice said.

"Because you have done so much of that in the past?" he teased her. He was not concerned his man of affairs would divulge any of their secrets—if he had been, he'd never have hired the man. "But I think you should help him with his research into the matter."

She finally lost her panicked air with that suggestion. "You would let me participate in the investigation?"

"I think the two of you could work together," Lucas said, making clear that she wouldn't be off chasing wild tangents on her own. He glanced at the time once more and pushed back from the table. "After I've talked with Harrington, we can discuss it. For now, I must leave you. Try not to get into too much trouble." He winked at her. He could feel her glare boring a hole in his jacket as he walked out the door.

Lucas pondered the previous night as he strolled the empty pavement in the direction of Gemma's residence. It was early still for the ladies of the *ton* to be out and about, calling on friends and enemies alike. It wouldn't be long before the sun began to cut through the chilling fog and society poured into the streets, but this was his favorite time to be out in London. When it was just him and the shopkeepers setting up for the day.

He'd yet to formulate anything resembling a plan. His mind drifted to the way Gemma's soft skin had felt against his hand, and the pull of her gown against her breasts. The way her eyes lit when she was annoyed with him.

From the moment he'd seen her at the Dorchester ball weeks earlier, he'd been intrigued. It had been three days after the first letter from the blackmailer had arrived, and reentering society after the solitude of his country estate had been a jolt. He knew the mamas of the *ton* believed him to be searching for a wife, and he was pleased with that assumption. He hoped it would throw off any suspicion about his sudden interest in the workings of society.

He'd been waiting for the right moment to slip out of the ballroom unnoticed when a sharp voice had pierced the air rather close behind him.

"He's such a bore, Roz. And what's more, I got the impression he wanted to open my mouth and inspect my teeth like one of his broodmares."

"The *on dit* is that he is on the prowl for a third wife. His first didn't give him any sons, and he's getting desperate," a second voice answered.

"He's old enough to be my grandfather! And he told me I had sturdy hips for birthing…stop laughing."

He'd angled himself to get a view of the amusingly candid women. He could think of several respected gentlemen of the *ton* that they could be discussing, none of whom would be happy to know he was the subject of such a conversation. He'd noticed her hair first—shimmering, unfashionable red, the candlelight bringing out its soft gold streaks. A few curls had escaped to frame her delicate face. Her gown had been a drab mud color that washed out her peaches-and-cream skin and disguised any shape. But when she leaned over to tap the other woman with her fan, he saw her gentle curves hiding beneath.

He'd forced an introduction later in the night, but when he talked to her, all the life he'd witnessed earlier seemed to be dampened. He'd found her to be a dull conversationalist, with little wit or personality. Still he tried, and still, he was disappointed.

"Miss Lancaster, have you been enjoying your season thus far?" he'd asked during their first conversation.

"Yes, my lord," she'd answered, looking at a spot just over his shoulder.

"And what have you found you like best about town?" he'd tried.

"The balls, my lord," she'd answered, not removing her gaze, obscured behind spectacles, from the fascinating sight just to the side of his ear.

He'd known, then, that she had secrets.

He didn't think he could have imagined just what secrets she had.

...

"You have a caller, Miss Lancaster," the butler announced, interrupting Roz and Gemma's lively discussion about the case.

"This early?" Roz exclaimed. The butler's disapproving expression turned even more censorious.

"Lord Winchester, my lady," he sniffed, without any of the reverence typically shown for a visit from such a high-ranking gentleman.

Gemma tamped down the excitement that sparked within her, and told herself it wasn't over seeing him again.

No. He's a nuisance.

But something told her that matching wits with such an adversary would be inherently dangerous—and invigorating.

She was no slouch in the intelligence department, herself, though. If it was a battle he wanted, he would shortly come to realize she would not give ground easily. She set down the paper she'd been about to read and skirted around Mr. Bird, headed in the direction of the drawing room. She was showing all the restraint of a schoolgirl in the first thralls of love as she hurried into the room.

Forcing herself to pause, she took a breath.

Lucas wasn't seated. He leaned against the window frame, lit from behind so his features were shadowed.

"My lord, good morning," she said and was immediately annoyed by the breathiness in her voice. It was just that he was so...large. And so handsome. She cleared her throat. "You're out and about early."

"Yes, I assumed you would be up. I see you are an early riser like myself, Lady Andrews." He tilted his head in the direction of Roz, who strolled into the drawing room with slightly less urgency than Gemma. "Apologies if I have interrupted your breakfast."

"We were finished and discussing Nigel's murder, so your timing was perfect, my lord. Please sit down." Gemma gestured to the delicate rose-patterned chairs near the window. He eyed them warily before lowering himself into one. "They're not going to break, my lord." She laughed at him.

"I would be forever disgraced and have to leave town, so I appreciate the reassurance. You are not wearing your spectacles," he remarked as he sat, turning the conversation without warning.

"Oh." She reached to her face, but of course she wasn't wearing them. They were part of the ruse and not necessary in her house. She had not been expecting him so early. "Well, I might as well be candid. I wear them so the *ton* finds me even more unfashionable than I am, and will thus pay me less attention. We imagined I could bend some of society's more autocratic rules if I could move about unnoticed."

"Clever," he said with an approving nod. She frowned, upset at the gratification she felt by the compliment. "Unfortunately the gossipmongers of the *ton* are unrelenting vultures, so I'm not sure you have emerged as unscathed as you think, or that your reputation is protected."

"I'm not concerned about my reputation, my lord," she assured him. "I have no intention of marrying, and as soon as this is over, I'm returning to the country." She sounded convincing to her ears, but she felt the now familiar sinking of her heart when she pictured returning to her bucolic life in Northumberland.

Lucas's face remained inscrutable, and he skipped over her protest. "I assume, Lady Andrews, that you are aware of everything that is happening?" He directed his focused attention at Roz, who had settled herself behind a desk, somewhat out of the way of their conversation.

"Indeed," her aunt confirmed. "Carry on with your discussions as if I am not here. I have letters to write to my dear friends. I have been putting them off for far too long." Roz proceeded to tuck her head down, and began writing with all the apparent concentration of a spy divulging state secrets.

Lucas' mouth tipped up at the corners, and he focused on Gemma once again. Each time he did that—turned his full attention on her—her tongue stopped working.

"Why Lord Howard?" he asked.

"I shall tell you why Lord Howard if you tell me as much yourself," she replied.

Just because he was as attractive as sin didn't mean she could let him distract her. It was time she got some answers, as well. Though she affected the impression of a wallflower with the *ton*, that wasn't who she was, and she refused to be cowed by the demands of an arrogant earl.

"That's fair." He paused, contemplating. He looked at a pointedly distracted Roz before glancing back at Gemma. She sensed he'd made a decision. "My sister is being blackmailed."

"Good heavens! And you believed Lord Howard is the culprit?" she asked.

"No," he said, and she could hear the frustration in his usually smooth voice.

It was a feeling she recognized well.

"But I'm following one of the more promising avenues that I have at the moment. No one knows the matter for which my sister is being blackmailed, apart from the two of us, and a gentleman who is no longer in the country. She does not believe he would tell anyone, and as the last I had heard from him he was headed to India, I am wont to believe her. Or I must choose to believe her, as the alternative would open too many possibilities."

"I can sympathize," Gemma commiserated. He met her eyes, and she experienced a moment of understanding and kinship she hadn't felt since Nigel had died. Roz was a continuous delight, but Gemma never quite felt that same connection—of knowing someone and being known in return.

"To make matters worse, my sister foolishly wrote about it in her diary, which was stolen sometime last month," he said quietly. Gemma cringed for the poor girl. She herself didn't keep a journal, but if she did, she would not like the idea of a villain poring over her innermost thoughts. "The only time anyone had access to our townhouse was during a party I hosted a fortnight ago. I have been going through the guest list from that night in hopes of narrowing down our suspects," Lucas continued.

Gemma gasped. "My lord, we have been on the same path, it seems." She drew up the skirts of her dress to reach a pocket underneath. Lucas arched a dark eyebrow at the sight of her ankles—and perhaps at the little blade she wore sheathed there—but Gemma refused to blush. She was too intent on her goal. She withdrew a carefully folded paper. "This is the guest list from the house party where Nigel was killed. I have been investigating the attendees for anything suspicious in their homes. That's why I was in Lord Howard's study, my lord. He was one of the guests." She held out the paper to Lucas, who reached for it. Their fingers brushed and hers tingled at the contact. She hastily withdrew her hand.

Such sensations were unfamiliar to her, as were the thoughts she had of where those sensations could lead. Roz hummed, a sound of doubt low in her throat, while Lucas scanned the list. They swiveled toward her in unison at the interruption.

"Roz doesn't approve of the plan," Gemma told Lucas. He glanced at Roz for confirmation.

"Well, dear heart, it's not that I do not approve, I just feel it might be problematic," Roz said with deliberate care, tiptoeing over the sensitive subject. The two of them had had several in-depth discussions over the best path to take. Roz worried she was chasing rainbows and fretted over the possible damage sneaking around could do to her reputation, but had been unable to come up with a better plan.

Gemma huffed out a dejected breath. "I am beginning to believe you are correct, Roz. I have made it through a majority of these attendees, and other than a few scandals and indelicacies, I have found nothing."

"I have also pointed out to Gemma—and I will remark to you—that one does not need to be on the guest list to gain entry to an event. It is even truer in your case, Lord Winchester, as someone could easily slip into an overflowing townhouse. It would take more work to pass unnoticed at a house party, but it was a rather large gathering, so I would not discount the notion."

Lucas surged to his feet and began to stalk around the small room. Impatience radiated off of him as if it was an aura she could actually see. He swung back toward them and halted almost midstride. "This cannot be a coincidence, our two cases."

Gemma's mouth parted in a slight "oh," and Roz sat back in her chair.

"Think about the chances of there being a murderer and blackmailer on the loose at the same time, attending society events," he continued, clearly warming to his revelation.

She rolled it over in her own mind. "But you do not believe Nigel was killed for any nefarious purpose other than the vengeance of an angry husband," she reminded him. But even as she said it, she knew the theory made a kind of macabre sense. What if Nigel had been caught up somehow in the blackmailer's scheme? Or had merely been in the wrong place at the wrong time?

Lucas studied her face for a moment. "Why do you think he was killed?" he asked, and for the first time it felt like he was ready to listen to her.

"I think he witnessed something he wasn't supposed to see," she answered. She could not believe Nigel to be a rakehell caught up in a scandal that had resulted in his death. Of the two of them, he was the calm, measured, sensible one, whereas she was the one who would go dashing off without much thought to propriety.

"Let us make a slight jump in logic. There are a few repeating names on our lists, at least from the ones I remember. Society is small, but that means several of the same members attended events in which our criminal deeds occurred," he answered and sat down again.

"That's not as rare as one would think," Roz chimed in sardonically. Lucas glanced at her, his mouth twisting up in a half smile, half grimace.

"Touché. But if one of the men on both our lists is the blackmailer, then he was also at the house party where your cousin was killed. The coincidence is too much, I think."

"I agree," Gemma said, planning how to communicate the idea she had been formulating since last night. She sucked in a deep breath. "We must work together." She leaned forward, bracing her elbows on her knees. "If we piece what we both know together, we could actually come up with a clear picture of the villain. And you have useful…skills." She paused for a moment. "*But* I must have your word as a gentleman that you will not hinder my efforts in any way."

"Yes, indeed," Lucas agreed. Was that a hint of a smile at the corner of his mouth? Gemma couldn't tell whether she was imagining it. Was he as pleased as she was at the notion of spending more time together? For her there was an anticipation that she hadn't felt in a long time. Of course, that's the moment Roz took to pop the bubble of excitement.

"If I may interrupt once more," Roz spoke from her desk, a strange look on her face. "It will be nearly impossible for you two to work together without creating a scandal. Even if Lord Winchester is thought to be courting you, that still limits greatly the amount of time you're allowed in each other's company."

Gemma sighed. It was true—young ladies out in society were monitored with an intensity that seemed better suited to Cromwell's time. And still, even with the tight restrictions, many ended up compromised anyway, at least in the eyes of the *ton*. Gemma had heard of girls forced into marriage simply for taking a breath of fresh air with a gentleman at a ball for too long a time. Society told them it was for their safety, but Gemma chafed at the thought. It had more to do with a need for control, something she could not countenance.

"Roz, I have no aspirations in town past finding Nigel's murderer. Let them gossip about me," Gemma said at last. She could think of no other way around the problem.

"No. I've been supportive of your wild chase because I think many have not taken note of your escapades, but this will be a scandal you would not live down. The gossip will be merciless, and you will be torn to shreds, my dear." Gemma could hear the steely resolve in her aunt's voice. "I have countenanced a great deal from you, but this I will not. I will *not* let you willfully toss your reputation to the wind."

That was unfair. She was doing this for her family. Her mind raced for a solid rebuttal, for Roz seemed unmovable in her conviction. She would rather not have to sneak around her aunt; in fact, it could prove impossible. But there was no way they could collaborate to catch a killer and blackmailer in the few minutes they would be allowed to be seen together at social events. At most, they could stroll in the park with a chaperone, but even that was limiting. Her plan was crumbling before her, and there was nothing she could do to stop it. There was no way she could work with Lord Winchester and go unnoticed. She would have had more freedom if she was a widow…but they'd already introduced her as unmarried. If only she had thought ahead.

The feeling of loss took her aback. How could she miss something she'd never had?

She glanced at Lucas, who had remained silent through the exchange. He was studying her, his face an inscrutable mask.

"The solution is simple," he said, his eyes not leaving hers. "We must announce our engagement."

...

Lucas had never proposed before, but he did not think the desired reaction was blind panic. He tried not to be insulted as the color drained from Miss Lancaster's face.

"Have you gone mad?" She leaped to her feet and began to pace.

His temper pricked. It was the clear solution to their problem, but she seemed to find the mere suggestion appalling. A blow to his pride, indeed. "It is perfectly sane. In fact, it is the most logical course of action. It allows us to be seen together, and for me to escort you around town so that I can protect you, and it will head off any scandal before it can gain legs."

"I don't need you to protect me," Gemma protested,

without pausing her fretful wanderings around the study.

Rosalind remained quiet, but they both tracked Gemma as she moved around the small room.

"What about me?" Lucas asked softly.

She finally paused and turned her fierce blue eyes on him.

"What do you mean?" she asked, wary. She was intelligent and sensed a trap.

"If we do not make our arrangement respectable in the eyes of the *ton*, and scandal ensues, my reputation will be in tatters as well," he said. He noticed Rosalind narrow her eyes, but still she did not interrupt. The idea to announce their engagement had not come from the blue. The possibility had occurred to him the evening before, when he was sneaking out of her carriage. Above all else, and as much as she protested against it, he needed to ensure her safety if they were to embark on this investigation together. The only way to do that was to be close to her far more often than the boundaries of propriety allowed.

"What are your objections?" Lucas asked. He believed he could knock down all her oppositions if given enough time. She was no frivolous society dilettante. She would see the logic of the idea.

"First, no one will believe it," she said, waving her hand in his direction.

"They will believe it if I announce it," he said firmly. *First notion dismissed.* "What else?"

"What will happen when we catch the killer?" She paused right after she spoke the words. Clearly a thought had just popped into her head. He braced himself for the inevitable madness that was about to come. "You will have to cry off," she said in a rush of words.

"No." It was a gut reaction—the only one he could muster in the moment.

"Don't you see, it's perfect," she said, clearly warming to

the crazed notion. "I was planning on returning to the country at the end of the affair. Or perhaps I will travel instead." She lit up with excitement as he scowled at her. This was not going as planned. Nothing ever seemed to when it came to Gemma.

"Gemma…" he began, not even sure where to start. Mostly because he didn't quite know himself why it mattered to him so much. She cut him off, however.

"No," she said, and the fire colored her cheeks and lit her eyes. "It is the only way I shall agree to our false engagement. I will not have you trapped into marriage with me simply to protect my reputation, when you have not actually compromised me in any way. I would rather return home this day than have that occur."

Her chin tipped up, and her hands clenched at her sides. She met his gaze unflinching. He glanced over at Rosalind, who was watching them with a bemused smile. She seemed unfazed by the wild scheme. He was smart enough to let this battle stand.

"You will not trap me into marriage at the end of this, Gemma," he said, the best promise he could make at the moment. She relaxed at that, a gesture he found intriguing and confusing. Any other girl in town would have been happy to trap a wealthy earl into marriage, he thought; several of them had tried. Gemma Lancaster was in a class by herself.

"It's settled, then," Roz said, rising from her desk. "I believe I left something upstairs…"

Amused at the ploy and grateful for the moment alone, Lucas moved closer to Gemma and did what he'd been itching to do since she'd tumbled into the room, all flushed skin and fiery hair—he touched her. His fingers found her hips and settled there for a moment, relishing in the softness, before he pressed his hand flat against the small of her back. She trembled beneath him, her startled eyes lifting to his.

"What is this?" she asked, gripping his upper arms.

"I think we should seal our engagement with a kiss, yes?" He watched her lips part on a quick intake of breath. He brushed a loose copper curl away and cupped her cheek in his rough hand. Something akin to fear showed on her face before curiosity settled upon it.

"Well, it wouldn't be a proper deal without sealing it," she murmured, her eyes on his mouth.

Her sense of humor kept surprising him. The odd mixture of amusement and desire was unfamiliar, and it was intriguing. It was something he would be haunted by later, but for now he pulled her flush against him. Every muscle in his body tightened as her subtle curves, the ones he'd known lurked beneath her dowdy dresses, molded themselves to his body. Groaning, he pressed his lips to hers, and lost himself to the feeling of her under his mouth.

It's just a kiss. Get a hold on yourself.

But even as he had the thought, he wasn't able to resist deepening it, his tongue exploring the seam of her mouth.

A small gasp, and then she opened for him. She tasted like warm honey.

Somewhere in the back of his mind, warning bells chimed. Too much. Too fast. The feel of her, her heat, her smell was wreaking havoc on his normally ironclad self-control. He was all but calculating the distance to the couch, so that he could lay her down, strip her naked and lose himself in her.

Rein it in, Stone. Rein. It. In.

He gentled the kiss, pulling back and nibbling on her freshly plump lower lip. He lingered there, waiting until her ragged breathing evened. Then, with what he swore was an act of God, he stepped back.

Her eyes were glassy, her cheeks flushed. It looked like he had claimed her as his, and something suspiciously close to satisfaction welled in his chest. He tamped it down.

"That should do it," he said, annoyed at the slight quiver

in his voice.

He had to get away before he forgot himself and took her right there in the drawing room.

"I shall see you tomorrow night," he said as he strode toward the door, not waiting for a response.

"Wait! What is tomorrow night?"

"Lord Conway's ball. He's on both of our lists."

Chapter Four

The minute Lucas left, Roz returned and went to work on Gemma. A new wardrobe and look were in order, she decreed. When news of their announcement hit, she would be the main attraction in every ballroom in town. She could no longer go unnoticed by society; she would have to make a splash instead.

Roz mustered her troops with the calm and command of a general.

"You should only ever wear jewel tones, dear heart," Roz informed Gemma as the dressmaker her aunt had summoned tut-tutted over her body, poking in pins she could swear drew blood. "Those eyes, that hair."

"Just days ago you were bemoaning the color," she reminded her aunt.

"That was back when you had to tone down its fire. Now you can let it shine," Roz said with a flourish. She turned to Madame LeCroix, who was about as French as the post outside on the street. "I know this is of the very last minute, but will you have something ready for tomorrow night? It is dire."

Madame reassured them that she could send something over in time, but warned it might not be to the highest standards with such short notice. But, on the night of the ball, Gemma couldn't find a single stitch out of place on the stunning ballgown. She smoothed a hand over the emerald silk, as she peered into her looking glass. She almost refused to believe it was herself staring back. Roz's maid had dressed her hair, and rather than fighting the wild mass of curls, she had simply pinned it up in a few places and let it run like a river over Gemma's ears and around her face.

She was foolishly glad Lucas would see her with her new look. She maintained to herself that her dowdy disguise had aided her in her investigations, but Roz was correct. Now she was no longer invisible, but she would still be hiding — this time it would simply be her relationship with Lucas providing the subterfuge. She had to remember that. When they caught the killer, they would go their separate ways. She steeled herself. It had to be this way. Never again would she be a burden to someone she loved.

And if she'd had any doubts, the answering buzz when she walked into Lord Conway's ballroom squelched them. Of course, none of the content of the whispers reached her ears, but the undercurrent flowed through the sparkling room. The news of her engagement had reached the ears of the *ton*.

Roz patted her arm, careful to make the reassuring gesture unnoticeable, and murmured, "Head up, dear heart." Then she whisked them toward the center of the room. They were soon surrounded by Roz's bevy of admirers, and Gemma felt her nerves calm amongst the elderly rakes. Long gone were their days of carousing, but their charm remained, untouched by age.

She'd almost relaxed when she felt a looming presence behind her. She pivoted to find herself face to chest with

Lucas. She took a shaky step back, trailing her eyes up until they met his.

Would the jolt she felt when she saw him ever fade?

"My lord," was all she could manage. He took her hand, brought it to his full lips, and brushed his mouth over her knuckles.

"Miss Lancaster," he said, making the words sound like a dark promise. He turned to the gaggle of men hovering around her and nodded to each.

"Winchester," came the chorus from the group as a series of heads bowed. Gemma smiled to herself. They looked like nothing so much as a group of puffins.

After paying his respects to Roz, Lucas turned back to her. "Is your dance card open for the waltz, Miss Lancaster? I believe it is the next song."

She refused to admit she was saving the set for him, lest he become even more insufferable, so she made a show of checking her card. "I believe I am free."

His eyes lit with humor as he led her onto the floor. Couples in beautiful silk and lace took their places, awaiting the quartet on the small stage by the terrace doors.

She had a thought. "Did you time your entrance to coincide with the waltz, my lord?"

"Merely a happy coincidence, Gemma," he said, letting her name melt off his tongue, a deliberate intimacy after the "Miss Lancaster" of earlier. The sweet strains of the strings began, and he swept her into a graceful arc. Colors and light swirled as they spun through the crowd on the dance floor.

Her pulse tripped as the warmth of his hand seeped through the gossamer fabric of her dress. She wanted more. She wished they were alone so he could pull her closer, maybe even kiss her the way he had done after they'd made their deal. She blushed at the memory—and at the urge to repeat it.

Where had these thoughts come from? She had always

had a fair appreciation of the male form. But this visceral ache, this need to be closer, ever closer was new and unfamiliar. Scary. But a little invigorating, too, if she were honest with herself. Her fingers dug into the soft fabric covering his broad shoulder.

Then she realized what it was. It was the waltz. She'd always heard it could inflame the senses and cloud logic. That is was sensual and dangerous. She'd laughed the warnings off. The waltzes she had danced before had all been staid, awkward affairs in which she'd been stuck with her partner for half hours at a time. But now she realized why the highest sticklers criticized the dance and restricted who could partake in it.

"Where are your thoughts?" he asked.

Her blush deepened. She hoped he would attribute it to their exertions on the dance floor. "I was simply thinking how much I enjoy the waltz."

"With the right partner it can be very…stimulating," he murmured, and she sucked in a breath.

Was he reading her mind?

"And how many times have you danced it with the right partner?" she returned.

His smoldering gaze held hers a moment before he said, "You told me attending balls is your favorite thing about being in London. Were you being truthful?"

She was confused for a brief second by the question before remembering the conversation. She laughed. "Oh, heavens no. The only way I survive them is by hiding behind the protective wall of the puffins."

"The puffins?"

"How I think of Roz's admirers," she said. She thought about the question. "I do enjoy watching society at these parties. I only wish I did not have to be a part of it."

"An observer of human nature," he mused.

"As are you, my lord," she said. "You do not see only what you are looking for. You see who people are. You saw through my ruse, after all."

"It was obvious to the most casual observer that you were not what you appeared to be." His grin was arrogant and peeved her a bit, even though she believed his words were meant to flatter her.

"No one else questioned it," she reminded him. "What gave it away?"

"Your eyes," he said. "You could never keep the humor from your eyes."

...

"Oh, do not fret, Lucas." Beatrice smiled over her breakfast, a ray of sunshine on the dreary morning. "I will not embarrass you."

Since he'd come to London, Lucas had enjoyed the routine he and his sister had fallen into, sharing their morning meal, but he was not in the mood to indulge her today. He and Gemma had searched Conway's house for any sign of extortion and had found none. To say he was frustrated with the lack of progress was an understatement.

But the night hadn't been a complete waste. He thought about Gemma's face when they'd waltzed, and the way her body had moved with his. He'd wanted to pull her hips flush with his, to bend and kiss that happy, mischievous smile from her lips.

He usually was able to show more restraint, even if it was just in his own thoughts.

That damn waltz.

That's what it was. It tested every gentleman's self control. He'd been able to hold her, but not properly. Not the way he really wanted to. The hum of arousal that thrummed along his nerves had been constant for the rest of the evening.

"There is no need for you to meet her," Lucas said, knowing he was going to lose the battle but refusing to surrender without a fight.

"Of course there is," Beatrice said, his stern tone not diminishing the glow on her face at all. He should not be surprised. He had never been able to intimidate her. "The *ton* will talk if I appear to ignore your fiancée, Lucas. Think about the stories that would cause."

She was right. But he did not want to waste a day on something he viewed as frivolous. Introducing the two women would not help solve the case, and would only serve to complicate matters further. Suppose Beatrice developed a genuine attachment to Gemma? Suppose this whole matter became too…believable?

"I am forever grateful that you are taking care of my problem, please believe me. But you do not need to treat me like a child," she said. "What do you think is going to happen during a daytime tea? If we are not introduced it will be much more of a spectacle."

The engagement was meant to lessen the talk, not add to it. Lucas sighed. "All right. I shall arrange it."

"Wonderful." Beatrice clapped her hands in victory. "What is she like, Lucas? I cannot believe you two have hatched this scheme. It will be dreadful when she has to call off. The gossips will be merciless."

He refrained from pointing out that he was doing all of it for her, and instead answered the original question. How to describe Gemma? She was fire and light. She was smart and had a sharp humor he admired. She was courageous enough to face down a potential murderer, but shy around society. She was a riddle at times and an open book at others. In short, she was Gemma.

But to the question of what she was like? To tell another

how he saw her and how she affected him?

"She is stubborn," he muttered.

She giggled at him. "Well, then you two have much in common. That is also your defining trait."

Lucas growled his displeasure at the comment, but she just laughed it away.

"Mr. Harrington is coming this morning to meet with you, yes?" Beatrice asked after a moment.

"Hmm," he affirmed, glancing at his pocket watch. "He is enthusiastic about the investigation."

Lucas himself was hopeful about young Harrington's help on the case. He was the fourth son of a viscount. His family had thought him destined for the clergy, but he had shown little desire for it. That same family had not been pleased when, in their eyes, Harrington had lowered himself to take a position as a steward.

But Lucas had been impressed with the man's cool-headed temperament and intelligence from the start. It had been with some reluctance that he'd called Harrington down to London to join the case—as he hadn't wanted to pull him away from the estate—but he knew the fresh pair of eyes could prove invaluable to their search.

Now he just had to finesse it without bringing utter humiliation to his sister, who was currently gnawing at her lower lip.

"He is a rather dull fellow, if I remember correctly," she said. "Very interested in mathematics and farming techniques."

Lucas thought about Harrington, and privately agreed with Bea's assessment. The man of affairs was a gentleman of average height and average looks. He did not seem to anger easily, nor laugh easily. He was quiet-tempered and staid. The perfect man of affairs. But Beatrice remained worried, he could tell.

"You may sit in, Bea," he told her, and she immediately brightened. "I told you I would not reveal your secret."

Before she could respond, the door swung open and admitted his butler. "A Mr. Harrington is in your study, sir. I informed him you were unavailable, but he said he would wait."

"Ah, good man." Lucas pushed back away from the table. "His timing could not be better."

He headed out of the room with Beatrice close at his heels.

Harrington turned from his position in front of the bookcase when Lucas swung into the study. His serious, brown eyes darted from Lucas to Beatrice as she crossed the threshold behind him. They widened slightly at her presence, but he showed no other outward emotion.

They exchanged a few pleasantries before settling in at Lucas's desk. He steepled his fingers to peer at Harrington over them.

"We are trying to find a man," Lucas started. Harrington's eyebrows rose, and he glanced at Beatrice. Lucas laughed. "Rest easy. We have not brought you all this way to help us marry off Beatrice." His sister blushed, and Harrington's lips pulled back in a ghost of a smile.

"I would not imagine you would need my help in that matter," Harrington said, and Beatrice's color deepened at the implied compliment.

Lucas smiled. "No, indeed. We are looking for a murderer," he said, and found himself amused that he was uttering the same words he had found so melodramatic and alarming from Gemma only a few nights earlier. There was really no other way to put it, he thought. To keep Beatrice mostly out of the story, Lucas had decided to focus only on Nigel's murder, hoping that if Harrington could help him find the perpetrator of that deed, he would identify the blackmailer as well.

Lucas quickly filled Harrington in on what details they

knew, but realized there were not many. "I keep returning to the pocket watch," Lucas finally said

Harrington regarded him for a few moments and then asked, "Why would the villain take it? Why would he risk that one indiscretion? If he had wanted to make it seem a robbery, then he would have taken everything. If he had wanted it to seem an affair gone wrong he would have taken nothing. But he took the watch."

"Perhaps he could not help himself for some reason," Beatrice chimed in. Harrington glanced at her with approval.

"A collector," Harrington said, finishing the thought Beatrice had begun. "This could prove to be a worthwhile path to investigate, my lord."

"It seems to have potential," Lucas conceded. He felt a flutter of excitement at the possibility that they had a lead for Harrington to follow already. He glanced at the clock on the mantle. "If you will excuse us, however, we have a call to make."

• • •

Gemma scolded herself for her nervousness as she paced the room. There was no logical reason to feel this way. She did not have to actually impress Beatrice. The girl knew their engagement was false.

And yet she had taken care to wear one of her new day dresses, an aquamarine muslin that brought out the copper in her hair, or so Roz had said. It brushed against the carpet as she paced the room. Her aunt glanced up as she made a pass by her writing desk.

"Dear heart, you are giving me a headache. Please sit down," she finally said.

Gemma grimaced at her and took a seat, only to shoot up when she heard a carriage in the streets. She rushed to the window to peer out. It was Lucas. Roz looked to her for confirmation and, when Gemma nodded wordlessly, went to arrange herself on the delicate sofa for their guests. Gemma joined her, clasping her trembling fingers together so they did not give her away.

Roz patted her arm. "It's only his younger sister."

"I want to make a good impression," she answered, though she did not understand why. Roz's eyes narrowed in a concerned look before resuming a polite expression as the door opened.

Gemma rose to her feet to greet the pair as Beatrice breezed into the room.

She was the sun if Gemma had ever seen it. She had white-gold hair, cut short in ringlets that bounced happily around her face. Few with her coloring could have worn her bright buttercup-yellow muslin without looking sallow, but on her, the color glowed. Lucas was a dark storm cloud behind her, dressed in shades of gray and white. He looked quite menacing next to his sister.

Beatrice walked straight to her, clasping both of Gemma's hands in hers. "It is so nice to meet you, Miss Lancaster," she said, without waiting for the proper niceties. "I cannot thank you enough for what you are doing to help me."

Gemma's nerves could not hold out against the genuine warmth emanating from her. The difference between the siblings was stark. But they had the same emerald eyes, Gemma noticed, and the same intelligence lurking in their depths.

They sat and made small talk until Beatrice stood abruptly. "I must see your gardens," she announced. "Miss Lancaster, would you care to give me a tour?"

Gemma bit back a smile. A bit too much personality? Stuff and nonsense. This woman was spectacularly fun.

"Of course, but you must call me Gemma," she said, intertwining their arms.

The rain from the morning had cleared, and the sun had

broken through the clouds. Gemma tipped her face back, enjoying the rare occurrence.

"I know you are not doing this for me, but I must thank you again for the help you are providing Lucas with this silly matter," Beatrice began quietly, as they walked among Roz's rose bushes.

"I just hope we are able to retrieve your diary before any damage is done," Gemma said.

"Did Lucas tell you his man of affairs, Mr. George Harrington, will be looking into the matter as well?" Beatrice asked.

"He mentioned he was planning to bring him down from his estate to help," Gemma said. "I do not know much about it otherwise. Have you met him? Does he appear trustworthy?"

Beatrice tipped her head to the side, thinking. "I have only met him a handful of times. He is new to the position. Lucas says he is quite brilliant." She paused. "He is rather plain, and his fashion is from at least five years past. And quite unremarkable at that. But there's something about him. Yes, I think I trust him, though that has landed me in trouble in the past."

"Appearance is rarely an indicator of what lies beneath," Gemma commented. "And I'm sure you have learned quite a bit from your past mistakes."

They strolled in silence for a moment. "You must think me so foolish." Beatrice sighed. "I know Lucas told you enough of what happened for you to think so."

"I do not find you foolish at all." Gemma stopped walking. "I find you extremely intelligent and delightful, although I'm sure many in our society have made you feel otherwise because you are beautiful."

Beatrice blinked at her, surprised. "You are not what I expected," she finally said. "Yes, I am often treated as if I have only clouds between my ears. I have yet to find a gentleman who will actually listen to anything I say."

"The man from your diary did not?" Gemma asked, knowing she was prying to a shameful degree but unable to stop herself.

Beatrice pulled her into step again, their soft slippers sinking into the damp grass. "He made me feel small, as though he was the only one who could love me. I was all wrapped up in him. He told me I was pretty all the time, and never once listened when I talked. It was destructive, but beguiling." She glanced at Gemma. "One doesn't believe oneself capable of being caught in such a situation. Perhaps you would never be, but I was. And I did not realize it until it was too late."

"It can be destructive," Gemma said. "Love, that is."

"Yes," she agreed. "But it wasn't love that we were in. I realized that too late, as well. Thank heavens for Lucas, though. He pulled me out of my despair last year. He helped me hide my disastrous choices and recover from a bruised heart. He has always been there for me. I want nothing more for him than to find his own happiness now."

Beatrice stopped, watching Gemma expectantly with raised brows.

"Yes, he deserves to be happy," Gemma said, unsure of what Beatrice wanted.

Beatrice huffed out a little annoyed breath. "Please do not hurt him," she said. "He seems strong and unemotional all the time, but he's had a lot of responsibility in his life. Our parents did not exactly lavish us with affection. And while I had him to protect me, he had no one. All I am saying is to be careful with his heart."

Gemma was stunned. "I do not have the power to hurt him. We have only just met."

Beatrice smiled sadly.

"Please do not disappoint me," she said before turning toward a particularly beautiful lilac tree. "Tell me about this side of the garden."

Chapter Five

Gemma hid a grimace when Mr. Collin Peterson's foot landed directly on her toes once again. The man was lovely, in a nondescript way, but she deeply regretted her decision to dance with him, as she did not think she'd be able to walk again. She attempted to concentrate on what he was saying instead of the pain radiating up her leg.

"And once I had heard of our shared interest in the Egyptian civilization, I knew I must seek you out, Miss Lancaster," Mr. Peterson said as he spun her around the floor. Gemma sent an apologetic smile to the pair they'd almost barreled into before she was swept in another direction.

"Mmm," she managed, most of her attention focused on staying upright, avoiding broken bones, and directing them out of the way of the other couples.

"Have you been to the British Museum to see the Rosetta Stone? It is quite fascinating," he said, charging forward on their problematic path. "I think you would find it very thought-provoking."

"Indeed," she choked as they came perilously close to a

manservant with a tray full of lemonade. She breathed a sigh of relief as the music drifted to an end.

"Invigorating," Mr. Peterson proclaimed, with a little bow of his head. She curtseyed and tried not to limp off the floor. He patted her arm as he led her to a quiet corner. The ball was not quite a crush, though Lord Perry's wealth demanded a turnout of some sort. It was the third event she and Lucas had dropped in on that week, and she felt she was becoming an expert on the attendance of society's affairs. Anyone at the center of a scandal would garner a large crowd. Money also brought guests out of the woodwork. If the hosts had both, theirs would be one of the best-attended parties of the season.

Lord Perry's status brought out a few high-fliers, but mostly men like Mr. Peterson. Of medium height and brown hair, Peterson was one of those that could easily fade into the background of any large gathering. He was pleasant enough to chat with the dowagers or dance with the wallflowers, which tended to garner him seat-filler invitations to events out of his social league.

"May I retrieve a glass of lemonade for you?" he asked.

"Should my fiancée require anything to quench her thirst, I will provide it," a low voice growled from the shadows as a dark figure emerged.

"Lucas!" Gemma was startled to see him there. She'd thought he'd be arriving later, but happiness rushed through her at the sight of him. A lock of his midnight hair fell across his emerald eyes. Where many of the other men donned bright frippery to peacock for the ladies, Lucas stood out with his head-to-toe black.

He is so solid.

In the past few days, they'd had to rely only on each other as they rifled through studies and libraries in search of answers. The trust one gained when standing guard while one's partner in crime broke into a safe was vast.

"Of course, my lord," Peterson stammered, glancing at Gemma. She took pity on him and patted his arm.

Lucas eyed her hand on Peterson's jacket. She wondered at his annoyance with the man. Although she was realizing Lucas was not one for society affairs, he was on generally good terms with many of the people who inhabited—or in Peterson's case, orbited—the higher levels of society.

Could it be that he was jealous?

She immediately scoffed at the notion. That would mean he had developed some sort of *tendre* for her, which was impossible.

She strove to break the tension between the two men. "Thank you both, but I do not require any lemonade. Mr. Peterson, I very much enjoyed our discussion about Egypt, and the dance was lovely, thank you," she said with a polite smile, not quite meaning it. As harmless as he was as a fellow guest, she couldn't foresee wanting to re-experience their whirlwind on the dance floor anytime soon.

"I believe my fiancée needs some air. Pray excuse us," Lucas said, with barely a curt nod toward Peterson. He placed a hand at the curve of her spine to direct her toward the doors, and her nerves tightened at the way he touched her so easily, as well as the idea of being alone with him.

"You were rude to poor Mr. Peterson, my lord," she chastised as they wove their way through the brightly shimmering jewels of the *ton*. Fake laughter rang out amongst the clinking of glasses and the buzz of gossip. She nodded to a few acquaintances as they breezed past.

"He'll live," Lucas grumbled. They'd made it to the French doors that opened onto a terrace and a surprisingly large lawn in the back, considering they were in the middle of London. There was a small gazebo off to the side, shrouded in rose bushes. Lucas steered her toward it once they were outside. Except for the times when they were sneaking around in studies, they had not spent any time alone together since they'd begun their ruse of an engagement.

Would he try to kiss her again? What would she do if he did?

The cool air nipped at her bare arms, and she shivered. Lucas shrugged out of his coat and wrapped it about her shoulders; she burrowed down into it as his smell engulfed her. Unlike the heavily perfumed society set in the ballroom they'd just left, his smell was earthier, redolent of sandalwood and something else she couldn't quite place.

They reached the darkened corner of the garden. The fragrance of spring was all around them. Gemma loved this time of year, as the gloom of winter was chased out by the hope of new life. Even the nights with a bite still in the air were invigorating to the senses. She hadn't realized how stifling the ballroom had become until they'd stepped outside.

She took a seat, but Lucas remained leaning against the entrance of the gazebo. The darkness and isolation settled around them, even though the noise and chaos were not far away. They were in their own little world. The danger of it, the promise of it, was exciting.

"You have a plan, my lord?" Gemma asked when he did not volunteer it on his own. Lucas glanced back at the lights spilling from the house.

"The library opens up onto the terrace, so it should be easy enough to slip inside." He paused. "I think I should search it alone this time."

Gemma shot up. "You say that every time, and I am growing weary of arguing with you. You know that if we are discovered it is safer to say we were searching for a quiet place to be alone. If you are discovered, they will suspect the truth."

"Are you worried about me?" he asked.

"Of course," she said, annoyed with the question. "You're my partner in this investigation. I must look out for you."

Lucas gazed off into the hushed night. "You're not like most women."

That stung.

Embarrassment heated her cheeks. She hadn't been raised like the ladies of the *ton*. When they'd been practicing needlepoint, she'd been learning from Uncle Artie how to fight with a knife; when they'd been taught the art of wielding a fan to flirt, she'd been learning survival skills in case she was ever lost in a tropical locale. It had never bothered her before. But now part of her wished she was more like the cultured ladies in the ballroom. They would never demand to be included in a crime against a peer of the realm. She made to push past him when his arms shot out, encircling her waist.

"Wait," he voice was urgent. "Gemma, wait. That was not a criticism. The farthest thing from it."

She searched his eyes and saw the truth there. Only then did she relax, feeling a bit foolish over her behavior.

"Uncle Artie was an explorer, you see," she said, wanting to explain herself to him. "In his younger years he'd take off on whatever ship was in port. He went to the Indies, Africa, the tropics, everywhere. He was the younger son, so he never expected to inherit, and his brother was generous and paid for most of Artie's adventures.

"When Nigel's mother died, Artie began taking him along, until they ended up in an alley in China, surrounded by criminals with knives. Nigel was four at the time. They escaped, but it caused Artie to reassess his travels. He ended up settling back in the north, to wait until Nigel got older—so that he could teach him the skills he'd need to live abroad. And then I came along and squelched that plan."

"It's not your fault he settled down, Gemma," Lucas said. She shouldn't be surprised that he had focused on the thing that haunted her the most. The guilt used to roil her stomach. There had been times when she was younger where she felt the need to prove herself worthy of her uncle's time. He'd given up so much just to raise her, and she would do anything to make him proud. "He had no business traipsing around dangerous locales with a young child, let alone two."

"I know. I tell myself he was happy raising us in that old rambling country mansion. He taught us all sorts of things, although none of them are particularly applicable to navigating society." She gave a rueful laugh. "Except perhaps the art of deception."

"Indeed," he agreed. "You want to travel?"

He really was one of the most perceptive gentlemen she knew

"I do, yes. I've read about so many fascinating cultures and civilizations. It would be lovely to be able to see them in person."

"Have you enjoyed the academic societies in London?" Lucas asked. "There are plenty you could get involved with in some capacity."

"Yes. I have found some of them quite stimulating. I was just talking with Mr. Peterson about that before he whirled us around the dance floor. He enjoys travel with a bent toward the historical. He told me about a lecture tomorrow with the Ancient Civilizations Society that I might find interesting."

"Did he?" His arms dropped to his side as he glanced toward Perry's house. "I think we should make our move," he said, an abrupt subject change. "We've delayed long enough."

She sighed as he led her from the gazebo. She refused to ponder if the sudden chill coursing through her was due more to disappointment, or the loss of his arms holding her.

• • •

It wasn't so much that Lucas had been a spy, but that he'd been tapped for favors by the government. He knew a surprising amount about chemistry, and during his year on the Continent following his schooling at Oxford, he'd managed to pick up a few useful skills that served him well. Now, as his boots sunk into the soft grass of Perry's garden, he was grateful and impressed that Gemma seemed to have similar finesse in the sneaking-about business. They were just two shadows slipping across the lawn.

They made it to the library's terrace doors, and he tested the handle. Unlocked. Gemma was close behind him, and they were quickly inside. She immediately crossed to the heavy door that was the main entrance of the study, pressed her ear against the solid wood, and tried to listen for any surprises. In the past few days they'd established a routine. Lucas trusted her, and so put her out of his mind while he scanned the room.

Something was off about the study—for one thing, there were only a few books on the shelves. Lucas knew that Perry didn't spend much time in town, preferring his country seat in the south. The desk was a delicate thing, with intricately carved flowers on skinny legs. The furniture was light and feminine. This wasn't Perry's room, he could feel it. Lucas thought of Lady Perry, a vivacious and charming hostess who spent most of the season in London. This was hers, it must be. If they were to find anything on Perry it wouldn't be in here.

He did a quick pass over common spots but quickly confirmed his suspicions. There wasn't even a safe in the room.

He looked over to see Gemma studying his movements. "There's nothing here," she said, more a statement than a question. He shook his head anyway.

"I need to get into his bedroom," Lucas said and braced himself. He needed her not to come with him, but knew it would be near impossible to convince her to wait in the ballroom. The scandal that would emerge if they were found in a bedroom together would be impossible to come back from. Let alone the safety risks if Lord Perry or any of his guards caught them in the act. If Perry was the blackmailer, he'd proven that he had no compunction about killing witnesses who got in the way.

"I believe there's a set of servants' stairs back toward the kitchen. I saw them when I pretended to go to the ladies' withdrawing room," she said without flinching. He found himself reluctantly admiring her courage. She never wavered, no matter how daring the task. Still, allowing her to come with him could be disastrous.

"Gemma, I need you to stay downstairs while I do this. Worrying about you will be a distraction that we cannot afford," he said, attempting to appeal to her logical side. For all that she wanted to be an equal partner, she would also listen to reason.

"Well, I suggest you get past that," she said, already reaching for the door. Before he could react, she'd stepped out into the hallway and headed toward the back of the house.

"Bloody hell," Lucas muttered, and hurried to follow.

• • •

The hallway was dim, as guests were not intended to be this far back toward the kitchens. Gemma decided speed took precedence over stealth. If she was stopped at a brisk walk, she could say she was looking for the withdrawing room. Being found skulking in the shadows would take a lot more explanation

She heard a soft scuff of boot on carpet and trusted it was Lucas coming up behind her. For a brief moment she had worried he would stew in the library. Men so often became stubborn when they didn't get their way with the ladies in their lives.

Not that he would leave her to snoop around by herself. He was a gentleman to his fingertips. But while he meant well, in his own overbearing, protective way, he needed to get it through his hard head that they were partners in this. Working together would yield far better results. It's what was best for the case.

She glanced back as she started up the servants' stairs. He was close, his features made starker by the sporadic candlelight. When he glared up at her she simply smiled and continued. Short of making a scene, there was nothing he could do.

At this point, they'd have to be more careful. She tried to step lightly, but every few stairs the wood would creak and settle. Somehow Lucas didn't seem to be having the same problem—he moved with the grace of a hunting cat, with nary a groan slipping from the trodden wood. She felt both jealous and impressed.

Could he hear her heart racing, she wondered as they reached the top. If they were caught, there would be serious consequences. She stopped, less sure of her movements now that she'd reached the upper hallway.

Lucas laid a hand at the small of her back, and the warmth seeped in like comfort. His lips grazed her ears. "We need to move. Now."

The upper floor was well lit, leaving them no safe place to linger. They needed to find Perry's bedroom immediately.

They opened the first door to a small, Spartan room they didn't even need to investigate. Not his. They moved on to the next one.

She let out a hum when they walked through the door. The room was large, with a heavy dark bed in the center. The wallpaper was deep burgundy, and there was a solid leather reading chair near the fireplace, a thick book put aside on the low table beside it.

Lucas scanned the room, as well, with a satisfied expression. They were in agreement, it seemed: they'd found

Perry's room.

Lucas crossed to the paintings on the wall, and she watched as he checked behind each, a move she'd now seen him complete many times. He didn't look at her when he finished, just shook his head. She swung in a slow circle, thinking of what she'd learned in the past couple of weeks and looking for the hiding place. Her eyes landed on an old globe. She assessed that it would be big enough to hold a small safe. She locked gazes with Lucas and nodded her head in its direction. He glanced over, eyes narrowed. He strode to it and prodded the equator.

A low click broke the sharp silence. She tried not to look smug when he pushed open the top half of the globe and revealed the safe. Lucas dipped into his pocket to retrieve his lock picks and went to work. She loved watching him this way. She let her eyes trace the hard line of his jaw, set in concentration. His five o'clock shadow made him look more dangerously attractive, and she ached to stroke his face and then run her hands through his thick shock of hair. She thought of him leaning closer, his lips seeking hers, and then jolted herself out of her fantasy. This was not the place, she laughed in her own head. For heaven's sake, they were in the middle of Lord Perry's bedroom.

He exhaled once, pocketed his tools, and eased open the door of the safe. She hurried over to peer inside and narrowed her eyes at the contents: pound notes stacked from top to bottom in two rows, a small bag of jewels, an expensive-looking gold pocket watch, and a leather journal. Her heart jolted at the sight of the timepiece. She took it with an unsteady hand, holding it up to the low light. The piece was old and intricate, but it was not Nigel's. She shook her head, replaced the watch, and reached for the journal while Lucas palmed the bag of diamonds.

There were only four lines written in the whole book:

locations, dates, and amounts of money stood out starkly against the white page. Lucas replaced the diamonds before looking over her shoulder. She felt his entire body tense when he saw what was written.

"It's the house party where Nigel was…where Nigel was shot," she whispered, and she traced a finger over the words, her stomach pitching as if she'd been punched. She tried to collect herself. "Do you recognize any of these locations?"

He nodded once and pointed to an address in an area close to the docks. "I had to leave the payment there after the first letter."

"You think he's the blackmailer?"

"This does not look good for him either way. Come, we must go. We've pushed our luck quite enough tonight."

"Yes," she said, memorizing the information to write down later, then replacing the journal. "And we finally have a lead."

She couldn't deny the excitement that rushed over her, potent even through the stab of pain at thinking about Nigel's death. This was the first time she'd felt like they were truly headed in the right direction, rather than on a fool's errand.

Lucas closed the globe and did a final sweep of the room. She knew he wasn't looking for another hiding place, but rather making sure they hadn't left anything disturbed. She'd watched him perform this ritual after each search, but it was especially important tonight. If Perry thought someone was nosing around, he might destroy any evidence and flee town, and then they'd be nowhere.

Nigel's killer. Lord Perry could be Nigel's killer. They might have solved the case. Could this really be over? So soon? Lost in thought, she didn't listen for footsteps before opening the door to the hallway and stepped directly into the path of a man. Surprise stole her breath.

He was a hulking brute, with short dark hair and beady

eyes. Between his stature and the fact that he wasn't dressed for the ball, she had to assume he was one of Perry's guards Lucas had warned her about. His eyes narrowed, darting between her and the door. Recovering, she shut it with as much nonchalance as she could muster, sending up a quick prayer that Lucas would realize she was better off without him dashing to the rescue.

"Oh, thank heavens, I am so turned about. Could you help me, sir?" she asked, flashing him big innocent eyes.

"What were you doing on this floor?" His voice was harsh and unrelenting. She nibbled her lip and realized he wasn't going to buy the lost lady routine. She pivoted back and burst into noisy, ugly tears.

"He's meeting…with…her," she sobbed. "I just…just…know it!"

The guard took a small step in retreat, so she pushed on harder.

"He snuck out of the ball." She gulped in air. "I am…so…humiliated." She added a wail to the last word to really drive it home. "Just let me be, sir. Please."

"You're not s'posed to be up here, miss," the guard said gruffly, looking unsure what to do with his hands.

She clutched her stomach in defeat. Was she overdoing it? In her experience, men tended to think women were always on the verge of a hysterical breakdown, so she might be safe.

"I'm so foolish," she whispered. "I thought if I caught him… I don't know what I would have done but…" She trailed off. "I am sorry."

This was the moment to make a move. She rushed by him, a whirl of tears and emotions. As she fled down the stairs, she sent up a prayer that Lucas had found a good hiding spot in Perry's bedroom. Since she didn't sense the brute behind her, she figured he was checking there next. She heard music and laughter as she neared the ballroom, and she stopped running. Once she got to the edge of the crowd she slipped in between a marquis and a viscount and lost herself in the press of bodies.

Her heart was in her throat. What if Lucas was discovered? The guard could be carrying a pistol. Dire thoughts chased each other in her head, so when a hand reached out and grabbed her bare arm, she almost shrieked. She managed to suppress it to an unladylike squeak, which caused a few of those closest to her to glance her way.

"Brava, my dear. That was quite an act," Lucas growled in her ear. She was so relieved that he was all right that she sagged back against his chest for a moment. His solidness soothed her nerves. "We need to leave, immediately."

"Indeed," she said. "I believe we have had quite enough excitement for this evening." And she slipped into the shadows with him.

Chapter Six

"There he is!" Gemma leaned forward to peep out the window of the carriage. Lucas smiled at her excitement and dipped his head to catch a view of Perry leaving the bookshop. It was on a busy thoroughfare. Multiple groups of ladies milled about on the pavements in their daywear. Lucas double-tapped on the ceiling of the carriage, a prearranged signal to his coachman to pull into the stream of conveyances. They should be able to keep pace with Perry, as the streets were clogged enough to slow them down to walking speed.

Lucas could see the tall man, just ahead, dressed in black with a bundle of books under one arm. He had a jaunty step, and he maneuvered through the crowds with ease.

"We still may not discover anything from this, my dear," he cautioned. She had settled back against the velvet cushions, but enthusiasm still lit her face.

"I know, but he will slip up eventually," she said. "We just have to wait for him to make a mistake."

"Or for us to," Lucas said. She had far too little regard for her own skin, in his opinion. When she'd walked out into the hallway the night before, his heart had frozen in his chest. He'd listened, helpless, as she confronted the armed guard by herself. He hadn't enjoyed the sensation, and he certainly had no desire to repeat it.

"You're such a ray of light, my lord," she teased him. Then her face fell. "Oh, bother."

He leaned forward to find the cause of her consternation, and caught sight of Perry headed into a distinguished-looking townhouse.

"His club," he muttered. "We'll be here a while, I'm sure."

"Hmph," she said, crossing her arms like a petulant child. He was amused by her show of impatience. "Well, we might as well make use of it."

His mind immediately jumped to their kiss in her study. He hardened as he thought of her soft lips under his, the touch of their tongues, her body pressed against him. He cleared his throat and shifted, trying to retain control. It was not like him to lose his head to passion in the middle of the day.

"To discuss the case," she said when he remained silent.

"Yes, of course," he somehow croaked out.

"My lord, may I ask a question?"

"You may, if you start calling me Lucas," he answered, pleased with the blush that painted her cheeks.

"How many payments have you made to our villain?" she asked, sidestepping his remark.

"Two," he said shortly, annoyed that he'd had to concede even that much.

"May I make an observation?" she asked, and he arched his brow. She obviously had something to say and had asked for his permission only to humor him. "Right, yes, well. You don't seem the type to give in to blackmail. What I mean to say is, I am surprised you paid anything at all."

"You think less of me because of it?" He had battled long against his nature before conceding it was the only choice.

Beatrice's future was at stake. He could not let pride stand in the way.

"No. Just curious is all. And if I were picking blackmail victims, you would not be first on the list. Or even on my list. I would immediately assume you would not play the game," she said, and he saw where she was going with her line of thought.

"So, why me?" he summed up.

"Precisely," she said, looking contemplative. "You would think there'd be easier prey in society."

"I believe part of it is that the blackmailer focused on Beatrice," he said. "If I were the actual target I would not pay anything. But if her secret gets out, she will be completely ostracized. The only marriage that she'd be able to make—if it were possible at all—would be to a fortune hunter I could buy off."

"Yes, she would be ruined in the eyes of society," she agreed. "You would go to lengths for her that you would never consider going to for yourself. And it's not about the family's honor as it would be for some. You truly care about her happiness. That is a rare quality amongst the gentlemen of the *ton*."

Lucas remained quiet while he watched her turn something over in her head. He liked the way her quick mind worked, the way she challenged and dissected the information she received.

"You are known to be stubborn and arrogant," she remarked with a matter-of-fact wave of her hand. He smirked. "But everyone knows you are protective of your sister. I suppose it would not be too much of a gamble to assume you would go out of your way to make sure her reputation remained unblemished."

She paused for a moment, and he knew she was parsing her next thought. "However. Everyone also knows you to be quite intelligent and in possession of considerable power. It would be like poking a sleeping lion."

"Perhaps the villain is not as adept as you are at gauging situations, my dear," he said. She might be onto something, though.

Why would the blackmailer target his family? It could have been a crime of opportunity, a random peep into a young lady's bedroom. But the chances that a villain would happen to find incriminating evidence by luck seemed unlikely. And that meant he must have known in advance that there would be something to find. Yet, even so, there was no reason to go after Beatrice.

"My God, Gemma," he muttered, floored not only by the realization, but that he hadn't thought of it earlier. "He's after me."

...

Beatrice had not needed the little bottle of perfume. Or the ivory-bone fan. Or the four bonnets she had sent back to the carriage with her long-suffering groom. She had not needed any of it, she thought as she strolled down Bond Street, her maid a discreet distance behind. She would not want to see Lucas's face when he received the bills for such frivolous expenses.

After Lucas had left to collect Gemma so they could follow Perry, Beatrice had lapsed into a sulky, bad-tempered mood. When she snapped at one of the maids—a sweet, shy girl new to the household—for dropping a teacup on the drawing room floor, she'd known she had to get out of the house. She had no business taking her frustrations out on innocents.

So she had gone shopping and tried to feel better about herself, but while usually each purchase would have lifted her spirits, instead it was like rubbing salt in the wound. She wished she could help with the investigation. It was all her fault, and she had been left waiting around.

Lucas kept her apprised of recent developments, but when she asked to be included, he had essentially patted her on the head and told her not to worry. He had offered for her to work with Mr. Harrington as a consolation prize, but she had so far heard nothing from that corner. Perhaps Mr. Harrington also thought it was too dangerous for a silly girl like her. It did not seem too dangerous for Miss Lancaster, however, Beatrice thought caustically. Then she chastised herself. Even she did not want to be around herself at the moment.

She wished she'd never laid eyes on Ralph Stockwood, Viscount Wallace. If she had not been introduced to him during her fateful coming-out ball, she would never have needed Lucas to fix her mistakes for her. Ralph, with his strawberry blond locks, which he wore fashionably curled, and his sparkling, bright green eyes. He'd always smiled at her as though they shared a secret. Even when they first met. She did not know why she'd taken complete leave of her senses when he smiled at her so, but she had. And now everyone around her was paying for it.

She was so lost in her dark thoughts that she almost did not see the gentleman stepping out of the shop directly in front of her. She stopped abruptly to avoid a collision and shot him a haughty glare before brightening when she recognized him.

"Mr. Harrington!" she exclaimed with a bit more enthusiasm than the encounter strictly merited. The gentleman in question, who had been walking away without a thought as to whom he may have trampled, turned back at his name. His clothes were the color of dirt on a road after a long spell without rain. He was only slightly taller than she, though he seemed solidly built. His hair was brown without a lick of blond or red to make it interesting. His eyes, though… His eyes were in fact remarkable, she noticed as she came closer. They were a very light hazel brown, flecked with yellow and green. They were inscrutable. She could not tell if he was happy or upset to see her there.

But, of course, he was a gentleman to his toes, so he bowed and greeted her.

She glanced at the door he'd emerged from and clasped her hands to her bosom. It was a pocket watch shop. "Oh, you are working on the case," she said excitedly, then glanced around to ensure the passersby had not heard her. His lips tipped up in the slightest of smiles.

"Yes," he confirmed. A man of few words. That was fine with her, as she was a woman of many.

"You are trying to compile a list of those in society who are known collectors of antique pocket watches?" she guessed, starting down the street again. He fell into step beside her before casting an approving glance her way.

"Yes, that is exactly it. Clever of you to realize," he said, and she warmed. So few gentlemen ever took the time to appreciate anything other than her looks.

"It is the smart path to take," she said. "It would require an enthusiast to recognize the value of an antique piece in the heat of the moment, and be compelled to take it even if it might jeopardize his anonymity."

"In my experience, collectors tend to be ruthless and single-minded in pursuit of their obsession," he agreed.

"Were you successful in your inquiries?" she asked with a nod back to the shop behind them.

If she had not been watching his face closely, she would have missed the imperceptible tightening around his mouth and eyes.

"I was not," he told her, confirming her theory. "I have built a small list but need more information. The owner was unable to help in the slightest."

"You will persevere," she said. She was confident in that. She had never before met someone who radiated the level of competence Mr. Harrington did. She had no doubt he would discover what he was searching for. She had a moment of unease. The man was intelligent, determined, and perceptive. It would not take him long to work out that they were pursuing more than just Nigel Thorne's murderer. And then he would find out. The appreciation in his eyes would turn to disgust when he discovered her secret.

"Are you off to another shop?" she asked.

"I am, yes." He glanced at her, his hazel eyes narrowing incredulously. "But surely you cannot wish to join me on such a dull undertaking. It is too fine a day for a young lady such as yourself to wander in and out of watchmakers' shops."

"Nonsense! I insist," Beatrice said, with a sunny smile few men could resist. He shook his head at her, but he did not attempt to dissuade her further. He probably assumed it was merely a girlish whim, she thought.

They continued on in silence, but her sulky mood, which had refused to budge with her extravagant purchases, had dramatically improved in the past five minutes.

• • •

"It does seem like a possibility that he particularly targeted you," Gemma spoke as gently as she could. She couldn't blame him for being shocked. The idea had been fermenting in her mind for a few days, so she'd had time to get accustomed to it. Impulsively, she slid over to his side of the carriage. She laid a comforting hand on his leg and patted it, feeling awkward. "It will be all right. We shall figure it out."

He glanced down at her fingers on his dark breeches and smiled. He seemed amused by her soothing gestures.

Embarrassed, she made to move her hand, but he covered it with his own, trapping hers against his thigh. Ignoring the warmth of his leg through his breeches, she tried to press on with her questioning. "Do you have any enemies?"

"Plenty, I am sure. I will have to think on this." his voice was dismissive, as if he suddenly didn't want to talk about it. Her suspicions were confirmed when he turned hooded eyes on her at the same time the pad of his thumb found and then stroked the sensitive dip in her palm. He wanted to distract her.

And it's working.

She tried to tug her hand away in a manner that wouldn't be obvious. When that didn't work, she shifted so that she wouldn't be tempted to lean into the cloying warmth of his solid body. His smile told her she wasn't being as subtle as she hoped.

"How many enemies do *you* have, my dear?" he asked, his voice silken, his thumb continuing that maddening pattern against her hand. There was something underneath the question, something persuasive that traced shivers along her spine.

"None," she whispered. Her voice had deserted her along with her common sense. She cleared her throat hoping to regain both. "Of course."

"Of course," he murmured, bringing her palm to his lips. The gentle touch was all it took to set her nerves aflame. This time when she pulled her hand back, he let her go. Amusement glinted in his eyes. "No broken hearts along the way?"

"Oh, a few dozen here or there," she replied, though her voice was still breathy. Not quite the carefree flirt she'd wanted to portray. *Back to the case. That was safe territory.*

"So as to the people who could be after you…" she prompted.

"I'm far more interested in the beaux you have left

mournful in your wake." His fingers trapped one of the loose curls that bounced around her face, sliding the strands between the pads.

Maybe he needed time. Time to think and time to digest. She could relate to that. She was stubborn, but she wouldn't press him. That's what partners did, she thought happily. They distracted or listened or prodded or helped. And when necessary, they backed off.

It was a nice feeling, that. Being needed. As a partner. She decided she wouldn't overthink it for now.

He wants banter? We'll banter.

"They were legion. But they were all honorable gentlemen—unlike yourself, I may add."

He gasped his faux outrage. "Are you saying my behavior is anything less than exemplary?"

She slid her gaze to the fingers that were still toying with her hair.

His free hand flew to his heart. She stifled a wholly unladylike giggle at his shocked and offended expression. "I demand satisfaction for this insult. Pistols at dawn," he roared into the swaying carriage.

She wrinkled her brow. "I believe, as the challenged party, I get to choose the weapon."

"A thousand apologies, my lady." He cut a small bow in her direction. "Would you rather it be slow and tortuous?"

"I am not cruel," she said loftily. "I can take mercy on you if you so humble yourself before me."

"What if *I* like it slow and tortuous?" he murmured.

Heat burned in her cheeks and in her belly. She may be an innocent, but she knew he was no longer talking about their fake duel. She wished she could be audacious and meet his gaze, and smile and flirt, but she couldn't quite muster up the courage. She faltered instead, and he rumbled with a low chuckle. "Is it just a glance then? You could fell a man with your eyes alone, my dear."

He wasn't letting her escape the tension that had fluttered to life between them. She felt it, like a palpable thing, almost as if she could reach out and touch the fire that burned in the spaces they didn't fill.

"Oh posh," she laughed, trying to douse it. It was getting harder to get air into her lungs; her breath kept catching in her throat. She'd wanted to distract him, but she hadn't quite pictured it going this far. It was the middle of the day for heaven's sake.

"Or your…mouth. Is that your weapon of choice?" His gaze dropped to her mouth as she wet her suddenly parched lips.

"I have been told it can be quite savage," she quipped, though with more bravado than arrogance. There was something dangerous in his answering smile.

"Shall we put it to the test?"

Before she could answer, he pulled her into his lap. She didn't resist. Couldn't think to resist. All she could think about was their kiss in the library. She wanted that again. Wanted his lips on hers, that slick rush of heat when his tongue pushed into her mouth. If that made her a wanton, well, she was finding it harder and harder to care. It wasn't as if she were planning to find a husband when this was over.

He tipped her chin up so that his gaze locked on hers, and the black of his pupils all but swallowed up the color in his eyes.

This is what I've been waiting for.

The thought was gone almost as soon as it flitted across her mind. It was preposterous. She hadn't been waiting for anything. Not for the way she felt when pressed against him. Not for the heat that pooled at her center. Certainly not for the way his finger traced along her cheekbone, making her feel precious and vulnerable in his arms.

She sucked in air as his lips finally lowered to hers, and she willed all the chatter from her head. She just wanted to feel.

The brush of his mouth against hers. The pressure of his tongue. The bump of teeth.

His hands cradled her hips as she shifted and settled, and his fingers dug into the soft flesh there. Her own fingers found the nape of his neck before burying themselves in his thick mass of hair.

He withdrew and she chased, and she was momentarily amazed at her own daring as she became a participant instead of just a willing spectator to the kiss.

It was only when his thumb brushed the underside of her breast that she pulled back, gasping.

His head fell back against the cushions, his eyes closed. It looked like he was in pain. But she thought she might look like that, too, if she could see herself in a looking glass. Silence filled the carriage, and she didn't know how to break it other than with her small, shuttering breaths as she tried to regain control of her faculties.

She moved to scramble off his lap, and only then did he grunt and release her from his embrace. It seemed more an act of self-preservation than an attempt to help her restore her modesty. Another minute passed before he finally opened his eyes.

She almost wished he hadn't. She looked away from what she saw there. It was overwhelming.

"Are you all right, my dear?" His voice was rocks and gravel compared to what it usually was.

She nodded, not sure she could form words at the moment.

He was about to say more, but his attention was caught by something outside the carriage window.

"Bloody, bloody hell," Lucas cursed. Gemma followed his gaze and saw Perry heading into the park. Just then, there was a double knock on the partition. He flicked his chin up toward the sound. "That is the signal if we cannot follow in the carriage."

He made a few adjustments to his clothing, then turned to survey her with a critical eye. She resisted the urge to pat her hair. He gave a little nod of approval.

"Would you care for a walk in the park?" he asked without a trace of irony.

"It seems like a beautiful day for it," she managed to respond.

He smirked and pushed open the carriage door, vaulting down and holding up a hand to help her out. She adjusted her skirts one last time before she stepped from the carriage.

She looked around for Perry, worried they'd lost him in the mist. She caught a glimpse of his hat and was thankful the man was so tall. She took off after him, but Lucas nabbed her hand and pulled her back.

"We can't just march right up behind him, my dear." He laughed and tucked her hand into the crook of his elbow. "We are an affianced couple taking an afternoon stroll in the park."

She pursed her lips in impatience, but conceded his point. They should strive to appear natural. The pebblcs bit into her soft shoes as they started into the park. Even with the poor weather, ladies and gentleman dotted the expanse. If one let fog deter them from outside activities in London, she supposed no one would ever go outside.

"Do you enjoy London, my lord?" she asked, trying to think of what she would say if they really were an affianced couple on an afternoon stroll in the park. Something that was not about what they had just shared in the carriage. He seemed recovered from the experience, she thought with a slight pout. She wasn't entirely sure she was, though.

Lucas furrowed his brow. "I do in some ways. I enjoy my club and the intellectual pursuits the city has to offer. I even enjoy Drury Lane and Vauxhall Gardens."

"Oh, I would love to visit Vauxhall," she said. She'd heard such wondrous things about the pleasure gardens.

"I shall take you to them," he promised.

They walked a moment in silence before she prompted him to continue. "But…"

"I miss the solitude of my country home. I would ride the land every morning, and there are few things that compare to a crisp English morning when you are the only soul about. There are too many people in London. It makes it hard to breathe sometimes." He paused, looking momentarily embarrassed by how much he'd shared.

"I crave the quiet of the country, as well. It is a bit freer there. You do not have to consider every move you make or thing you do. Sometimes you can just *be*, and I haven't found that in London." He glanced at her, his eyes soft. "Do not mistake me, though. I adore many things about the city. It is quite stimulating," she said in a rush. Her face felt flushed and hot.

He murmured a low sound and inclined his head to two older ladies walking toward them. The women acknowledged them, and Gemma glanced over her shoulder to see them put their heads together and chatter.

"People are perplexed as to why you are with me," Gemma stated. Lucas looked confused but then followed her gaze.

"People will gossip about anything in the *ton*. It is their favorite pastime," he said easily.

"It's more than that. A wealthy, handsome lord announces his engagement to a woman of low rank and less beauty—a peculiar bluestocking at that. It's a wonder no one has questioned its authenticity to our faces," she mused. She was more entertained than insulted by the whole matter. Of course, people would think it strange that she could land herself an earl. She was sure in clubs across the city there were bets about a possible pregnancy or secret inheritance. Why else would Lucas Stone, Earl of Winchester, lower himself to make such an unsuitable match?

Lucas turned to her and gripped her shoulders. She met his eyes and found his expression fierce. "If anyone dares say anything to you, you will tell me immediately."

"Oh, I do not think anyone would say anything to me directly," she said hastily, a bit taken aback by his ferocity.

"Gemma," he said, his voice low and deadly serious. "Promise me, if you hear anything, you will tell me. I'll take care of it."

"I promise," she assured him. He let go of her arms and fell into step beside her once more. "We will soon give them a great deal more to talk about anyway."

"What do you mean?" he asked.

"When you cry off. The *ton* will be aflutter. I'm sure many people will say they knew all along. Busybodies, the lot of them."

He shrugged dismissively.

She tried not to think about never seeing Lucas again. She'd gotten strangely used to having him around. She would miss the thrill that shot through her whenever she saw him, their engaging conversations…and, increasingly, their passionate interludes. But that prospect was still a ways in the future. They still had a blackmailer-murderer to catch. She refocused on Perry, who was a bit in front of them. He did not seem to be meandering through the park; rather, his purposeful strides gave him the air of a man on a mission.

She was about to redirect their conversation toward Perry—Lucas seemed uncomfortable talking about their false engagement—when the sound of rapid hoof beats interrupted them. She stepped a bit to the side to make sure they were not in the way of the rider.

"Miss Lancaster!" The man atop the muddy brown horse called out in excitement. She felt a jolt of confusion at the voice's confident familiarity and turned to peer up at the rider.

"Mr. Peterson, how lovely to see you," she said once she recognized him.

"Indeed," he said with a jovial smile as he slid off his horse to walk with them. "I spotted you down the way and thought I must come see if you've read the most recent edition of John Calderon's series in the Times. He wrote it from South America."

"I did read that," she said, her delight in having found someone who shared her interest in faraway cultures temporarily distracting her from the true purpose of their stroll. "The Mayan civilization there is utterly fascinating, don't you think?"

He nodded, excited, before launching into a rendition of Calderon's piece, replete with hand gestures and exclamations. He was such a dear, but as she'd read the piece already, her mind drifted to how far Perry was getting out of view and then to the brooding man beside her. He had held out longer than she expected.

Lucas interrupted Peterson midsentence. "You will excuse us, Peterson. My fiancée and I must continue on."

Peterson stumbled to a stop, hands spread, his face frozen in a moment of bafflement before he shook it off. "Ah, of course, my apologies for keeping you so long. I may have gotten carried away in my excitement. Winchester." He curtly nodded at Lucas. "I would be delighted to continue this conversation sometime in the near future, Gem—er, Miss Lancaster."

Gemma could feel the thrum of Lucas's frustration as he grasped her arm tighter. "I am afraid our schedule is quite packed for the foreseeable future, and such a conversation may prove impossible. Come, my dear." Lucas strode forward along the path without a backward glance and dragged her along with him. Gemma cast a quick, apologetic smile at Mr. Peterson, whose normally mild face bore a strange expression.

"Lucas! That was unbelievably rude to poor Mr. Peterson," she hissed as soon as they were out of earshot.

"You will not talk to him again, Gemma," he growled, not looking at her.

"Excuse me?" She struggled against his grasp, but he was far too strong for her. "You cannot dictate with whom I have conversation, my lord. You are not my husband." She was reaching her breaking point with his high-handedness. She knew he had a stubborn, autocratic side, but enough was enough. She would not be bullied.

"No," he said, stopping and swinging around to stand in front of her. He towered over her, but she met him toe-to-toe. "I am your fiancé."

"*Fictional* fiancé," she corrected. She felt her jaw clench and she wondered if she'd lost her mind. Here they were, trying to blend into their surroundings and instead they were making a huge scene in front of the beau monde.

They stared each other down for several beats before he broke the gaze. "This is not the time or place. Come along."

...

He'd never met such a hardheaded, stubborn woman in his life.

He guided her toward one of the circuitous paths leading to the edges of Hyde Park. He'd kept an eye on which direction Perry had headed.

He didn't know why Gemma couldn't see that Peterson was drooling over her like a lovesick puppy. She was too naive regarding the predators of the *ton*, no matter how mild-mannered they appeared. It was his duty to keep her safe while they were on this case, whether it was from a blackmailer or a lecherous rogue in sheep's clothing.

It wasn't jealousy. It wasn't.

They didn't talk any further as they pushed their way through the growing mist. By this point, they'd left many of their fellow park-goers behind. Droplets dotted his face, and the hair on the back of his neck rose. He could not see enough in front of him to comfortably continue forward with Gemma.

"I believe it's time to turn back, my dear. We shall try again tomorrow," he said as firmly as possible. He was not surprised when she argued.

"But we've come so far. Should we not continue a bit farther to see if we can find him again?"

"No. It is time to leave."

"Actually," a voice purred from behind a cluster of trees, "I believe it is time for the two of you to explain what you are doing following me." Gemma gasped as Lord Perry emerged like a specter from the fog—with a pistol pointed at Lucas. "And I believe you should do it quickly."

Chapter Seven

Lucas took a swift step in front of Gemma, placing himself between her and the pistol, and put his hands up and clearly in Perry's view.

"We weren't following you, my friend," Lucas said. He calculated that he wouldn't be able to reach Perry before he could shoot. At least Gemma would be able to escape before Perry could draw a second weapon.

"Do not try that, Winchester. I heard you and your lady talking. You were trying to find me." Perry's hand was as steady as his voice. "What is your purpose?"

Lucas weighed the options. If this man was the blackmailer, there was a distinct possibility that he'd killed before and seemed to have no compunction about it. However, if he were the extortionist, it was not the most likely scenario for him to plead ignorance on why they were following him. He imagined that confrontation would have looked rather different.

He decided to gamble that he was correct.

"Are you by any chance being blackmailed?" Lucas asked. Perry's face turned white. Certainty settled over Lucas in the same way it used to when he dealt with the best liars in the world. Perry was not the villain, but a fellow victim.

"How…how did you know that?" Perry asked, jerking the pistol higher, seeming unsettled for the first time since he'd materialized from the trees.

"I am being blackmailed as well," Lucas said in soothing tones. Even if he was not the criminal they sought, he still had a pistol, and his hand had become decidedly less steady. As long as he had it pointed anywhere near Gemma, Lucas would remain on guard.

"It's true." Gemma stepped out from behind him. Perry's pistol swung in her direction. Lucas growled. His heart clenched and lodged in his throat. What the devil was she doing? If they made it out of this alive, he'd throttle her himself. Lucas braced to move as Perry's eyes darted between him and Gemma.

Gemma's words spilled out in a single breath. "Sir, we erroneously thought you might be the perpetrator of this evil deed, and were trailing you to prove or disprove our theory. It seems we may be on the same side in this matter."

"You are not the blackmailers?" Perry asked slowly, and Lucas watched as the tension of fear and excitement seeped from him. His hand drooped and shook, and finally the pistol's dark mouth pointed to the ground.

Lucas's heart unclenched. He had faced danger in his life, but never had he been so affected. The image of Gemma standing before Perry without a touch of caution would haunt his sleeping and waking hours for quite some time, he was certain.

"We are not," Gemma said, even though it had not been much of a question.

"Do you have proof of that?" Perry demanded. Lucas sensed more than saw Gemma glance at him. He considered.

"Do you? This could be an elaborate act," Lucas pushed.

Could Perry be trusted? The consequences could be fatal if he was wrong.

"I have the latest note. I had just finished delivering a payment when I realized you two had followed me. I circled back, and here we are," Perry said, reaching into his overcoat with his free hand.

"Yes, here we are indeed," Lucas parroted the gesture, retrieving the letter he kept tucked away in an inner pocket. He held it out first in a gesture of goodwill. But he also knew that Perry would have to pocket his note or his gun to accept it. He studied him, waiting for him to make his move.

Perry looked from his note in one hand to his gun in the other. Finally, he pocketed the weapon and exchanged letters with Lucas.

Gemma stood on tiptoe and gripped Lucas's arm to peer over his shoulder. He tipped the paper so she could better read it. Upon a cursory glance, it looked authentic. It was addressed to Perry, the handwriting appeared to be similar, and the blackmailer signed off in the same odd way: *Inveniam viam aut faciam*.

"I shall find a way, or make one," Gemma translated in a whisper.

Perry looked up at them. "I believe we should discuss this further. Perhaps in a more comfortable setting? No doubt you know my address."

A trap? Although not impossible, Lucas didn't believe it to be the case, and after a moment assented. "We shall meet you there in one hour. It may be best not to leave this location together." If Perry had come from making a payment, there was a good chance they were being spied on even at that very moment.

"I agree. I will see you then." Perry traded letters once again and then melted back into the fog as quietly as he'd come.

...

She did not want to like him.

Beatrice cast a glance at Mr. Harrington as they exited yet another shop specializing in antique watches. No, she did not want to like him, but she could not help herself.

When Lucas had informed her of Mr. Harrington's involvement she had been terrified. If another person discovered her secret, she would be humiliated. Once she was reintroduced to Mr. Harrington, though, she knew she would be more than that. She would be devastated.

"You are quite good at this business," she commented now to the man in question. She could tell after spending the afternoon together that he was too sharp not to eventually work out the real reason he was involved in the case. It was not *if* the shoe would drop, it was *when*. She wondered why she cared what her brother's man of affairs thought of her.

He glanced over at her, a half smile tugging at his lips. They were walking back toward her carriage, and she did not want the afternoon to end. He had vastly improved her mood. He was certainly amusing, with his dry observations of everyone around him. He always toed the line of humorous rather than scathing, which she appreciated. But it was not just that. It was something about the way she felt immediately comfortable in his presence. The way he listened when she talked, no matter how inane the topic. She slowed her pace, and he fell back in step with her.

"I like mysteries," he finally said, after some consideration of her praise.

The coach was up ahead, and she wondered if he would ride back with her if she suggested it. He might find it improper, but he would need to talk to Lucas about their afternoon anyway.

"What was the first mystery you solved?" she asked. She

wanted to know more about him, although she could not exactly explain this desire.

His head tipped back in surprise. He was silent a moment, and she wondered if she'd asked a stupid question. She held her breath. But then he smiled, a full-on smile, and she felt a weight slide from her. His smile made her feel as though she'd been granted a special gift. "I have three older brothers," he began, and she nodded. "One day when I was very young I came into the library, and our mother's favorite vase was scattered in pieces on the floor."

"Oh no! Your poor dear mother," Beatrice said.

He laughed full out at that. "The 'poor dear' raised four hellion boys. A broken vase was hardly a surprise," he said. "But it was her favorite, so she promised there would be consequences. She thought I was to blame, because I was standing over it when she found the disaster. She told me no pudding for a month."

Beatrice gasped in faux outrage for the small boy, and squeezed his arm where her hand rested. "It was not even your fault."

"She refused to believe me," he said, shaking his head. They had arrived at her waiting carriage.

"You must want to inform Lucas of our afternoon," she said. "Please let me provide a ride back to our house."

Mr. Harrington stared past her at the horses and the waiting coachman. It took him a few moments, but when he turned back to her, he had made a decision, it seemed. "Thank you, yes."

They climbed into the coach as her maid scrambled up to sit beside the driver. "How did you convince her you were not the culprit?" Beatrice asked as she settled into the seat, intrigued by the picture he was painting of his childhood self.

He chuckled. "I made her believe it was one of my brothers, of course. A servant would have spoken up by then.

My parents were not harsh, and the punishment would not have been great. For members of the household who weren't her sons, that is."

Beatrice lifted a hand to cover a smile. "For you, that must have been a fate worse than death."

He lounged against the seat and slowly nodded. "You will never know the pain I suffered."

She giggled at the absurdity of it, and his eyes gleamed with humor in response.

"Once I had narrowed it down to one of my brothers, it was easy," he said. "James had recently received a new ball for Christmas, and he frequently talked Theodore into playing with it inside, even though the rules only allowed outside play."

"If they were both known to break that rule, how did you know which one it was?" Beatrice asked, glad she had pursued the line of questioning.

"Ah," he said, adopting a wise tone. "That is where some knowledge of the suspect comes in handy. Theo was the bowler in the family. But James was the hitter. They may have both been culpable, but James was the one who took out the vase, and I knew it."

"Did you tell your mother?" she asked.

He smiled his half smile. "Never. You never betray a brother in need," he said. "But I made him sneak puddings to me for the whole month."

She laughed even as her heart turned over in her chest. Oh yes, she was in trouble.

• • •

It was a strange feeling, returning to the scene of the crime, Gemma thought as she glanced about Perry's study. Light streamed in from the doors leading to the gardens, bathing the delicate furnishings. She and Lucas sat on a rose-colored chaise, while Perry perched across from them looking rather like an uncomfortable elephant amidst doll furniture.

"The Latin phrase," she said, when she could no longer bear the tense silence. "Does it have some meaning to you?"

"I cannot shake the feeling that I have heard it before," Perry said. "I have been turning it over in my mind, but every time I get close to some sense, it flutters away."

Gemma glanced at Lucas. He shook his head. "I am not familiar with it outside of history books. It clearly is important to him, but I wouldn't weight it too much. He might be suffering from grandiose delusions." He looked at Perry. "How many payments have you made, thus far?"

"That was my fifth. I do not know how long I can continue. The amounts he demands are reasonable, as if he knows how much I can afford to lose. I do not know when, but I do know he will escalate to the point where I am unable to pay him," Perry said.

Gemma agreed with his assessment, from what she knew about the crime. Before she had met Lucas, her experience with the crime of blackmail had been limited to Uncle Artie's old stories and sensational novels, but she understood it well. Many times blackmailers started off with small demands, but as they grew either more confident or desperate—depending on their situation—the amount would grow exponentially. Eventually it would reach the point where the victim could no longer afford the secret.

"Do you have any thoughts on who it could be?" Gemma asked.

"I confess, I do not. Much of my focus has been keeping my wife from finding out about what is happening." Perry dropped his head into his hands. So, Lady Perry did not know the secret. It could be an illicit affair, but she did not think that would warrant blackmail. Most lords—and ladies—of the *ton* were engaged in liaisons with partners who were not their spouses.

Gemma changed tactics. "Did you by chance meet a Nigel Thorne during your stay at the Waverly country house a few months ago? It may have been one of the locations at which you made a payment."

Lucas touched her hand, a quick, light gesture of comfort. How had he come to know her so well so quickly?

Perry's head shot up. "Yes. Nigel Thorne. Tragic, that was. He was shot dead in the library at the house party."

Gemma blinked. "And did you not find that odd, sir? That he was murdered in the same location as you were instructed to produce a blackmail payment?"

Perry's head swiveled back and forth between them. "Well, no. The investigators assured us it was a common housebreaker. There was no reason to not believe that."

Gemma could not believe the man's obtuseness. She was not without her doubts that Nigel's murder was connected to the extortion affair, but she at least heavily weighed the coincidence. This man did not even grasp it while they were asking him directly about it. She met Lucas's narrowed eyes and wondered if they were completely wasting their time.

"Was anyone in attendance at the house party acting suspiciously?" she asked, switching from the previous line of questioning. She was not inclined to explain to him why Nigel was probably connected to the case, and it did not seem as though that would prove successful enough to warrant opening herself up to the pain of it all.

"I have been turning that over and over in my head, believe me," Perry promised. "But it was the normal circle. It was a larger gathering, certainly, and there were several nights Lady Waverly opened the house to more guests, including the third night—when I was to make my payment in the library."

The night Nigel was killed.

Lucas squeezed her hand, and Gemma let the warmth of it soothe her battered heart. Most days she was able to soldier on, the act of hunting for her cousin's murderer enough to keep her moving forward. It was nice, though, in the moments where grief caught up to her, to have Lucas nearby.

But how was she going to live without it when they went their separate ways?

She needed to cut herself off from it. To distance herself, so that the end wouldn't hurt so much. But not yet. She'd take it in this moment when she wasn't strong enough to resist.

Soon, though.

"I wish I could point with certainty to someone who was a guest, but in truth it could have been anyone on that night," Perry continued, unaware of her inner turmoil. "There were people in and out of the house—it is a wonder anyone can keep track of that."

A dead end again. Gemma tried to remind herself that Perry had been the result of a supposed dead end, but then she thought about Perry.

Dead end, indeed.

"Do you have any enemies, Perry?" Lucas asked. "Anyone who would want to target you or your family?"

Perry's expression turned bewildered, and he ran a hand through his thick blond curls. Gemma was thankful Lucas had not taken up that particular fashion style.

"I cannot imagine why anyone would. The offense for which he is blackmailing me happened long ago and affected only two people, neither of whom is out to destroy me," Perry said. A child, Gemma thought. An illicit child, it must be.

"Do you know when or how the person obtained this information?" Gemma asked.

"I don't. But I know he must have dug rather deep. It is extraordinarily well hidden."

"Until now," Lucas murmured and exchanged a look

with Gemma. This didn't feel like opportunistic blackmailing. As with Lucas, it seemed as if the extortionist first chose the victim, then the damning secret.

"Perry." Suddenly Lucas's whole body tightened like a coiled spring. "That ring you wear…"

The blond man looked down at his hands as if he'd forgotten what was there. On his right middle finger he wore a thick gold band with a ruby inset.

"My father's." Perry twisted it in what seemed a familiar gesture. "He died several years ago. He gave this to me before he passed."

"May I see it?" Lucas asked. He stretched out his hand, and Lord Perry placed the ring in his palm.

"My lord…" she began, curious, but he just shook his head once and ran a finger over the jewel. In a swift move, he flipped the ring to examine the underside of it. She saw his muscles stiffen further under his jacket as he stared at whatever he had found there.

"I have this ring," he finally said.

"You mean one similar to that," Perry said.

"No. Not one similar to it. One exactly like it. My father gave it to me as well. It has this same engraving on the inside." He handed it to Gemma.

The metal was still warm from his hand. She checked under the band and saw a symbol engraved on the gold.

It was amazingly intricate. The center was the head of a lion wearing a crown; surrounding it were four symbols.

"Do you know what the images are?" she asked, and Lucas shook his head. She looked from him to Perry.

"No, I am not sure I even noticed them, to be honest. I thought the lion was a nice touch, but didn't think much of it further," he said.

"Of course you didn't," Gemma murmured. "Do you think your fathers knew each other? Is that what this means?"

"I never heard my father mention Lord Perry, other than in passing perhaps," Lucas said, and Perry nodded his agreement.

"And now you are both victims of the same blackmailer. In your words, my lord, this cannot be a coincidence," she said, goose bumps rising on her arms.

"No," Lucas agreed, "No, it cannot."

• • •

"Well," Gemma said as they settled into Lucas's carriage. "That was…something."

"You mean Perry's a bloody idiot," Lucas summed up, stretching a booted leg to rest on her bench—what she was coming to realize was his favored position. Her stomach clenched as she remembered what had taken place not long ago and not far from where she was sitting. He gazed at her now with hooded eyes, and she wondered if he was remembering the interlude as well.

She cleared her throat and tried to ignore the insistent throbbing between her legs. One look from him reduced her to a quivering pile of mush.

The carriage jolted forward into the quiet street.

"How do you think we should proceed, my lord?"

"Are we back to 'my lord' even here, then?" Lucas's deep voice stroked over her skin like a silk glove. She shivered and tried to steel her nerves.

"Oh, do stop teasing me and be serious, Lucas." The man flashed her a wicked grin and she felt her heart thump harder in her chest.

"Of course, my dear. We must be serious," he said, still eyeing her as if he wanted to eat her up in one bite.

She tried to ignore the heat prickling at her skin and charged forward, though she was sure the slow burn rising in her cheeks gave her away. "I think we must discover how your fathers knew each other, and what happened to make them drop out of each other's lives."

"We are looking at this as if they were the only two with rings. Perhaps the connection is more tenuous than that. Maybe they were acquaintances who went their separate ways, and that's why I never heard they were friends," he said.

"Correct me if I am wrong, but that ring looked expensive, and the engraving quite intricate. Even if there were more than two of them, it could not have been a large number. It seems notable, at the very least, that both your fathers owned one. Do you think you would be able to find any information your father had about it?"

"Possibly at the country house, but not in London, no." He stared out the window, contemplative. "I have an idea," he finally said slowly. She could tell he was hesitant to suggest it.

"We've come this far, my lord. We have survived a fictional engagement and encounters with both a pistol and a dimwit. I am confident we can handle whatever you may suggest," she said, hoping to lighten the mood.

He flashed a genuine smile, not his usual smirk or sardonic grin, and her heart fluttered. When he truly smiled, his eyes lit up and crinkled slightly at the corners, and the fine contours of his chiseled face became more defined but somehow softer, too.

"This is true." He paused and grew serious once more. She immediately missed the crinkles around his sharp green eyes. "I have an old friend. I think she would know if there were a connection from long ago that may have been forgotten by others."

"Someone from your espionage days?" Gemma queried, all innocence.

"I do not have espionage days. But yes, someone who deals in information. I shall try to arrange a meeting with her," he said.

"I shall come, too, of course," she said, lest he think he was going to cut her out of what seemed like a fascinating interview. She continued before he could disagree with her. "What on earth do you think is going on, my lord?"

He peered out of the carriage to the fog-shrouded gray streets of the city. His brow furrowed as he sank deeper into the shadows, as if he were completely lost in thought.

"I think someone is bent on revenge," he finally said, not looking at her. "For what, I cannot guess."

"That all seems so dramatic," Gemma said.

"Yes," he agreed. "I have plenty of enemies who would wish to hurt me, I have no doubt. People of my station always have enemies. But it is difficult to ignore the ring, which seems to imply that my father and Lord Perry's are wrapped up in this somehow. Perhaps even the true targets of this villain." She wished she were brave enough to slide across next to him and offer him the comfort he had done for her. But fear and uncertainty held her rooted in her seat.

"What was he like, your father?" she prompted when he didn't continue further.

Lucas did not answer and for some time the only sound in the carriage was the muffled clop of horse hoofs on cobblestones. She worried that she had pried too far into an uncomfortable subject, and she twisted her peach silk gloves in her hand.

"We were not terribly close," Lucas finally said, and she paused her silent fretting. "Until today, the word I would have used to describe him was honorable. Very hard. Distant. But honorable. There was a time, when I was about eight or nine, when a horse thief stole one of my father's favorite mares. He was captured by the local magistrate. His sentence was, of course, death—the mare was very expensive, after all. My father took me into town, though, to the magistrate's.

He asked to see the thief, who turned out to be a boy no more than a year older than I was then. His father had been killed a month earlier by some bandits, and his family was starving. He had five younger sisters and his mother to look after. The magistrate was a bastard. Not of birth, of course, but of disposition. I was terrified of him and tried not to show it. My father confronted him and told him to release the boy immediately. The magistrate was furious—I think he perversely enjoyed the power of taking someone's life."

Gemma cringed at the picture he painted. She knew men like this magistrate, men whose little portions of power teased out all their existing demons to wreak havoc on their own little world.

"The magistrate refused to grant him leniency, until my father told him that he'd given the boy permission to take the horse. That he'd forgotten until just then, but that the boy couldn't be punished for my father's mistake, and that my father would bring in witnesses if necessary."

"He committed perjury," Gemma said. "Did the magistrate relent?"

"He had no choice at that point," Lucas said. "Either he accused one of the wealthiest and most powerful gentlemen in the land of perjury, or he let the boy go. My father placed him in a lose-lose situation, and he hated him the rest of his miserable life for it. But the boy was released."

"And did he steal again?" Gemma asked.

"No. My father gave him a job in our stables, where he still works as head stable master," Lucas said with a slight smile. "He's a good man, and wonderful with horses. But that is what I think about when I think of my father. He may not have been a loving father, or even a good one. But the memory of that day at the magistrate's has stuck with me. Not everything in life is black and white. Lying can be honorable; saving a thief can be the ethical choice. He could be harsh, too, certainly. But I will not forget the lesson of his mercy."

Gemma shook off her self-consciousness and reached over to place a hand on his knee. He looked at her with sadness in his eyes.

"I do not want to believe my father could have done something to incur so much vengeance," he said. "But that does seem where this is headed, does it not?"

"I think," Gemma chose her words delicately, "that even our heroes are often flawed. That does not make them bad people. It makes them human. When we look up to people, we make them into caricatures rather than appreciating them as a whole. When we see them making poor decisions or disappointing us in some way, we feel as if the whole of them is invalidated. Instead, we should view them as more valid. A misstep off the path to a moral life does not make one evil. Only if one steps off and does not return are they a bad person. Remember, for whatever your father did, he not only saved a life, but he shaped yours. The world would be less had he not done so."

Lucas reached for her hand, intertwining their fingers. "You are quite wise, my dear," he said. She searched for any hint of sarcasm in the words, but found none.

"A complicated man raised me," she said in response. "My views of the world tend to be a bit more fluid than your normal society lady."

"To Uncle Artie," he said, raising their joined hands to his lips. He kissed her knuckles, and she felt a flutter race into her stomach. They locked eyes. The carriage rolled to a stop, and she pursed her lips, disappointed. Lucas laughed at her petulant expression. "Timing has never been our strong suit, has it?"

Chapter Eight

Gemma shifted in her seat in hopes of relieving the strain on her back. And Mr. Matthew Cooke continued to drone on about West Indies trading policies—a topic that could be fascinating in the right hands. Mr. Cooke's were not those hands. While she did not expect every Travelers Society lecture to have her on the edge of her seat, she'd had higher hopes for one titled "Adventures on the High Seas: My Life Among Pirates and Natives of the New Lands." From what she could tell, Mr. Cooke had had a tame journey to the West Indies and then proceeded to live an uneventful life once he was there. They were an hour into the presentation and not a single pirate had made an appearance.

The two ladies behind her chattered about the latest gossip, and an older gentleman several seats down was snoring, a soft rumbling she was sure could be heard even several rows ahead.

"Can you believe he offered for that little country mouse?" The whisper grabbed her wandering attention. It came from the women who had long since given up on poor

Mr. Cooke. With a sideways glance she was able to determine that they were well dressed in deep blue and green day gowns, and evidently a few years older than her own twenty-five.

"She's connected to Lady Andrews, but it is too distant a relation for it to weigh on the decision. And she's a homely little thing, isn't she? It couldn't have been her great beauty that hooked him," the second woman murmured. Gemma stiffened. They had arrived later than she had, so they must not realize she was in front of them.

"There were rumors a few weeks back that they were caught in an indelicate situation, and that is why…"

"No! I had not heard. Well, that makes more sense—she trapped him into it. Did you hear about the Thatchery miss?"

Loud buzzing filled Gemma's ears as the ladies turned their attention to some other unfortunate soul. So, people did gossip about the engagement. This was not unexpected, she told herself. However, there was something about hearing just how unsuitable she was for Lucas that shook her. Logically, it should not bother her. The engagement wasn't real, and maybe they were right. The only way she could catch someone like Lucas would be to trap him. That's why the sooner she solved Nigel's murder and returned to the country, the better. The more she was around Lucas, the harder it would be to walk away. She already had difficulty maintaining her logical composure, of which she was so proud, when he looked at her in that certain way. She imagined the two women clucking over the news of their broken engagement and struggled against the embarrassment, even as her face heated.

The smattering of polite applause stopped her emotional spiraling. She held her breath as Cooke asked for questions, and she did not think she was the only one who let out a sigh of relief when there were none. Cooke seemed disappointed, but he rallied as a small group of devoted society members encircled him. She popped open her delicate fob watch. Lucas was picking her up at a quarter past three for a stroll and some iced cream. A perfectly respectable and unexceptional afternoon for an affianced pair. That gave her several minutes to chat with her friends in the society before she was due outside.

That also meant standing up and confronting the two gossips behind her. She wondered if she could slink off without their notice, but anger was overtaking mortification. She gathered her courage around her like a protective cloak, rose, and turned to look them directly in the eyes. Theirs widened in recognition, as though they were running through what they'd said, checking if anything was beyond the pale.

"Ladies, I do not believe we've been introduced," she said, her voice as sweet as sugar as she gracefully extended her hand. "Miss Gemma Lancaster."

"Congratulations on your engagement, Miss Lancaster," the woman in the deep blue dress said. Gemma noticed that the other could not help but smirk knowingly.

"Thank you. We are overjoyed to have found one another. Lord Winchester just goes on and on about how bored he was with the silly, insipid, and…perhaps I ought not say…*plain* women who were offered up to him before we met." She let her eyes trail up and down the two ladies. "Oh," she said softly, as if coming to a realization. "You set your cap for him a few years ago, did you not, Lady Matthews? I'm *sure* he was not talking about you. Well, I must be off. You ladies have a wonderful afternoon. Good day." Gemma turned on her heel without awaiting a response.

Her departure was somewhat ruined when she smacked into a solid wall of man standing a few feet behind her. She might have tumbled to the ground had he not steadied her with his strong, rough hands. She looked up and met amused emerald eyes. "Lucas! You cannot just stand in people's way!"

He grinned down at her without releasing his hold on

her arms. "Darling, you rammed into me. I was standing here minding my own business, basking in the prospect of our joyous union"—she blushed at the realization that he had been there long enough to hear her attempt to cut down the busybodies—"when I was almost toppled at no fault of my own."

"Oh posh!" She swatted at his chest. "As if I could hurt you."

"I wouldn't be too sure about that," he said in a slightly different tone. She did not know what to make of the words, which had all of a sudden lost their playful edge. But before she could delve further, his eyes shifted to the now empty space behind her. "They were bothering you?"

She glanced back as well and wished he hadn't heard any of the exchange. "They were vacuous gossips. Apparently our engagement was a delicious morsel they were examining thoroughly before devouring."

"They upset you? What did they say?" His voice turned downright dangerous.

"It was nothing I did not expect. They simply did not realize I was sitting directly in front of them, the little fools. It's all right, Lucas, I handled it." She steered him away from her seat and toward a group of members with whom she'd had fascinating conversations before.

"Hmm." Lucas still looked ready for a fight, but he let himself be directed toward the group of men near the front of the room.

"Really, you would think you're about to challenge them to a duel, my lord. Here, let me introduce you… Mr. Afton, how lovely to see you. And you, Mr. Tiddle." The group tumbled into a lively discussion on a lecture from earlier in the week, each member eager to give his take on the American West.

• • •

The day had turned sunny and bright, a true rarity in the city of fog and rain. Gemma tipped her face up toward the light, and Lucas let himself soak up the sight of her happiness. She had begun to wear her emotions closer to the surface since she had abandoned her dull wallflower act, and he could now read her easily.

Or maybe he was someone with whom she felt she could show her true emotions. Someone with whom she could be herself. The thought pleased him.

When he'd walked into the lecture hall that afternoon, she had been radiating upset. The casual observer might have seen her as composed when she confronted the two gossipers, but he'd seen the tenseness in her shoulders, the barely contained anger in her tightened mouth, the flush of embarrassment on her delicate, pale skin.

The intensity of the rage that burned in his stomach on her behalf surprised him. It was as if her anger and his were inextricably tied. He'd wanted to cut down the two ninnies with a withering remark, and at the same time kiss Gemma until all the hurt and unhappiness was replaced by passion.

He'd done neither and seethed at the missed opportunity. Though, he had to admit she had handled herself well.

They strolled now on the crowded sidewalk. Much of the beau monde was out enjoying the mild weather. They walked in a comfortable silence for a stretch while Gemma enjoyed her iced cream. He realized this was the first normal excursion they'd had since they'd begun their investigation, and he enjoyed the feeling. He even let himself a few fleeting touches of the soft skin of her arm. Nothing improper, of course. Just. Sometimes he needed to touch her. Even if it was just her hand. Her elbow. He laughed at himself. If someone had told him a month earlier he'd be all but writing an ode to an elbow he would have thought the person mad.

He was in uncharted territory with this woman, and for

some reason that didn't terrify him.

"Have you traveled to many places?" she asked. They had talked at length with her friends from the society, and she had lit up when he mentioned some of the destinations he'd frequented.

He slid his gaze to the side, assessing her profile. "I have traveled, although not so widely as some of my acquaintances."

"Was it during your years in espionage?" She turned her face toward him, eagerly curious. He wanted to laugh at her persistence.

"I did not have years in espionage, my dear," he told her. "But, yes, when I was younger I traveled. I spent a year on the Continent after Oxford. I met a good friend who turned into a mentor. Benjamin Slack. He taught me what I know about… travel."

"Are you still close?" she asked, the smile gone from her face. She must have heard something catch in his voice.

"He died," Lucas said, no longer choking on the words as he had in the early days of it. The sharp stabbing pain under his left rib cage had turned into a dull ache. He did not want to tell her. And yet, he also wanted it more than anything.

I trust her.

The realization was jarring. Trust meant vulnerability. At its most dangerous, it meant weakness. A fatal flaw.

He turned the thought over in his head, examining it, before letting it shift and settle into an empty space in his chest. Then he met her eyes. Trusting her didn't feel like it made him weaker. It was entirely possible that it did the exact opposite. It made him strong.

"It was my fault."

"Oh, Lucas," she murmured, squeezing his arm. "What happened?"

He was quiet for a moment.

"We were…travelling. I put my faith in the wrong

person." Her fingers pressed into his forearm again, a gentle reassurance. He dragged in a breath. "I was new to the game. Arrogant, maybe, thinking that I knew everything. The attack happened too fast. It was too fast. I couldn't get to him in time. They weren't after me. They didn't care about me."

"I held him when he died," he said, and she leaned her head slightly to rest against him for a brief moment. Warmth spread from that point on his shoulder. It didn't erase the pain, but it was a balm against the sting of it.

"Did you…" She paused and cleared her throat. "Did you find the men responsible?"

"Yes."

He didn't justify. He didn't explain. If she was horrified by his actions so be it. She wasn't the only one who could be driven to seek vengeance.

"Good."

The answer shocked a dry laugh from him, more from surprise than any type of humor. He met her eyes. They were deep pools of liquid, the tears there but held back. Her chin was set, though, her mouth a resolute line. He wanted to kiss her. He settled for squeezing her hand on his arm.

"I came home to Beatrice," he said.

"I am sure she was thrilled to have her brother home and safe."

"Yes. I am not sure I did my best to protect her even then, but at least I was there to help clean up the mess," he said, still frustrated with himself over it. The ache at having failed to protect his partner abroad had only been echoed and magnified when he'd come back to find that he was just as powerless to protect his sister at home.

"Believe me, there's only so much you can do when it comes to a young woman in love," Gemma said with a smile in her voice. "They are rare, unpredictable creatures. But Beatrice has turned into a lovely young lady, and that is partly because of you."

He swallowed hard past a lump in his throat. He would not argue with her. Beatrice was a bright spot in his life.

They walked a few more streets in silence once more, but he knew he had to tell her his news. He'd been putting it off, but the longer he waited to inform her, the more upset she'd be.

"I received another blackmail demand last night," he finally said, wishing he didn't have to bring a dark cloud to their sunny day.

Gemma stopped midstride and had to sidestep when the couple behind them almost plowed into her. She murmured her apologies to the disgruntled pair, but then she swung her piercing sapphire eyes back to him.

"Details," she snapped out. Lucas pulled her back into step with himself, so they were not making a spectacle.

"I came home to the envelope on my desk. The amount was double the last payment, and the date it is due is the end of the week," Lucas said. "Three days, or else he releases Beatrice's journal to the hungry hounds."

"How is she taking it?" Gemma asked.

"Better, I believe, than she would have taken it a day or so ago," he said. "She talked her way into helping Harrington with his research of shops that sell antique pocket watches. They have not found much yet, but I think being a part of the investigation has given her a new energy."

"Oh," Gemma exclaimed. "That is wonderful. She must have been feeling so impotent."

He raised a brow at her choice of words, but decided not to tease her over it.

"Yes, I only realized she must have been feeling out of sorts over it when she came back from her outing yesterday," he said, and he swore he heard her utter something that sounded like "men!" under her breath. He would not defend himself or his gender. He *had* told Beatrice that she could work with Harrington, after all. True, he had made no move to promote their collaboration, but, well…no man was perfect.

"They did not find anything useful, though?" Gemma asked.

"A few names that repeat on both our lists are on theirs. Peterson's on all of them. As are some of the members of the society we just left," he told her. Before she could rush to any of their defense, he made sure to add, "However, there are a shocking number of collectors in society, and I am not sure the current list will help us much. Perry is on it."

"I do not think he was lying to us, though, do you?" she asked, distracted from the implication that any of her new friends could be the villain.

"I think he is hardly clever enough to pull off so brilliant an act, but I have been wrong before." He smirked. "It is rare, but it has happened."

She fluttered her eyelashes at him. "Oh, sir, it is so brave of you to admit such a thing."

He laughed, and they continued their stroll.

"What if we never catch him?" Gemma finally asked, breaking the silence after a few moments of contemplation on both their ends.

"We will," he said, and the words hung over them both with a solid certainty.

• • •

The missive arrived early the next day. Gemma was sitting at her writing desk in her aunt's study when Bird trooped in.

"You've a letter, miss," he said, offering up a silver tray. Gemma snatched it and tore it open:

Gemma—
  Meeting has been arranged. I shall pick you up

at two this afternoon.
— W

Gemma squealed with excitement and clutched the paper to her heart. She imagined it was how other women reacted when they received their first invitation to a ball.

She laughed at herself then dashed past a curious Bird to find Roz in the drawing room, sifting through the post.

"We are to meet with Lord Winchester's informant," Gemma cried out to Roz, unable to contain herself.

"Well, this is exciting news." Roz reached out for the letter and gave the lines a quick glance. "But, dear heart, you are being careful, are you not?"

Gemma sank into the opposite chair. "Why, of course, Roz. You know I can take care of myself, and Lord Winchester certainly is no slouch in that area, either."

Roz peered at her over the unfashionable spectacles she only wore in the privacy of their own home. Her deep brown eyes were full of concern. "That is all well and good, of course. But I mean to ask whether you are being careful with Lord Winchester. I do not want you to emerge from this devastated, with not only your reputation in tatters, but also your heart."

"Oh, Roz, that is not going to happen." Gemma tried to reassure her aunt even as her stomach dipped. Was she truly being careful? Last night she had not been able to sleep. Images of him had kept her tossing and kicking at her bedsheets. She refused to remember or acknowledge the throbbing in a part of her body she had just recently become aware of in his carriage. But it was more than that. She wanted to tell him about little things she noticed. She'd wanted to share humor over Mr. Cooke's dreadfully dull lecture, or secret smiles across crowded ballrooms. She was convincing herself it all stemmed from the bond over the investigation. Being in dangerous situations with only each other to rely on would necessitate a connection deeper than the normal friendship. But what if it was more than that? Was she really guarding her heart? Or would she end up crushed in the end? She pushed the thoughts away.

"I took responsibility for you from the moment you stood on my doorstep and asked me to help you with this wild case," Roz said. "I may not have kept you from a path of completely ruining your social standing, but it would break my heart to see him crush yours."

"Where is this coming from?" Gemma tried to hide her dismay. When even one of her biggest champions could not foresee a positive outcome to this affair with Lucas, she knew it was hopeless.

"I see how you are when you talk about him," Roz said gently. "I just want you to be happy, Gemma."

"Pish posh." She put on a front, waving her aunt's concerns away. She would have to deal with her own feelings eventually, but now was not the time. Nor did she particularly want to delve into it with Roz. "I will be happy when we catch Nigel's killer. I am excited because we are making progress. I have developed quite a bit of admiration for Lord Winchester's intelligence and investigative skills, but that is all. At the end of this, we shall go our separate ways without a single thought," she said, ignoring the little clutch around her heart at the idea.

"Hmmm." Roz searched Gemma's face for a moment before shaking off the topic. "Well, tell me about this informant."

"Lucas—I mean Lord Winchester—says she knows much of the old gossip that flowed through the town like the Thames. He says even if most people have forgotten an event, she usually recalls something of it," she said.

"And who is this again?" Roz asked.

"That's the mystery of it! I have no idea, and Winchester

simply calls her an old friend. I think they met during the days he worked for the Crown." She leaned in, elbows on knees, and dropped her voice. "He does not admit it outright, but I am sure he worked in some capacity in the art of deception." She paused. "For God and Country, of course."

Roz tipped her head in a knowing gesture. "Of course. God save the King."

"I get the idea that this woman deals in information. It is all very cryptic, but Winchester seems to believe she will indeed know something about his father," she said.

"I am devastated that I am unable to help in that regard," Roz said, a little pout in her voice. "You know I pride myself on my intimate knowledge of everything that happens in society."

"Well, you know boys, they like their secret clubs. Maybe they were able to keep everything hush hush," Gemma said.

"Quite," Roz said with a laugh. "Boys and their clubs. But I have never heard even a whisper of scandal surrounding Lord Winchester's father. Perry was a bit more of a rake than Winchester, but the normal nonsense. Some gambling, a few affairs. Nothing out of the ordinary for a gentleman."

"Well, I suppose that is why blackmail is effective," Gemma commented. "They've managed to bury the secrets so deep in their gardens, no one has a clue."

"Yes, but they are not being targeted for their fathers' secrets, they are being targeted for their own," Roz paused. "Or, in Lord Winchester's case, his sister's."

"True. So it is possible we are going about this in the wrong fashion, and their fathers' connection will have nothing to do with the case!" Gemma threw her hands in the air then let them fall back into her lap. "This whole investigation feels like we are chasing our tails. Every time something seems promising, reality comes crashing down."

Roz reached out and patted Gemma's hands. "Dear heart,

this could be the very key to unlocking the whole mystery. At the very least, do not give up until you have spoken with this woman."

Gemma heaved a breath. "You are right, of course. I am sorry. In any case, she must be more helpful than Lord Perry."

Roz chuckled. "Do you know what his secret is, by chance?"

"No, I do not. How he is able to dress himself in the morning, perhaps?" she said, a bit caustically.

"Oh, that's no secret. I am sure his valet dresses him," Roz answered and they dissolved into laughter.

. . .

At precisely five minutes to two, Gemma was in the foyer, peeking every few seconds through the heavy beveled glass by the front door. Then she paced the length of the floor to the stairs and back again. Bird stood stoically by, watching the mad march.

If only they were closer to getting a handle on any part of the case. What she had told Roz earlier was true: they were chasing their tails, forever making deductive leaps that did not turn up results. The only progress they had made was to discover even more questions. She had to keep tamping down her rising frustration and panic. This next step needed to be the break for which they were waiting. She peered out the glass once more before resuming her pacing.

Her aunt lived on one of the quieter circles in one of the most fashionable boroughs of London, so she was able to hear Lucas's carriage roll to a stop in front of the townhouse. Bird's sharp look was the only thing holding her back from dashing out the door without a thought to propriety. But she dare not challenge Bird on social etiquette. They would wait for Lucas to fetch her to the carriage himself.

The moments dragged on, and Gemma tapped her foot on the floor with unladylike impatience. The act earned her another glare, but she was beginning to think Bird's face was set in permanent disapproval, and really, there was nothing she could do about that.

Finally, the heavy knocker echoed through the room, and the butler made his way to the door.

"Good day, Mr. Bird," came Lucas's voice from around Bird's stout body. "I am here to retrieve my fiancée for a drive in the park."

She pushed her way forward. "Yes, yes, here I am, my lord. What took you so long?"

Lucas made a show of pulling out his pocket watch and checking the time. "I believe I have arrived two minutes early, my dear."

Gemma waved off the facts. "Irrelevant," she said, all but skipping down the steps toward his carriage. The coachman stood ready to help her up the little stairs, but Lucas was there to steady her.

"I do have to warn you about something, my dear," Lucas said once they'd settled into the velvet benches and the carriage rolled into the street.

"It seems to be the day for that," she muttered to herself.

"What was that?" he asked.

"Nothing, my lord. Please continue," she said, cheeks blazing. The last thing she wanted to bring up was any tender feelings she might be developing toward him. He would leave a Lucas-sized hole in the carriage door just to escape her, she was sure.

He narrowed his eyes, and she could tell he wanted to pursue the conversation. Instead he left it alone and said, "The woman we are meeting…I should have mentioned this to you before we were on our way."

"Yes, my lord?" Gemma prompted as he trailed off, her

patience expiring.

"Well…" He cleared his throat, clearly nervous. She was fascinated as to what would cause Lucas to feel such discomfort. He was usually so composed. "She was a well-known brothel owner back in the day."

"How interesting." Gemma sat forward. "I have never met a brothel owner before."

"I should hope not," Lucas said, a trace of amusement in his deep voice.

"That is why you think she might know something?" she asked. "She was privy to the private lives of influential gentlemen?"

"Yes, most of the men of significance in society have ventured through her doors at one point or another. She knows many secrets."

"I would imagine so," she murmured, thinking through the ramifications of what he was telling her. She remembered the intimacy she had felt after simply kissing Lucas. She might not have spilled her closest held feelings, but it would not have taken much to pry information from her in that state. The amount of knowledge the women in a brothel could gather was probably astonishing. She wondered why she had not thought of that before. "The implications are astounding, actually."

"The women have to be careful with the secrets, though, you must remember," Lucas said, following her thoughts as usual. "They would not last long in the business if they were blackmailing their clients. Rose would not allow it, either."

A heavy silence descended in the carriage, and Gemma shifted in her seat. She huffed out a breath and crossed her arms over her chest. A man would only know of business at a brothel if he had reason to be familiar with their services.

Lucas raised an eyebrow. "Do you have something to ask me, my dear?" He sounded amused.

"No," she responded shortly, even more irritated, and

refused to look at him. She did not want to know.

Did. Not. Want. To. Know.

And she certainly did not want to see his smug smile. She would not give in to either the curiosity or the jealousy that clawed at her stomach.

The silence stretched on for several blocks as they left the more posh part of town. She oriented herself to their location—they were not in the rough section near the docks, but the quieter area where many merchants and businessmen lived, the ones who were wealthy, but because they worked for a living were not welcome into society. Except when they were serving the upper class, she thought.

She supposed she shouldn't be surprised at the neighborhood—this Rose was a businesswoman, and if Lucas was to be believed, a rather successful one at that.

"I have never availed myself of the services of one of Rose's girls," Lucas finally said, the amusement still in his voice. "I know you were not wondering, of course, but I thought perhaps we should all enter this interview with the same knowledge."

So this was something of a joke to him. She no longer cared. The effect of what he'd said, joke or not, washed over her. She tried to ignore the warmth that the reassurance brought her, but it was there whether she wanted to admit it or not.

"I care not what you did or did not do," Gemma protested, a little too vehemently. She paused as a thought struck her. "Does she know I will be coming with you?"

"She does. She seems intrigued to meet a lady of the *ton*. She has plenty of experience with the lords, but I'm not sure how many gentlewomen she has encountered in her long career. I am sure it is one of the reasons she took the meeting," he mused.

She gasped. "So you are using me? Is that what you are saying, my lord?"

"Yes, the only use I have for you is to leverage the status

of your birth to acquire a meeting with a notorious prostitute," he said with a straight face. She swatted at him, and he grabbed her hand, interlocking their fingers. Her breath caught at the intimacy of the gesture. She bit her lip as he squeezed her hand once and then let it go, and felt a surprising sense of loss as he released her fingers.

"Surely she would have met with you because you two know each other from the past?" Gemma asked once she composed herself again.

Lucas considered the question. "I think to make it to where she is now, she has not let herself be pulled into situations that might disrupt her life unduly. We helped each other at one time, so I was useful to her and worth the risk of divulging highly sensitive information. However, I have nothing of real value to offer her now. She does not need money, as she sold her businesses and retired several years ago an extremely wealthy woman. I have no power that interests her. To her, information is the only currency that matters now. I come with none of it."

He locked eyes with her. "But you—a gentlewoman lowering herself to meet with a brothel owner. She would find that impossible to pass up."

"I understand. I do not know why more women would not want to meet such a fascinating person, but the rules of society are rather strict, are they not? Infuriatingly so, I think. It has improved greatly for me, though, my lord, since we announced our engagement," she said happily.

He mimicked her earlier gasp. "So you are using me? For the freedom to move about unrestricted by rules developed for your protection? Is that what you are saying?"

"It is precisely what I am saying. Your only usefulness to me is your status as my fiancé."

He snatched her into his lap and laid a quick kiss on her lips, cutting off her surprised gasp. "Ah, then. I shall strive to do my best in the role."

Chapter Nine

The carriage pulled to a stop outside a large townhouse. Lucas had grudgingly deposited Gemma back in her seat. There was a time for everything, and on the way to visit Rose Stephens was not the ideal moment for engaging in a passionate tussle.

He glanced at her now. She was a bundle of nerves and excitement. It was both amusing and endearing. He could not imagine any lady of his acquaintance behaving in the same manner. In fact, he could not think of one who wouldn't be horrified. He had clearly been associating with the wrong people.

They disembarked from the carriage, and he told his coachman to return in an hour. While he had no qualms about his visit to Rose, he did not want to court gossip, especially with Gemma's name so closely connected to his own. Gemma's eyebrows rose at the order, but she remained quiet.

They made their way up the steps and rapped on the door. It was opened promptly by a tall, stately woman in expensive but tasteful clothing.

"We have an appointment with Miss Stephens," Lucas

said, producing a calling card for the housekeeper in a practiced move. "Lord Winchester and Miss Lancaster."

The woman stared at Gemma, eyes narrowed, as she ran a finger over the expensive paper. She stepped back after a few tense moments, and Gemma gave her a quick smile as they followed her into the house.

The Amazon led them to a small, well-lit parlor near the entrance. Rose was a seated general, in control of her battlefield, but she stood gracefully as they were announced.

"Lucas," she said, both hands held out in welcome. She grasped his and squeezed them before turning her attention to Gemma. "And Miss Lancaster. Welcome, both of you."

"Thank you so much for having us, Miss Stephens," Gemma said as they settled into chairs opposite of Rose's.

"Please do call me Rose. Mrs. Darling, we will have the oolong," she said, calling out the order to the Amazon as she returned to her seat.

Rose had easily slipped into the life of a high society lady, or at least the trappings of one. If he didn't know better, he would find it hard to believe the woman sitting in front of him had grown up on the streets of East London. But her smile gave her away. It was too cunning, too sharp. It told those watching closely that it would be dangerous to underestimate her — or forget that she'd run a business that pulled desperate women into the same lifestyle that she'd hated so much.

She was ruthless. He just hoped that trait would be of use to them.

"Shall we forgo the small talk, Lucas? I can see you are well, and I am the same." She waved a dismissive hand at her expensive surroundings. Nothing in the room was audacious or gaudy, but the furnishings clearly showed her good taste and wealth. Even her gowns were the height of fashion. He knew it meant more to her than she was letting on.

"We do not want to waste your time, Rose," he said as she

poured them the tea that her housekeeper had placed on the table between them. "We are looking for information."

"Of course you are," she said, her lips curling up as she sipped from her fine china. He answered with a sardonic smile.

"Did you know my father?" He had many questions he could ask, but he went with one of the most basic ones. He could not very well ask more prying questions when he did not yet know what answers he needed.

She thought for a moment.

"Yes," she said slowly. "He was not a frequent customer of my establishment. By then he had set up in your country seat, for the most part. But I believe he had his favorite places in his younger days." She glanced at Gemma, as though checking to see if she was scandalized.

"Most men right out of school go through a rabble-rousing phase," Gemma said, and he couldn't help but admire her composure in the face of the risqué subject matter. "Nigel did."

Lucas nodded, unable to deny his own slightly sordid years when he was a younger gentleman. "I think that's the time we would like to know more about. Have you heard of Lord Perry?"

"I know him well," Rose said without hesitation.

"His father—did he…" Lucas stopped, wondering the best way to phrase it. "Was he connected to mine?"

Rose slowly placed her cup in her saucer and tipped her head as she considered the question. "Now that you mention it, they did associate. For a short period, a long time ago, they ran in the same crowd."

He sensed Gemma's heightened awareness, though not through any perceptible movement on her part. Rose didn't even seem to be aware of the shift. It was as if he were acutely attuned to her every breath, her every emotion, her every reaction.

"I do not think I would have even recalled it had you not mentioned both men," Rose continued. "It was about forty years ago, and I had just gotten my own room in a house. Neither of them were customers at the time, but another gentleman came by frequently. He mentioned Perry and your father a few times."

"Impressive that you remember this after so much time has passed," Gemma murmured.

Rose turned her sharp eyes on Gemma. "I have always had the gift of an excellent memory. It has served me well in the years. But as it happens, I still might not have remembered except this gentleman was a lifelong client up until a few years ago. The thing is, he always wears a ring, I've never seen him without it. I asked him about it in the early days. I'm not sure at that point I'd seen much that was as expensive as that ring."

All of Lucas's instincts came alert, but he kept it hidden behind a smooth mask and a calm voice. "And that has something to do with my father and Perry?"

"Mmhmm. On the underside of the ring was an engraving of some sort."

"A lion?" Gemma asked.

"Yes. That was it exactly." Rose glanced between the two of them, appraising. She wanted to see if her information was hitting its target. "This means something to you?"

Lucas considered how much to give up. He did not trust this woman in the slightest. She was more than likely filing away the entire conversation to benefit her at a later date. But he wanted to retrieve as much from her as possible. He had to give her something. "We think it might be a connection. Did he say anything about the ring in particular?"

"He said he and three of his friends had commissioned it right after they finished their education. He said they called themselves the Kingsmen. Grand plans they had, he always said. It was strange. The club fell apart after a season. But even toward the end of our time together, which was only a few years ago, he was talking of them. They had shaped his life, and they could have shaped all of England's future, socially and economically. If only they'd stuck together, they would have taken over the world," Rose said. "That is what he said."

"Did he say why they were not still the Kingsmen?" Lucas asked.

"No, and I did not ask. Many men have silly delusions of grandeur. That is all this seemed to be. And a few friends who were no longer as close, well, it is a common tale. Like I said, the reason I remember it is because of the ring, and that he would bring it up on occasion, usually when he had been in his cups."

"Would you be able to tell us the names of the two other gentlemen of the Kingsmen? Other than Perry and Winchester's father?" It was Gemma who asked the crucial question.

"I can," Rose said, but first looked at Lucas. "On two conditions. One, you get me into the investor group for the Winthrop building project."

"Done," Lucas said, relieved at how easy the demand would be to fulfill. The man running the investor group was a good friend of his. Which Rose would have known. She did not quite smile at his response, but she assumed a victorious air.

She switched her attention to Gemma. "Two, you tell me why you are here."

Lucas started to answer, "We—"

Rose cut him off with a sharp gesture, not even looking at him. "Not you, darling," she said.

He shifted closer to Gemma, but she seemed to be taking the turn in conversation with aplomb. He should have known not to be worried. She handled most things with equanimity.

"A few months ago, my cousin was murdered," she

answered. Her voice was steady. "We believe...well, now that we know the story...that the Kingsmen are involved in the business somehow. Before we came here, we knew there might be a connection between Perry and Winchester, but we could not determine it for certain. I am searching for justice for my cousin."

"But what are you doing *here*?" Rose asked again, without blinking at the mention of murder. "You could have let Lucas come alone."

Gemma paused, clearly pondering that for a moment. "Well, in all honesty, Lucas did not inform me of who you were until we were on our way here," she admitted. "But I think he knew I would insist on coming in any case. I am invested in finding my cousin's killer, at any cost. It is my sole purpose at the moment."

Rose nodded, a respectful acknowledgment of her statement. She also looked somewhat disappointed by the answer.

"But I would have wanted to have tea with you either way, Miss Stephens," Gemma continued. "The fact that you built yourself a life out of a dire situation, when, I am quite sure, you faced harsh opposition, is admirable. I would not pass up an opportunity to meet such an intelligent and enterprising woman, and learn whatever I could from her."

Rose leaned back in her seat, her first real reaction of the visit. "Well," she said with amusement. She looked at Lucas, who simply smiled at her.

"You would like my advice?" Rose asked Gemma. When she nodded, Rose said, "Stay away from men."

Gemma dissolved into laughter. "Well, it's a little late for that," she said, glancing at Lucas. He noticed Rose tracking and registering the moment. Who knew when the information would come in handy, he thought, but Rose was the type of woman to gather and catalogue any bit she received.

"Indeed," Rose murmured. "Well, the names, yes? Let's see, the three friends were Lord Winchester, Lord Perry, and Lord Dalton. And the gentleman who told me about them was Lord Rathburn."

Gemma watched Lucas from the corner of her eye. He shook his head almost imperceptibly. He did not recognize a connection with any of the names. Rose was watching them carefully as well. "Not who you were expecting?"

"We did not know whom to expect," Lucas said. "But no, those names mean nothing. I know Rathburn and Dalton are still alive, and have encountered both of them briefly here and there. That is all, though."

"I hope coming out here was still worth your time," Rose said.

"It was," Gemma assured her, though Rose did not seem concerned either way. "It brings us a step closer to solving our mystery."

"Always happy to help my friends," Rose said.

• • •

"She is fascinating," Gemma said once they were ensconced back in Lucas's carriage. "You would never guess how she acquired her wealth."

Lucas gazed back at her, a curious look on his face. "I would like to take you to Vauxhall Gardens."

Gemma laughed at the sharp pivot in topics and then clapped her hands. "I would adore that more than anything. I have read about the pleasure gardens, of course, but we have yet to venture out to them."

Lucas smiled at her enthusiasm. "Then it will be done. Perhaps tomorrow?"

"Yes. This is so exciting," Gemma said. One of the things she'd wanted to do most in London was pay a visit to

Vauxhall. She longed to see the fireworks, attend a mesmerist performance, and hear the orchestra perform for the mixed masses. The most wonderful part of the experience, it seemed, was that the classes merged and mingled. Anyone could attend, and you could be anyone when you attended.

"But, my lord, you are distracting us from the case," she chided. "We have learned valuable information today from Rose."

"My apologies, my dear," he said, though he did not seem sorry at all. "You are correct, we have a clear path to follow now, and we should devise a plan on how to traverse it."

Gemma pondered their options. "There seem to be two ways we could approach this: be stealthy or confront them. You said they are both still alive?"

Lucas inclined his head toward her. "Well summed up, my dear. Yes, they are still with us. Getting on in years, but still about in society. I do not know much about either one of them, other than some vague generalities. Dalton has not made a name for himself in the House of Lords, nor in the investment realm. Rathburn, on the other hand, has the reputation of being viciously cunning when it comes to both. He votes in favor of his wealth, it has been said. Even so, neither has had much scandal attached to his name."

"That seems to be a trend in this case, does it not?" Gemma said, considering all the pieces they had thus far. "If we were not digging around in the past, I would never guess any of these gentlemen were involved in something nefarious."

"It does seem like an innocent boy's club. The Kingsmen. How lofty of them," Lucas said with a laugh. "My father never mentioned it in connection with the ring. I did not realize it carried any significance."

"You do not wear it," she commented, glancing at his hands, though she knew it wasn't there.

Lucas looked down at his hands as well, and he clenched and unclenched them. "No."

She wanted to ask him about it, but she stopped herself. She'd already pried enough into his relationship with his father. It seemed complicated at best.

"What do you think we should do in regard to Dalton and Rathburn?" she asked instead.

"If one of them is the blackmailer, it could be dangerous to confront him. I do not think that is likely, however," he said.

"Because of the timing?" Pleasure tingled along her nerve endings. She had been thinking along similar lines. They were in such sync when it came to the case.

"Yes, it does not make sense. If they wanted to punish my father and Perry's they would not have waited until years after they'd died. My guess is they are victims as well. In which case, it might be more efficient to ask them directly," he said.

"Shall we pay our calls now?" Gemma was eager to continue their forward momentum. But Lucas flipped open the lid of his gold pocket watch to check the time and shook his head.

"It is getting late. I think we have missed our window today."

A wave of disappointment crashed over her, but she realized he was correct. They could not call on someone without warning at this time of day. Lucas seemed amused by her discouragement.

"Mayhap we could go by Lord Dalton's house, to take a look before we try again tomorrow," he said, and Gemma brightened.

Lucas opened the divider to the coachman's perch and gave him an address on the outskirts of Mayfair. They should be able to blend into the flow of traffic and passersby.

He shook his head as he settled back into his seat. "I should not let you talk me into such things."

"But how else would anything be accomplished?" she replied as the carriage made a sharp turn toward central London.

• • •

Something was wrong.

They watched the house for more than a quarter of an hour, but they saw no sign of movement.

Even though they were stopped two houses down from Lord Dalton's residence Lucas could see that no one passing by seemed to pay the house any attention. That was perhaps a sensible reaction for a nondescript home among others of the same kind, but this house was dark and shut down, whereas the ones around it were lit up with activity as servants were preparing dinner and the occupants were getting ready for their evenings out on the town.

Lucas could sense Gemma's disquiet as well. She had not said anything since they had pulled up to the address. She bit her lush lip and kept glancing in his direction, which he could see from the corner of his eye even as he kept his attention focused on the house.

"He may not be in town," Gemma said, breaking the tense silence that had filled the carriage.

"I remember seeing him only a few days ago," Lucas responded. "Perhaps he has gone off to a country party, though." For some reason he did not feel confident that was the case. He had learned to trust his gut a long time ago. There was something wrong.

"You don't believe that," Gemma noted, reading him correctly. When had that happened, he wondered. It had been a long time, perhaps never, since someone was able to discern his thoughts with such ease.

"No."

"Should we go check on the house?" she asked. "We could walk right up and knock on the door. I think it is time for society's calling rules to be tossed in the bin."

"I agree with you on that front, but we do not know what we will find. I would prefer to come back under the cloak of darkness. I do not want you tied to this at all. Who knows who has seen my carriage here as it is? I will come back at night when I can have a better look around," he said, even though he knew she would protest.

"I will come with you, my lord," she said, as expected. "I know how to be stealthy as well, or have you forgotten?"

He weighed the possible dangers. As long as they weren't seen, it might be beneficial to have a lookout in this case. And he did not underestimate her ability to be useful in such situations. If something went wrong, though, he would never forgive himself if he failed to protect her… But it wouldn't. The chance of real harm seemed extremely low.

He nodded and smiled at her sigh of relief. "We shall come back tomorrow, after Vauxhall."

Chapter Ten

Mr. Harrington was to come to the house after breakfast, Lucas had told her yesterday. Beatrice peered critically at herself in the looking glass, not fully understanding why she'd put extra effort into her appearance that morning.

Her maid had woven a pretty, light pink ribbon through her short blond curls. It complemented the dress she'd slipped on—her favorite—and both highlighted the color she'd pinched into her cheeks.

She turned slightly to get a different angle then nodded at herself, content with what she saw. Not that it should matter anyway.

Still, she hurried downstairs into Lucas's study so she would not be late. Her brother glanced up when she barged through the door unannounced. He raised his brows but quickly went back to poring over the documents he'd been reading, without so much as a greeting.

"Well, hello to you, too, my dearest brother," she said as sweetly as she could manage. His lips curled up at her tone, but he continued to ignore her otherwise.

"When is Mr. Harrington arriving? And will Gemma be by, as well?" She quickly asked the second question so as to not seem too interested in Mr. Harrington's coming and goings. Her brother heaved an outsized sigh and made a show of placing his papers aside. She bit back a grin. No matter how old they grew, she could always manage to be a thorn in his side.

"I have somehow convinced Gemma not to attend this gathering," he told her. "It would not be quite the thing for her to call on me, especially at this early hour, even though we are betrothed."

"I never fancied you to be such a stickler for propriety, dear brother," she said, unable to resist teasing him.

"I had not realized the depths to which I could be driven until I got a fiancée who cares not a whit for propriety." He smiled. "Who would have ever believed *me* to be its enforcer?"

"Certainly not the person who knew you when you stole kisses from every pretty girl in the village," she commented, and they grinned at the shared memory of a young boy's mischievousness. She really did not know what she would do without Lucas. She so wished she were not the cause of all his problems.

The sharp rap on the door pulled her out of her troubled thoughts. Lucas called out an order, and the footman let Mr. Harrington into the room.

He made a slight bow in greeting to Lucas and then turned to her. Their eyes met, and the world stopped, and she knew instantly why she'd worn her favorite blue dress.

A ghost of a smile flitted over his lips, but it almost seemed mocking. "Lady Beatrice," he murmured.

She curtsied and tried to shake off the sensation that her life had changed. She had certainly enjoyed their day together researching the pocket watch shops, but nothing earth-shattering had happened. They had talked on all matters, mostly trivial, and laughed a bit. He was quite serious, but he had a wicked sense of humor, if one paid attention. Most people might miss it, but she caught it under the dryness in his voice. They lowered themselves into opposing seats.

I am not in love with him.
I am not.
I.
Am.
Not.

Love was fireworks and passion and devastation. With Ralph, it had been a fire that burned through her against her better judgment. And in the end, when he'd abandoned her, it had left her scorched. Panic clawed at her throat, threatening to cut off her air.

No, what she was experiencing now was friendship. When she saw Mr. Harrington, the pleasant glow that coursed through her was nothing like the passion she'd carried for Ralph. She just had never experienced such a thing with a member of the opposite gender.

"I think the more information we collect on this case the better," Lucas said from behind his desk, drawing her attention back to the matter at hand. So much for any preamble, she thought, amused at her brother's abruptness. She hoped Mr. Harrington would not take it personally. "Although we have not crossed anyone off through the pocket watch connection, we have corroborated that there are those on our suspect list who are collectors."

Mr. Harrington nodded, his shoulders taut. He was clearly frustrated he had not progressed further with his questioning. He waited for Lucas to continue.

But instead of speaking, Lucas reached into the upper left-hand drawer of his desk and withdrew a small, emerald green box. Without warning, he tossed it lightly to Mr. Harrington, who, with a surprising grace, snatched it out of midair. She scooted to the edge of her seat so she could see what was inside when he pried open the lid.

"It was my father's," Lucas said. Beatrice saw that it was a heavy gold ring, with a ruby inset at the top of the band.

"Your father was connected to Nigel Lancaster's murder over a pocket watch?" Mr. Harrington asked, his brows raised.

Lucas did not spare her a glance, and she was thankful. If he had, Mr. Harrington might have looked as well, and then both men would have seen that her cheeks were the color of tomatoes. Secrecy and deception had never been her forte. She left that to her brother, for better or worse. Instead, she was allowed to sink into her misery without notice. But it was a good thing she was not in love with Mr. Harrington. Otherwise, she might care if he found out her secret. Yes, it was a good thing indeed.

"We believe Nigel's death is connected to a revenge scheme involving something that took place decades ago," Lucas said, without any mention of her blackmail.

Mr. Harrington took a moment to process the information. "And it's tied to this ring?"

"The ring was bought by four gentlemen who called themselves the Kingsmen," Lucas informed him.

"Lofty," Mr. Harrington commented, his mockery dry and only partially hidden. Beatrice smiled, and Lucas smirked.

"Yes, well, from the sounds of it they weren't exactly modest in their view of themselves," he said. "Apparently they formed the club right out of Oxford. It lasted for a Season at most. I would guess it was focused on typical rakish behavior favored by young bloods of the *ton*. But I think something happened to cause the men to stop associating with each other for the rest of their lives. Something that may have been responsible for tearing the group apart."

Mr. Harrington nodded. He had not taken his eyes off the ring. "You want me to figure out what happened," he said.

"I want you to find out more information about the club," Lucas corrected. "We may never figure out what happened, but I plan on confronting the surviving members over the next few days. But having information when doing so would be immensely helpful."

"Of course," Mr. Harrington said. He finally looked up, and when he did, it was directly into Beatrice's eyes. She caught her breath at the unexpected move. "Is there anything else I should know about this case before I proceed?" he asked, still looking at her, as if peering directly into her soul.

He knows.

Lucas cleared his throat. "Why would you ask such a question?"

"I find myself to be most efficient when I have all the information available," Mr. Harrington said, clearly choosing his words carefully. The room was taut with tension, and all three occupants were on high alert. She felt it in the air. "I would not want to duplicate efforts or chase down dead ends unnecessarily."

Beatrice interrupted before either could say any more. "I want to help you, Mr. Harrington. I was helpful the other day, was I not? I think we could get more information if I accompany you today, and Lucas did say I could help you, even if he does not really think I am clever enough," she said, her words tumbling out in a rush. Both men would try to discourage her, so she hoped to overwhelm their senses enough that they didn't realize they'd agreed to let her participate in something potentially dangerous.

"You do not know how I intend to spend the day, Lady Beatrice," Mr. Harrington reminded her in an even voice. "You might not wish to join me if you knew where I was planning to visit."

"I do not care," she proclaimed, and she meant it. He would protect her wherever he took her, of that she was certain. And she wanted desperately to help with the case again. She had finally been useful the other day. She wanted to feel that way again. Especially since it was her fault they were in the predicament.

They both turned to Lucas, who was leaned fully back in his chair. He watched them over steepled fingers.

"I have promised Gemma a drive in the park to keep her informed of our status," he said. "So I will not be available to provide any further information Harrington might need in the course of his questioning. It might be useful for you to go along, Bea."

She was afraid if she thanked him she would give him time to change his mind. Instead, she shot Mr. Harrington a victorious look and rushed to the door. She'd need only a few minutes to prepare for the outing. He wouldn't have time to leave without her.

• • •

Lucas tamped down his frustration at the pace of the curricle in front of theirs. He and Gemma had arrived in Hyde Park just before the truly fashionable hour, but the drive was still packed with vehicles and single riders making their social rounds for the day. Hyde Park in the afternoon was the place to see and be seen, and any desire to give his horses their heads had to be curbed.

He concentrated on the woman beside him instead of the urge to pummel the driver in front of them. She had her face tipped up to the sun to welcome its rays, a position he had noticed she often adopted while out of doors.

He realized it made him happy to see her happy. He caught his hand as it went to reach for her, remembering at the last minute that they were in public.

"Harrington and Beatrice went off to interview a few of

Harrington's older acquaintances and a jeweler or two," he said after filling her in on the morning.

"They will be successful," she predicted optimistically.

Lucas smirked. "You can be so sure?"

Her eyes snapped to his. "I can be. Beatrice is so very curious and smart. And Mr. Harrington seems quite competent, from what you have told me. What is he like?"

Lucas thought about it. He knew part of the question came from her anxiety over the investigation. He wondered where the other part came from. He tried to reassure her on the first front. "He is perceptive."

Gemma nodded, but clearly she wanted more. "What is he like, though?" she asked. "Is he humorous, is he serious? What does he look like? Is he a handsome young man?"

Lucas took his eyes off the drive and narrowed them in her direction. "What are you about?"

She nibbled on a delectable lip and cast a sidelong glance his way. "Well, Beatrice is a lovely young woman," she said finally. "They are being placed in a situation with high tensions. It would be natural for them to form a…" She trailed off, searching for the right word but not quite finding it. He followed her train of thought, and his hands tightened on the reins. His horses protested, and of course Gemma noticed. "Do you oppose the thought because he is your man of affairs?"

He clenched his jaw. "I am not a snob."

"I did not say you were one," she soothed. "Simply that it may not be looked upon as the most suitable match for your sister, even though he is the son of a gentleman."

"The fourth son," he bit off. Though he had been truthful—he was not a snob—he also knew his sister would not be happy in a life of poverty. It might seem romantic at first, but it would destroy her light soul. He would never want to see that for her. But Harrington was not impoverished.

He wore old clothes, but it seemed to Lucas to be more of a deplorable lack of fashion sense than because of his fortune or lack thereof. Lucas, himself, paid very well, and Beatrice would bring a considerable dowry into any match she made. And Harrington's father was a viscount.

"They have met only a handful of times," Lucas said, wondering how she'd even made him think of it. "They have shown no partiality toward each other."

"That you have noticed," Gemma replied tartly.

He opened his mouth to form a retort, but at that moment, a young, redheaded gentleman stopped alongside their curricle.

"Mr. Tidwell," Gemma cried out. "How lovely to see you this afternoon."

Mr. Tidwell beamed jovially back at Gemma. "Good day to you, Miss Lancaster." He eyed Lucas. "Winchester. Fine horses you have here. Very fine, very fine."

Lucas smirked. The young pup was nervous. Tidwell immediately directed his attention back to Gemma, engaging her in a lively debate about the latest Travel Society fellow to present a lecture. Gemma had missed it, she informed the lad, but she had read his works and found them stimulating.

"You simply must try to attend Lady Underwood's salon next week," Tidwell said earnestly. "Jones will be there, along with many of the members of the society."

"Oh, that sounds ever so delightful," Gemma said, clasping hands to bosom. "I shall endeavor to attend."

"I look forward to that greatly." Tidwell touched his whip to the brim of his hat and rode off with barely a nod to Lucas.

"You have an admirer," he commented as Tidwell faded into the throng of horses and conveyances.

"Pish posh." Gemma swatted his arm. "He is a nice young man, but barely out of the schoolroom." She laughed at that. "Anyway, I am not some great beauty. I am hardly one to collect suitors."

She said it lightly, but he could tell she believed it. "You are, though, my dear. A great beauty," he said. This time he let himself brush fingers over her knee. Just a quick, comforting gesture to make sure she knew he wasn't teasing. They locked eyes for a brief moment, before he returned his to the path.

"Well…" She cleared her throat. "It will be interesting to hear about Beatrice's day. Shall we await for them in your drawing room?"

"Yes," he said. "But you should put match-making out of your mind. If not, you should remember why we are in this mess in the first place. Beatrice is convinced no man will have her now, and I cannot reassure her."

Gemma smiled away the warning. "Ah, but you never know what life will throw at you, my lord. Young love can overcome many obstacles."

Lucas simply shook his head, then started laughing, which drew many a curious eye to them. He did not care.

. . .

Beatrice huffed out a frustrated breath as they stepped out of the jeweler's shop without having made any progress in uncovering the origin of the ring. It was the third one they'd visited that day.

"Research is not quite as elegant and charming as you may have imagined, Lady Beatrice," Mr. Harrington said, with enough condescension to raise her hackles.

"Yes, and my only pursuit in life is glamour," she snapped. "I could hardly bear something, no matter how worthwhile, that was not for pure enjoyment and laughter."

"Prickly," he commented, with that peculiar half smile of his. She was growing to hate it. She did not know what it was about him that brought out the worst in her. She certainly never snapped at anyone else that way.

Even though she knew she was being childish, she refused to make polite conversation as they walked the distance to the fourth store. She had wanted her silence to speak volumes about her irritation, but he seemed unaffected—if not downright cheery—at her lack of communication. Which only served to make her more irritated.

She couldn't quite hold on to her ire, though, when the fourth jeweler, after examining the ring, pushed his glasses up on his head and smiled at them. "I know this work."

Beatrice bit back the exclamation that sprung to her lips. This was not the vague praise they'd received at their previous stops. This might actually be progress. She took her cue from Mr. Harrington, though, and remained quiet.

"My memory is not what it used to be," the jeweler prompted.

Mr. Harrington simply raised a brow. "I am certain if you try hard, some name will come to mind."

Beatrice's glance darted between the two men. They seemed to be in a standoff of sorts. "I believe he wants to be bribed," she said, out of the corner of her mouth to Mr. Harrington.

Mr. Harrington turned full on toward her. His face was blank for a moment, but she saw humor in his eyes. It made its way to his mouth, and he tipped back his head in a full out roar of laughter. Surprised at the outburst, she actually took a step back; she had not seen him display any emotion in her short acquaintance with him, let alone something as ostentatious as what she had unwittingly provoked.

He took a deep breath a few moments later, wiping moisture from his eye. "You are quite correct, I believe, Lady Beatrice. And you are right that the pretense of it is just a waste of our time." He pulled a handful of coins out of his pocket and dropped them on the dusty countertop. The shopkeeper swooped them up with a practiced move, tucking them into his work apron.

"Ah yes, ah yes, it is all quite clear now," he said, as if thinking deeply.

"I thought it might be." Harrington had returned to his detached, sarcastic persona. It would be a long time, though, before she forgot the image of him almost bent double in laughter—even if he had been having fun at her expense. It was a sight to have seen.

"You want Mr. Adams on Ox Street," the shopkeeper said. "It is a few blocks over."

By the time they swung through the door of Mr. Adams' shop, Beatrice could barely contain her excitement. Some of it dimmed when they came face to face with the shopkeeper, however.

Mr. Adams' disheveled appearance was a sharp contrast to his pristine shop, Beatrice thought, eyeing him. She wanted to take a discrete step back, but held her ground. She would not show any signs of unease, lest Mr. Harrington send her on her way. She had a feeling he would pounce on any sign of perceived trepidation.

She turned her full attention to Mr. Adams as he examined the ring. He was a crooked old man, probably made so by years spent hunched over, shaping and creating rings and necklaces and other baubles. He had a smell she could not quite place, but wished to avoid. She wondered if it would be rude to breathe through a handkerchief. Even if it wouldn't, it would earn her a sardonic glance from Mr. Harrington, so she refrained.

Mr. Adams's clothes seemed to have a layer of dust on them, while the store itself was spotless. She wondered at his life. Mr. Harrington did not seem affected either by the sight or smell of the man. He stood casually against one of the tables, looking around the shop. Was it possible to love and despise someone at the same time? She supposed it was, they were two emotions that shared the same coin. He caught her watching him and graced her with that small half smile again, the one that said he was mocking the world behind his quiet reserve. She turned from him abruptly.

Mr. Adams peered up at them and said, finally and simply, "This is mine."

She locked eyes in triumph with Mr. Harrington. "Do you remember who commissioned it, sir?"

His heavy, lined face looked up to the ceiling in thought. He seemed to truly be in his memories, however, and not after a bribe.

"It was one of four," he finally intoned. His deep voice resonated throughout the shop. "They paid handsomely for me to never replicate it again. I did not. Even when a young man came in asking about it."

Mr. Harrington straightened, a sharp movement in the corner of her eye. "Someone wanted you to create a copy of it?"

"Hmm? Yes, a young man. Quite polite. His father owned the ring. Lost it right before his untimely death. Such a shame. Some of my finer work." He twisted the ring in the light again.

"Did the young man talk about his father?" Beatrice asked. Even if the story was false, it could provide clues. People tended to interweave truth into lies.

"Hmmm? Ah, just that he was a bit of a rake in his day. Was part of a club. I remembered that part," he told them proudly. "Can you describe the young man who came in?" Mr. Harrington asked.

"Hmm? Yes, let me see." Mr. Adams looked skyward. She considered doing the same to ask for patience. "Yellow hair. Walked with a slight limp. A little cockney in there. Not sure where that came from if his Pa was a lord. Which those boys were."

"Did he look at anything else in the shop?" Beatrice

asked.

"Hmm. Now that you mention it, he stopped by the watch case," Mr. Adams answered with a nod toward the far side of the shop. "He asked the price. Didn't buy, though."

Mr. Harrington pulled out a banknote this time and slipped it to Mr. Adams. "For your time, sir."

"Oh not necessary, not necessary," Mr. Adams muttered as he tucked the note away. Mr. Harrington gestured for Beatrice to go ahead of him.

"Well, that did not get us far," Beatrice complained as they stepped out into the small alley. She waved him off before he could make a comment. "I know, it is not all exciting and flashy as, of course, I must think it all is. But we came so close to being useful."

"I was not disparaging you, Lady Beatrice," Mr. Harrington said quietly after she finished her rant. "This sort of investigation is tedious and often fruitless. But every time you turn up any information it is helpful and useful. I was offering comfort and reassurance." He glanced her way, and this time his half smile was self-mocking, she could tell. "I do not appear to be very good at it, though, do I?"

Before she could reply, there was a rumble at the far end of the alley. She turned to see a carriage thundering down on them, with no apparent intent to stop. Beatrice froze as the hooves on stone grew perilously close. She felt a tug on her arm and let herself be jerked out of the way as the horses roared by. She found her back flat up against the brick of one of the buildings. Mr. Harrington had pulled her into an entryway and then proceeded to protect her with his body. If he had not done so, she would have been trampled.

She was breathing fast, as if she'd run very quickly up a hill, but she had not exerted herself one bit, other than to let herself be saved. He lifted his head to look down at her, but he did not pull away. She became aware that their legs were intertwined, that his body was pushed into hers, and that hers was pushed into the wall behind her. The wall did not give at all, and his body barely did. He might look unassuming when viewed from a distance, but when she was pressed against all his sinewy strength, she went weak at the knees. His eyes flicked down to her parted lips, where she still gasped for air far too quickly.

He lifted a hand and traced a thumb over her bottom lip. The movement quieted her breathing. They were so close, she could see all the flecks of color in his eyes. He lowered his head even closer and laid his mouth on hers. She tilted her head and opened her mouth, willingly accepting his probing tongue. Someone moaned as he explored, and she was fearful to admit that it was probably her. Her arms lifted on their own volition to wrap around his neck, her fingers resting on it.

He pulled away after a few moments.

"Are you all right?" Mr. Harrington—no, George, she could not think of him as Mr. Harrington any longer—asked, after studying her face. She dropped her arms back down as if she'd been burned. He stepped away from her, but did not go far. She immediately missed his comforting warmth.

"Thanks to you, I appear to be in one piece," she said, smoothing shaking hands over her dress. "What a careless driver that coachman was. He could have killed us."

He turned and looked down the alleyway from where it had come. "I'm not sure careless is the word I would use to describe that incident."

She drew in a sharp breath. "Are you saying that may have been deliberate?"

"I am saying I would be surprised if it was not," George said. "Come, let's get you home."

• • •

"Do you think they have discovered anything?" Gemma

asked for possibly the fourteenth time. Lucas glanced over his shoulder, one eyebrow raised. "I know I am being silly. We will just have to wait until they arrive home. They have been gone for some time though." She took a deep breath. She was babbling. Lucas, on the other hand, was calm and composed. She glared at his back, and considered hurling her teacup at him just to draw out a reaction.

Just as the evil thought flitted into her mind, the door burst open with no warning. Beatrice whirled into the room, a flash of color and noise in the quiet salon. Mr. Harrington trailed behind in her wake, a quiet and understated contrast to her.

"Someone tried to kill us," Beatrice announced dramatically then melted onto the love seat, clutching at her bosom.

Lucas turned sharply toward them. "What do you mean? Explain yourself."

Gemma knew in his worry he showed the worst of his arrogant earl self, biting out commands in a way that made him seem devoid of any feeling. But she could see the concern in his eyes. She shifted her focus to his sister, moving over to sit beside her. She placed a gentle arm around her shoulder, feeling a kinship with the girl even though she'd only met her once before.

"Are you all right?" Gemma asked her, glancing toward Mr. Harrington. He was watching Beatrice with an inscrutable expression, until he caught Gemma's eye. Then he turned toward Lucas.

"We were almost run down by a carriage outside one of the jewelers we visited," he said gravely.

"We are only alive thanks to the quick actions of Mr. Harrington," Beatrice exclaimed. "I would not be here now, otherwise. He heard the horses and pulled me out of the way to safety."

Lucas walked to Harrington, hand outstretched. "My good man, I owe you a great debt, it seems," he said.

"You owe me nothing," Harrington said quietly, but took

Lucas's proffered hand.

"Was the carriage out of control?" Gemma asked, pouring a cup of tea for Beatrice, who locked eyes with Harrington across the room.

"We do not believe it was," Harrington finally answered. "The alley ended on one side, and the carriage was clearly lying in wait for us to exit. It charged us down, not with the reckless abandon of a runaway horse, but with the speed of a directed team. I believe it was deliberate."

"Is it our killer, my lord?" she asked Lucas.

"It sounds like a possibility, yes," Lucas said. He gestured toward the chairs for Harrington to sit. They gathered around the small table in the middle of the room. "Tell us, did you discover anything today?"

Beatrice clapped her hands, cheeks flushed in excitement. "We found the man who crafted Papa's ring."

Gemma drew in a sharp breath and shifted forward, her eyes intense on Beatrice. "Did he know anything?"

Beatrice sagged a bit at that. "Well, no. Not much about the club other than it existed and that they commissioned the rings for it."

Harrington was studying his hands while Beatrice spoke. He glanced up when she finished, his little half smile tugging at his lips. "I was telling Lady Beatrice that any information on a case such as this is a step forward. I do believe we discovered several things today. Important or not, they could lead to the right clue in the end to help solve the mystery."

Beatrice narrowed her eyes dangerously, seemingly recovered from her brush with danger. "You are right, of course, Mr. Harrington," she said, sounding as if she wanted nothing more than to be able to say the opposite to him. "The jeweler also told us that a young man had come in asking about the very same ring."

Gemma's muscles bunched. "Our villain," she murmured.

Lucas's eyes slid to hers and their gazes held.

"Possibly," Mr. Harrington cautioned.

"What did you learn about him?" Lucas asked.

"He is not a wealthy man." Beatrice turned to Lucas and Gemma when she spoke. She missed Harrington's approving nod, but Gemma did not.

"Why do you say that?" Gemma asked. They suspected it was someone who ran in their circles of the *ton*, but that did not mean that he was necessarily rich.

Beatrice glanced at Harrington, who remained quiet, letting her share the information. "The young man visited the jeweler to try to either force him to make a replica of the ring, or to simply get information out of him," she said. She shrugged, though, an unladylike gesture that Gemma found endearing. "It does not matter, for I would wager he was unsuccessful on both accounts. The jeweler would not make another ring, and, as I said, did not seem to have a depth of knowledge about the men who had commissioned them. But, our villain—if we are to assume he is our villain—stopped to admire a pocket watch on his way out. When told the price he continued on his way."

"If he were a collector and had the blunt, I believe he would have purchased what he was admiring," Harrington added.

Lucas nodded. "That has sound logic to it, and fits with other aspects of the case. We believe he is blackmailing a number of people," he said, without revealing he was one of the victims. Poor Beatrice, Gemma thought, before Lucas continued. "Just as much as they can afford, and not more. It might be paying for the villain to be able to keep up appearances. A Season in London is an expensive endeavor."

"He also had a description of the man," Beatrice informed them.

"Oh!" Gemma exclaimed, sitting forward on the edge of the seat. Why they had not mentioned that fact first?

Harrington cleared his throat. "It was a young man. Blond, curly hair. He walked with a limp and had a cockney accent."

Lucas sat back, steepling his fingers. "Ah."

Beatrice, though, looked as confused as Gemma felt. "That is wonderful, is it not, Lucas? That will help us narrow down our field of suspects dramatically."

Lucas and Harrington exchanged a knowing glance. "Does it not seem a bit too easy, my dear? For us to have a very precise picture of the villain," Lucas drawled. "My guess is we are in fact looking for the opposite of that descriptor."

"You see, Miss Lancaster, they are quite obvious traits," Harrington added. "They are something a witness would see and remember, and then remember nothing else. The person could be invisible in plain sight."

"The accent, though, I wonder at," Lucas said. "If he is not a wealthy man and can affect a cockney accent at will, then perhaps he was not raised a gentleman."

"And you learned something else today, too," Gemma said, after they had spent a few moments in contemplation. "You learned that we are on the right path with the ring. Our current predicament has something to do with the secret club your father helped start years ago."

"We also learned that you ladies should not be involved in this case any further," Lucas said, his face set.

"That is enough, my lord," Gemma said with barely controlled temper. "This is my case, too. More so mine than yours. And I will decide for myself if it is safe enough."

"Hear, hear, Miss Lancaster," Beatrice cheered. "This dreadful experience only made me want to find the culprit more. Now tell me, you are to visit Vauxhall tonight? Are you ever so excited?"

The men exchanged a meaningful glance Gemma was sure Lucas thought she had missed. But she did not. High-handed, arrogant... She turned to Beatrice. "I cannot wait."

Chapter Eleven

Gemma was buzzing by the time they arrived at Vauxhall. They had taken a boat across the river to get to the pleasure gardens, and she had never felt more exotic. She'd wanted to draw a lazy hand through the river, even though she knew that would not have been a smart idea.

But it wasn't just the excitement of the adventure that was making her blood hum and her pulse skitter. It was him.

She hadn't even tried to deny it or justify it to herself. She just let her eyes have free rein over his features. Something pulsed deep within her when a lock of dark hair fell over his eyes. The feeling was so new to her that she could barely put a name to it. But in the quiet of the night she recognized it for what it was.

Desire.

They joined the mass of people streaming into the pleasure gardens. Some were masked; others were decked out in marvelous gowns. The excitement of the crowd shot through the air like lightning.

She was determined to enjoy the night and put the

investigation out of her thoughts as they strolled toward the brightly colored tents. Music and laughter floated by. It was similar to a ball, Gemma thought, but she preferred the gardens. Being outside under the blanket of stars and inky night sky felt somehow magical, like anything could happen here, and did. A small child dashed by, a lolly in hand, giggling wildly; an older man helped his wife onto a bench to wait for the fireworks; a group of young men guffawed and punched each other's arms, putting on a show for the ladies who had just walked by with their chaperones. And underneath it all was an undercurrent of wildness—a sense of inevitability since they were all free from many of society's strict rules.

"Do you come here often when you are in town, my lord?" she asked, nodding to an acquaintance she recognized.

"Almost never, actually. My parents brought us when we were children, of course. But I have only been back a time or two since then," he answered.

"Why did you want to bring me here tonight?" she asked, curious.

It was as if he were courting her.

The fanciful notion was captivating but dangerous for her heart to believe. They were partners on a case, nothing more—regardless of the desire that sparked across her skin when he touched her, or the feeling that blossomed in the pit of her stomach when he turned those emerald eyes on her.

He was quiet for so long she thought he might not answer. "One of the last times I came here I had just finished my education. I was about to take on all the responsibilities of an earl's heir. I knew all my life that was what I was destined to do—run our estates, take care of the family name." He paused. "I am not resentful of it, but at the time I was feeling…a bit stifled, as young men can. I was unaware of all the privilege I was afforded, and instead focused on all that I would not be able to do."

"That seems natural," Gemma said, pulling him to a stop at the edge of a small crowd. A vibrant canary and crimson canvas was sprawled on the ground, attached to a large woven basket. A small man with a large gray mustache and very little hair under his tall top hat was gesturing frenetically at the contraption.

"You can kiss the sky!" His voice boomed over the crowd as he bounced and danced around. "Fly with the angels, sing with the birds, look down on your fellow man as if they were the smallest of creatures!"

"I would think you would want to avoid flying with angels, as that would mean you have been called to your reward a bit early," Lucas said under his breath.

Gemma laughed. "Oh, hush. It does look amazing, does it not? I have always wanted to go up in a hot air balloon. Perhaps we could share the experience with someone a bit saner, though, yes? He seems like he is about to turn cartwheels."

Lucas smirked, and they continued on.

"Please, my lord, finish your thoughts from earlier," Gemma prompted.

"Yes, right. Well, I came here one night with some chaps from school, I don't even remember who anymore. But when I got here…" He trailed off, seeming hesitant. "It was a different world. Dock workers, dandies, whores, families. It was like traveling to a different country, to an exotic land—England felt continents away. It made me want to travel." He glanced at her out of the corner of his eye. "And by that I mean travel, nothing more. I wanted to see the world. I thought you would like to experience that. As you are committed to staying in London until we solve this case, I wanted to give you a taste of adventure."

She felt a long, slow swoop in her chest and wondered how long she'd been in love with this man. Had it been from the moment he'd forced an introduction? From when he found her hiding in the library? From the moment his lips had touched hers in that sensuous glide? She didn't know. She had never experienced the feeling before, but she was absolutely sure that she loved him. There was a quiet acceptance and certainty there. This man who wanted to give her adventure, even if it was just at a pleasure garden in the middle of London.

She cleared her throat, shaken. "Well, you have given me that. And I will always remember it."

"'Tis nothing, really," he said, embarrassment coloring his voice.

"It is, though," she said. They entered into a covered walkway that was painted with detailed scenes of lively revelry. She smiled at the image of a curvaceous blond coquette offering wine to a besotted lord. "As much as I consider myself a woman of the world, I have not seen much outside the bounds of our small village. Uncle Artie instilled in me a need to travel and see as much as possible, but my circumstances have tied me to the English countryside. You may think this is nothing, but to me this is everything. I am getting a taste of adventure tonight."

She smiled up at him, trying to control her emotions. She refused to fall apart just because she realized she was in love with Lucas.

This was not the night to worry about the future. It was not the time to think about how hopeless a true match between them might be. She would not despair over the inevitable end, but cherish the moments that she had with him. Savor the look of him, his smile, the way he made her laugh…even if it was just for this one night.

A loud crack brought her back to reality. She giggled out her nerves and turned toward the sound: the fireworks had begun.

The dark sky exploded with golds and blues; greens and

purples. She leaned against Lucas and let his warmth seep into her as she enjoyed the display. She'd thought falling in love would be like the fireworks, a riot of noise, color, and light. It had been more of a slow burn.

They clapped at the finale, sparks raining down like falling stars. Gemma never wanted it to end, and was happy there was still more to see.

"Oh!" She let out a happy exclamation and pointed toward one of the tents. "Look, Lucas, it is a tightrope walker. Let us go watch."

After the demonstration, Lucas pulled her to her feet, and they joined the crowd pushing toward the exit. The audience was being herded into one path and people were jostling about, eager to get on to the next attraction. For the first time all night she began to feel claustrophobic. A gentleman bumped into her from behind, and she felt a catch in her throat. She was not prone to discomfort in large crowds, but she was getting desperate to reach the cool fresh air.

A moment later she felt a hand push something into hers. She clutched at it without thought, glancing back to catch a glimpse of who was behind her. She saw a flash of blond hair, but before she could see a face, a pair of hands on her back propelled her toward the hard ground. It happened so fast she did not have time to brace for the impact. Lucas grabbed her arm before she hit the dirt, hauling her up and close to him. He pulled her to the side and out of the flow of the masses.

"Are you all right?" His eyes roved over her face, searching for signs of injury as he maintained his grip on her.

She felt out of sorts, but conducted a mental inventory on herself. "I am unhurt, my lord." Gemma glanced back toward the entrance. "I did not trip, though. I was pushed."

Lucas went still. "Someone knocked into you?"

She shook her head. "It was not an accident. Someone wanted me to fall. I felt the hands on my back. It was deliberate."

Lucas's eyes shot back to the crowd, scanning faces. "He is probably long gone, my lord," she told him. His fingers clenched on her arms for a brief moment, his face a hard mask. "I think it was because of this." She held up the folded slip of paper she'd managed to hold on to during the incident.

He studied her face. Outrage shown in his eyes, but his gaze caressed her skin. Her own breathing was returning to normal, and she waited patiently for his adrenalin-fueled anger to subside as well.

Finally, his gaze slid to the note in her hand. "What is it?"

"I do not know. Someone slipped it to me moments before I was pushed. I turned to see if I could identify the culprit, and that's when I was shoved to the ground," she said.

He took the paper she held out to him, his jaw clenching as he read it. She reached over and snatched it back to read it herself.

Dearest Gemma,

Abandon this reckless path you have set upon. Stay out of this affair. If not, someone will end up hurt. Or worse. You do not want that on your conscience, do you, my darling?

She exhaled and met Lucas's grim eyes. "The writing. Is it the same?"

"It looks similar to the blackmail demands," he confirmed.

Excitement hummed through Gemma, at odds with what she thought she should be experiencing at such a moment.

"I cannot say I enjoyed the encounter, but between the carriage incident this afternoon, and now this…well, now we know one thing," Gemma said.

"What is that?"

"We are doing something right."

...

Lucas tapped the roof of the carriage, a signal they were ready for their next destination: Lord Dalton's residence.

To her credit, she appeared in good spirits after the encounter. He had been watching her closely since her lithe body had crashed into him on her way toward the ground.

He would not forget the terror soon. The fact that she was unhurt was irrelevant; someone had been close enough to slip that paper into her hand. If the person had wanted to, he could have slipped a knife between Gemma's ribs and been gone before Lucas even realized she was injured.

He had to do a better job of protecting her. She was so willing to march directly into danger and that meant it was up to him to keep her safe. Sweat beaded on his palms at the thought of not being able to keep her out of harm's way. He'd lived through that before. But for some reason he knew he wouldn't be able to survive it, if something happened to Gemma. He didn't want to delve into why he knew it would be different. He wasn't ready.

He watched the moonlight play along the soft contours of her face. Something about her pulled at him. There was attraction there, especially in his heightened state of awareness. He wanted nothing more than to sink into her soft body, to reassure them both they were very much alive.

But that's not all.

It was the tenderness. The way her happiness was his. The way her pain was his. Tonight had been a sharp reminder that this was not a woman he could walk away from easily.

Gemma did not attempt to fill the silence, for which he was grateful. It gave him time to think. By the time the carriage clattered to a halt at the end of the alleyway behind Lord Dalton's house, he had formulated a plan. While he did not think Gemma would particularly like it, he knew she would come around eventually. It made sense. He would mention it to her tomorrow, though, after all the emotions surrounding her assault had calmed. As it was, she would be upset. She might even believe he'd tricked her. She would not want to feel he'd been pressured into the decision by outside forces.

He shifted his attention to the alleyway. He had instructed the coachman to stop around the block so they could enter through the back gardens without being noticed. He considered telling Gemma to stay in the carriage, but he knew she would not follow such orders. And it would be better to keep her close, he told himself. He could keep an eye on her that way.

He made a few adjustments to his clothing, stripping off the crisp white cravat from his neck, turning up the collar of his dark greatcoat. He eyed Gemma's apparel with approval: she'd chosen a dark green gown with a black cloak. Her hair was slicked back and out of the way, and she'd worn sturdy boots instead of soft, ineffectual slippers.

"That was impressive, my lord," Gemma commented from her darkened corner of the carriage. "You fade into the night as if you were a shadow."

He raised an eyebrow. "The skill has come in handy a time or two."

"I'm sure," she said, nodding that she was ready after adjusting her skirts one last time.

He jumped to the loose pebbles below, not bothering to lower the carriage's steps. He landed with the grace of a hunting cat and spun to grasp Gemma by the waist, lifting her down from the cab. He let his fingers skim up to her rib cage almost to her breasts before dropping away. Her eyes were deep pools in the dark night. Focus, he told himself.

He closed the door and rapped on the side once. The carriage meandered off down the narrow lane, and he pulled Gemma with him into the shadows of the alley.

He leaned in close, catching her sweet scent. "From here on in, no talking unless absolutely necessary." She nodded her acknowledgment, and he felt a deep certainty in his chest. It had been quite some time since he'd had such complete trust in someone. Although she could be stubborn beyond anything he had ever experienced when she felt she was right, he knew with absolute faith that she would do what was necessary to keep them both safe—even if it meant following his orders.

Dalton's house was four in from the start of the lane. He counted to the correct one and eyed the fence. It would be easy to make it over the flimsy barrier. He scanned their surroundings to see if it was safe to leave Gemma unguarded for the few moments it would take to scale it, and then gripped the wood and heaved himself up. Two more swift moves and he was dropping into the hushed gardens. He unlocked the gate, pushed it open, and tugged Gemma inside.

The house was dark and the night was cloudy, so not even the moon gave them away as they made their way to the door. The garden was overrun, providing plenty of coverage in case a neighbor happened to glance out a window. They ducked between rose bushes and lemon trees, pausing only when a clatter arose from the alley. He held up a hand until he heard the telltale screech of a cat. The fighting animals scattered after a few moments, and they continued onward.

They made it to the door without further incident. He tried the knob to test if it was open, but it did not budge. He withdrew his tools and ran a finger over the metal. He did not need light to pick the lock; he could do it with his eyes closed. He made quick work of it and slid the door open.

The smell hit him first, a fist to the stomach.

He knew the stench well. He reached into his pocket to retrieve a handkerchief for Gemma. Her eyes were wide, but she still had not made a sound. They locked grim gazes. There was no mistaking what they would find inside. He raised his eyebrows in a question, and she grimaced but nodded her head. She would come with him.

They made their way through the deserted kitchens into the hallway. He nudged open the door to the dining room and did a quick sweep. Empty. He repeated the moves on two parlors toward the front of the house. There was nothing out of order—no signs of distress anywhere.

The unnatural quiet of the house told a different tale, however.

They reached a closed door that Lucas presumed to be the study. He withdrew the small pistol he carried in his pocket. He did not think the villain remained at the scene, but the weight of it was reassuring in his hand, especially with Gemma coming in behind him.

It looked as if Dalton was waiting for them. He was propped up in his chair behind his desk, dressed for a night on the town, in slightly outdated but expensive clothes. A thick crystal glass halfway filled with Scotch sat in front of him.

Gemma clutched his handkerchief to her nose as they stepped closer. Lucas saw the pistol in Dalton's hand, dangling down toward the floor. He slipped his own back into his pocket. There was no need for it here.

There was no sign of struggle. Dalton's drawers were tucked in place, his papers untouched on his desk. He did not look like he'd been in a fight for his life, either, his body only slightly askew in the deep leather chair. Lucas gathered from the single glass that Dalton had not invited his murderer in for drinks before the crime, which might have indicated a familiarity with the man.

If not for the hole in Dalton's head, it would be an ordinary scene.

Gemma waved a hand to get his attention and pointed to the letter directly in front of Dalton. Lucas leaned over to read it, careful not to touch or disturb anything. Gemma mimicked the move.

> *Forgive me my weakness, for I have sinned gravely. I cannot bear the guilt any longer. I am sorry to all whom I have hurt with my cruel actions. I hope my death will make it right. Inveniam viam aut faciam. D.*

"I shall find a way, or make one," Gemma whispered, meeting his eyes.

Lucas nodded once, and scanned the desk for any other clues. "We need to leave. We've lingered long enough." He would not want to have to explain to a night watchman what they were doing breaking into a dead man's house.

"I do not need to be told twice," Gemma said, heading for the door without a backward glance.

Chapter Twelve

Lucas kneeled by the fireplace to coax the coals into flames, while Gemma poured them both a healthy serving of brandy from Roz's decanter. They had ridden back to the house in silence, caught up in digesting the events of the evening. But they had much to discuss, so she'd invited him in. Because of the case, she told herself, not because she desperately longed for his company after an emotionally fraught night.

She held out his glass then slipped off her heavy-duty boots, removed the knife she had strapped to her ankle, and tucked herself into the corner of the couch. She took a sip of the amber liquid and relished the way it burned down her throat and warmed her belly. There was a chill there, and it would be a while before she could close her eyes without seeing Lord Dalton's sightless gaze.

Lucas took his glass to the window and leaned a shoulder against the frame. He made such an imposing figure against the darkened glass that she smiled. He was a large man, sculpted like Michelangelo's David. Not that she'd ever seen it, of course, outside of books. That was Lucas though—all sinewy muscle and strength. A lion amongst the peacocks of the town.

"A penny for your thoughts," he said, and she struggled to contain a giggle. She could not imagine his reaction if she told him where her mind had wandered.

"I'm thinking brandy was a good decision," she said, raising her glass to her lips.

"Tonight did take a shocking turn, did it not?" he agreed and took a long swallow of the drink. He rolled the glass in his hand, catching the flicker of the firelight in its bevels. "So now we have at least two murders."

"You think it was a murder, and not that he killed himself."

"I do. The killer was methodical, but it still looked staged. And the writing did not quite match the other papers on the desk."

"What do you think happened to the servants?" Gemma asked the question that had been nagging her since they first encountered the scene. "You would think they would have reported the death. He had to have been there for at least two days now."

"I am sure they took off the moment they found him," Lucas said. "No servant in England would want to report his employer's death, if the circumstances appeared suspicious. Investigators would immediately target one of them, perhaps paint the picture of one pinching the silver."

"But the scene was not suspicious, at least how it was staged," Gemma pondered, though she saw his point. The lower class was quite vulnerable when it came to giving surviving family members satisfactory answers. She would not have wanted to linger in Dalton's home had she discovered him. In fact, they hadn't.

"Perhaps one of them saw something," he said, considering her point.

"I shall ask Mrs. Bird, as well. Housekeepers are a tight-knit group, and we do not live far from Dalton's residence. Perhaps she knew some of the servants," she said. "But do we alert the authorities?"

"I'll send round to a friend—a Bow Street Runner. I'll tell him I have tried to stop by Dalton's house several times to no avail, and that I am worried about the man. He knows that I would not send him on a fool's errand," Lucas said. "That should take care of it."

"They will rule it a suicide, won't they?" It was not that they were always incompetent, but the investigators tended to take the easier routes when it came to crimes dealing with the upper class, Gemma knew. They had no sway over members of society and they often ended up with dead ends. If the scene appeared to be a suicide, they would not go chasing the idea of murder.

"Most likely. Dalton had no close relatives—the title will go to a distant cousin. They will want that to go as quickly and smoothly as possible. No one will press for a thorough investigation," Lucas said matter-of-factly. "I think the best chance for justice is that we find the blackmailer."

Lucas pushed away from the window and began to pace the length of the room. "I do not like the feeling of being one step behind him."

Gemma tracked his restless movements. "We are learning more each day, though, my lord. We are getting closer to him, and he knows it. He would not bother with warning me off otherwise. Or with chasing Mr. Harrington and Beatrice down."

Lucas removed his coat and sank into the chair across from her. "You are right, my dear. He is getting nervous. Which means he may make a mistake. One that could prove to be his downfall."

"He might have done so tonight," Gemma said. "Why would he take the chance to contact me?"

"There's a chance he's observing you from afar and has become infatuated," Lucas said slowly, considering. "However, the way the letter was written…"

"It seemed like he knew me," Gemma finished for him.

"Yes," he agreed. "It does not narrow the field down by much. You have many acquaintances in town. It would just take a small introduction for him to become attached to you."

"Please, I am no siren," Gemma said, unable to fathom that a man would become infatuated with her within moments of meeting.

Lucas shot her one of his feral grins. "You are, my dear, but that is not what I meant. There are madmen out there who latch on to the smallest thing about a person and become fixated. Perhaps your eyes are the same color as someone he was close to, or your hair, or the pattern of your speech. I simply mention this because it will not help us narrow down our field of suspects."

"Always a ray of optimism, my lord," she teased him.

He saluted her with his glass. "At your service, madam."

"Well, if that does not help us, everything else we have learned will," she said, refusing to be discouraged. "This man has likely killed two men now, and blackmailed who knows how many. He must be stopped."

"He seems bent on a mission that we do not understand yet," Lucas said, rolling up his shirtsleeves.

"We understand that he is probably out for revenge against the Kingsmen and their families," she said and tried not to gaze at his tanned forearms, dusted with dark hair. "But why now? We were right, I think, that neither Dalton nor Rathburn would have waited so long to act. So why would whoever is doing this strike now? Two of the men he's after died long before any of this started."

"Perhaps he did not have the means before now to seek revenge," Lucas pondered. "That would seem to align with

Harrington and Beatrice's observation from earlier. One can make a pretense of wealth if it was once there, but infiltrating society from the lower class would be near impossible."

"So perhaps it is someone who just recently entered society, either this season or last. If he does not have much money, he would not be able to keep up appearances for very long. Even with an influx of funds from the blackmail payments, the cost of a season is astronomical. I can ask Roz if she knows anyone who stands out to her. She is tuned in to the comings and goings of everyone."

"I shall think on it as well," Lucas said, crossing a booted leg over his knee. He was settled in, and did not look like he would be vacating the spot any time soon. "I confess I do not pay much attention to society anymore. I am happier ensconced on my estate than in a crowded ballroom making chit-chat with marriage-minded mamas."

"Ah, I serve another purpose then," she said. "Keeping the beasts at bay."

"I never realized how much freedom being affianced affords the man as well. I no longer have to take cover when I enter ballrooms," he said.

"Yes, well, don't get too used to it. I am sure they will come flocking once we announce the engagement is broken," she said, reminding herself more than anything else. The easy smile slipped from his face, and he dropped his eyes to his glass. "So, what is our next course of action?" she asked to cover the sudden awkward silence.

She did not think he was going to let her switch topics, but after a few beats he answered. "Rathburn."

"I hope he is all right," Gemma said. She did not particularly want to relive their experience with Dalton.

"I believe he went to his club today, and then to the Merryweather ball this evening. I had put feelers out for both of them since we talked to Rose," he said, acknowledging her raised eyebrow. "I had not heard back regarding Dalton — now we know why. But Rathburn has been carrying on normally for the past day, from what my sources can tell."

"Well, that's a relief," she said. "Shall we call on him first thing in the morning?"

"That would be best, I believe. If at all possible, I do not want the killer to get wind of the fact that we found Dalton. If we can get a jump on Rathburn before the news breaks, we may be able to get in front of our killer for once in this investigation."

"Do you think Rathburn will be able to tell us anything?" Gemma asked.

"If anyone can, it will most likely be him. He may be hesitant to admit to whatever wrongdoing is involved here, but if we can convince him he is in mortal danger, perhaps he will divulge it."

Lucas reached up and casually flicked open a button on his shirt; she found she could not tear her eyes away from the small patch of chest the move exposed. "Once we inform him of Dalton's demise, we may have our leverage."

"He is the last of the Kingsmen now. And the remaining family members are being blackmailed," she said. "If he knows what is good for him, he will tell us what we need to know. We already have a great deal more information than we started with, though."

"True," he nodded. "We know something happened about years ago that involved my father, Perry, Dalton, and Rathburn. We know they were in a secret club together, and that it disbanded after only one season. We believe the person affected by this event has now resurfaced to wreak havoc on the Kingsmen and their families. We believe he killed Dalton, and also your cousin for interrupting his blackmail plan."

"And we believe I have encountered him sometime during my outings in society," Gemma added. "Although some of these facts are actually leaps of logic, my lord."

"They may be leaps, but I believe they are sound," he said. He cleared his throat. "About your admirer…"

"I think you are right, my lord, best not to focus on that and get distracted," she said in a rush, worried he was going to suggest she remove herself from the investigation.

As he studied her through narrowed eyes, she tried not to fidget. She had relaxed into an unladylike position, but if she moved now she would make it obvious that his scrutiny made her nervous. She slid her ankles farther under her skirts, but then told herself she could not be more immodest than he was, half undressed and lounging in the chair like a predatory animal.

"Perhaps you are right for now, my dear," he finally said. "Did you enjoy Vauxhall before that incident?"

"It was more than I could have imagined," she assured him. "I'm only disappointed that it was cut short."

"What else would you have liked to have seen?" His voice was low and husky, and it stoked the small fire that had been burning in her all night long.

The situation was precarious. It was true that as far as the world was concerned they were engaged. But they weren't. And even if they were, the situation was still not quite on the right side of proper.

It didn't feel wrong, though. It felt safe.

Their embrace in the carriage flashed into her mind, and she longed to feel his lips against hers once more. If they were going to risk their reputations by flirting so recklessly with the boundaries of propriety, shouldn't she at least get another kiss out of it?

One brow slid up, and she realized she was staring. Heat stung at her cheeks, but she didn't look away. She'd made her decision. "Have you heard of the dark walks?"

His eyes took on a seductive glint, but his lips tipped up

in a smile. "I think the better question is, how have *you* heard of the dark walks, my dear?"

She cleared her throat. "I've done my research."

She winced.

Research. Very alluring, Gemma. Might as well talk farming techniques next.

"Not first-hand, I trust." He was teasing her, she knew, but there was a sudden air of alertness around him that was a sharp contrast to his lazy pose only moments earlier.

She peeped at him under her lashes like she'd seen other ladies do when they wanted to flirt with their partners, and hoped she didn't look as foolish as she felt. "I was hoping tonight I would be able to augment my education with a trip along the walks."

"What has your research told you about them?" The amusement had died from his voice, only to be replaced by something she couldn't name. Something sensuous.

"Oh they sound magical." Her own voice turned dreamy as she pictured strolling with Lucas under the stars, through a maze of lush green walls. The scent of flowers and the thrill of expectation would make the air thick around them. "Almost like another world, where you can lose yourself in the beauty of the night without thought to consequence."

"There are always consequences," he cut in, dousing her fantasy.

"But imagine for a moment, if you will, that you could pretend there were not." This was not quite going as she had scripted it in her head. They would have already kissed by now if had been. And then she would have a sweet memory to tuck against her in the dark of the night when she tried not to think about death and warnings and blackmail.

"That's a dangerous proposition, Gemma," he said quietly. "That's not real life."

"That's what the dark walks are for," she countered.

"We're not in Vauxhall, though, are we?"

She lost her patience with subtlety. She didn't know why she tried it in the first place—it clearly wasn't her strong suit. "But what if we were. Would you embrace the magic? Or would you continue to talk at me about consequences?"

He narrowed his eyes then deliberately set his glass on the small table beside him before crossing over to her. The look in his eyes made her question her sanity for provoking him. He drew her up until she was standing in front of him.

She'd wanted him to kiss her, but she hadn't been prepared for the heat that burned in her belly, in the air between them, in his eyes.

"Magic," he murmured, stroking the pad of his thumb along her jaw. Sparks followed in its wake, sending shivers along her skin. "I choose magic."

• • •

It was a warm summer night of a kiss at first. Gentle. Romantic. It matched the dreaminess he'd seen in her eyes when she talked about lovers bathed in starlight.

She couldn't know what she did to him when she had peered up at him, a mixture of sweet innocence and curious desire all at once. He had waged a war within himself. He should leave, he'd thought. If nothing else in his life remained true, he was a gentleman. And gentlemen did not ravish young innocents in their guardian's library.

But when her milky skin flushed pink, he'd lost the battle. Even their talk of consequences had done nothing to tamp down the need that consumed him. For just a taste.

Just a taste.

She moaned, though, her fingers digging into his shoulders, and he wanted more. His hand tangled in her curls, the other finding the soft flare of her hip.

Only then did he lower his mouth to hers, closing the distance between them so that they were body to body with no space in between. She clutched at his shirt and sighed into the embrace.

The kiss turned deeper when she walked her fingers up to his shoulders, and used them as leverage to press even closer to him. Their tongues danced against each other, a slick slide. She shivered in his arms when he licked his tongue against the roof of her mouth, before pulling back to nibble on her plush bottom lip. Her whimper when he sunk his teeth in was the most alluring sound he'd ever heard

He pulled back to study her. Her eyes were glassy, her lips freshly plumped from his attention. A flush rode along her high cheekbones.

"All right," he murmured. "I shall help you with your research."

She was dazed, and he watched her clever mind work to catch up. She smirked once it had, with a womanly arrogance that hadn't been there moments earlier. "Oh, how noble of you, my lord."

He glanced around as if he were taking in some scenery. "You'll have to use your imagination. The real dark walks are shrouded in shadows and secrets. A far cry from a well-lit library."

"It is a good thing I have such an expert with me," she said. "I'm sure you'll be able to set the scene."

He laughed and shifted so that when he sat back on the couch she followed into his lap. He had needed that lightness to help him regain his control. There had been a moment when she'd mewled after he'd bitten into her lip that he'd been genuinely worried about disgracing himself like an eager schoolboy.

Even now, as her bottom settled against him, he wondered if he would go mad before the night was out. When she dipped her head to kiss him, he thought he might already be there.

"Do you hear the music?" he whispered against her neck. She tipped her head back and he knew she wanted his mouth on her.

"I only hear the fireworks," she murmured, and he groaned, giving into her wishes, his tongue teasing the delicate skin beneath her jaw.

"Mmm, beautiful. Do you smell the roses?" He moved lower, his lips finding the dip of her clavicle, the curve of her shoulder.

"They smell so sweet," her voice was muffled as her face was buried in his hair.

The delicate sleeve of her dress put up no resistance as he nudged it from his path. He made quick work of the other side, until the fabric pooled at her waist. She wasn't wearing a corset, and he thanked God for her unconventional soul as he took in the sight of her in his lap.

He couldn't breathe. Her skin was firelight. It was with reverence that he reached out to cup her. He almost didn't want to touch. Didn't want to mar her perfection. But he slid a thumb over one of her nipples, and she gasped. She liked the raspy slide of calloused fingers over silky skin. He repeated the motion, and then he bent to take her in his mouth.

Rational thought fled. All he had left was the feel of her. The hard tip against his lips, the murmurs that escaped, the pulse that raced against his hand as he cupped her. His whole world narrowed down to the sensation of having her.

He pulled back, desperate for control. "Do you see the stars?"

She met his eyes. Something shifted there. Something he couldn't decipher. "All I see is you."

The words struck him like a blow. She wasn't flirting. She was laying herself completely bare for him. Making herself utterly vulnerable. And he knew in that moment she was much braver than he would ever be.

It was the last straw. "Gemma, do you want this?" He needed to know, needed to make sure. He wondered if she truly realized what this would mean.

She nibbled her lip, but didn't take her gaze off his. "Yes."

That was all it took. He shifted, laying her on the couch and ridding her of her dress in one quick movement.

Her hands tugged at his shirt. "Not fair," she muttered. He was amazed he could laugh in that moment. He stripped out of it, but kept his breeches on, not wanting to overwhelm her. He went slow. Trailing his fingers up her calf, dipping into the space behind her knee, sliding up the silk of her thigh until he cupped her warmth. She was wet already, and he groaned into her neck. Fingernails bit into his bare back as he nudged at her. His mouth was on hers then, swallowing her gasp as he pushed one finger in. So tight. So ready. For him. He strained against his breeches, his hips pressing against the couch, desperate for friction.

His thumb found and toyed with her most sensitive spot, and she turned molten beneath his machinations. A second finger joined his first, and she clutched at his shoulders. She didn't know what she needed. But he did.

He slid even lower, his lips trailing down the soft curve of her belly until he was where he always wanted to be.

"Lucas?" He heard the nervousness in her voice.

"Shh, love," he murmured, and then dipped his head until his lips were placed where his thumb had just been. She went taut, her hips rocking against his mouth. He was thankful she had enough of her wits about her to bite back the cry he'd heard start in her throat. "That's it. Beautiful."

She was building toward her release; he could feel her on his fingers, beneath his tongue. His lips nuzzled her inner thigh, and he bit down slightly against the soft skin. This time she wasn't able to silence herself. He'd had an inkling she'd like that. But he couldn't torture her anymore. For that was just torturing himself, and he wasn't sure how much longer he'd last with her taste on his tongue.

"There we are, love. Just let go," he murmured against her, feeling the muscles tighten. "I want you to see the stars, Gemma."

She was whimpering, her fists balled against the couch, her eyes shut. He almost came from the sight.

Control it.

He dragged in a ragged breath then nibbled at her sensitive nub. She arched back and then shattered around his fingers.

He shifted over her, undoing his breeches with an unsteady hand. He pushed into her as the last waves of pleasure washed over her. He didn't want to hurt her, but he knew it was unavoidable. He leaned down, his mouth against her ear. "I'm sorry, love," he murmured before breaking through the barrier of her innocence. His vision blurred and faded at the edges as he sank to the hilt. Sweat beaded along his spine. Everything in him told him to move. But he couldn't hurt her.

He met her gaze. She was biting her lip, but she didn't appear distressed. More curious. He, on the other hand, had lost the line between pain and pleasure. "Are you all right, Gemma?" he gritted it out.

A little wrinkle furrowed her brows. "I think so," she said. Then, as if she hadn't already tortured him enough, she rocked her hips against his.

"Gemma."

"Did I hurt you?" she sounded genuinely concerned.

He groaned into a laugh. "No. Just hold on."

He began moving. Slowly. Letting the friction build again for her. He watched her carefully with each shift, keeping them deep and even. He watched as her eyes drifted closed in pleasure. He watched as her breath caught and she bit on her lip. And when he saw the flush of desire deepen her skin to rose, he reached between them.

"Look at me, Gemma," he said. It was all he could manage. Her eyes locked on his and he pressed his thumb against her just as he buried himself to the hilt. When she shivered around him, he finally let go.

He saw the stars.

Chapter Thirteen

Lucas was brooding. He was ensconced in his corner of the carriage as it hurtled through the busy streets toward Lord Rathburn's house. He had not said more than a handful of words to her since he had collected her at precisely ten o'clock. She wondered if she should feel affronted that he was not lavishing her with poetry and romantic words following the events in the study. He had not said much to her the night before, either. They'd both realized he couldn't linger. If anyone in the household had come upon them, there would be no hiding what had occurred.

He'd kissed her, though. Right before he left. He'd pulled her to him, and his mouth had played over hers in a way that was more caress than passion.

"We'll talk tomorrow," he'd murmured. Then he'd laid his lips against her forehead. The affection in the gesture had tripped at her heart, and she hadn't been able to reply. She'd simply nodded.

She wondered if he was regretting their night, now they were in the harsh light of day. If anyone should be having second thoughts about their interlude, it was she. She was effectively ruined after all. But she couldn't muster up the will to care.

All she could think about was the way it had felt so completely right to be in his arms. The way it had felt like home, in a way that she'd never had before.

And she refused to regret that.

Gemma grimaced as a sudden thought crashed into her. He might even be feeling some sense of responsibility to follow through with their engagement after last night. She would burst from mortification if Lucas felt pressured into marrying her. She had specifically forbidden it when they had first made the damnable agreement. Her back went ramrod straight.

"Please tell me that you are not thinking about doing anything rash after the events of last evening," she said, unable to tamp down the fires of rising panic that the notion fanned. It was not that she thought marriage to Lucas would be a disaster; in fact, she could see the prospect being quite diverting. But he would view it as something he had to do rather than something he wanted to do, and that she could not bear.

He considered her for a moment, his eyes roving over her face. "I rarely do anything rashly, my dear," he finally drawled, confirming her worst suspicions.

"I knew it!" she cried out. She would not be a burden or a frivolous debt of honor. Society might insist that a man marry the woman he had despoiled, but she refused to participate in such idiocy. Why should a man sacrifice his freedom and happiness for a lunatic social nicety? She would not have another man bound to a life with her as his burden—even if she had to sacrifice her own happiness to save him. "You are no more responsible for last night's actions than I was. I dare say even less so."

He arched an elegant eyebrow, the picture of arrogance. "Is that so? How is that, my dear?"

"I seduced you." She blushed as the words seemed to expand and fill all the space in the carriage, but she refused to show weakness on the matter. She knew he would pounce if she did.

"Well, then, I believe it is you who needs to make a respectable offer to me this morning," Lucas said, without a hint of irony in his deep voice.

"Oh, be serious. I know you are feeling responsible for me now, but there is no need. Our…encounter was my decision, and I am not your problem to solve," she said.

He cocked his head, studying her. His lips parted on a reply, but he glanced out the window before the words escaped. The carriage slowed, and she turned her attention to the street as well. They'd arrived. Their carriage rides really did have horrible timing.

"We shall discuss this topic later," he said without even looking at her. She wanted to continue the argument even though she knew he would be stubborn about it, but they couldn't sit outside Rathburn's house bickering in the carriage. She reluctantly gave in and kept quiet as he turned to exit the carriage.

Side by side, they studied the door for a beat before heading up the short flight of stairs in lock step. The stony-faced butler who greeted them did not seem happy with their appearance on his doorstep at such an early hour. He plucked the calling card out of Lucas's hand and studied it before admitting them.

The entryway was dark and oppressive. The little hairs on the back of her neck stood up, and she inched closer to Lucas. She couldn't explain her feeling of unease, but she realized most of the windows were shrouded with heavy black curtains and supposed that could be one of the reasons.

She nudged Lucas with her elbow, and he dipped his head in acknowledgment. Not all was right in the Rathburn household.

"Milord will see you now," the butler intoned in a heavy, resonating voice. Her first, slightly hysterical thought was that his funereal demeanor fit the setting. They followed him into a dark room off the side of the foyer.

Rathburn was standing at the window, his back to them even as the butler announced their names. He gazed out at his garden, a dark silhouette against the bright morning sun that streamed in through the glass.

They both sat as the butler went for tea and closed the door with a soft click. Only then did Rathburn turn from his post. The man had aged well, Gemma thought, and must have been quite a rakehell in his younger days. He had raven hair threaded with silver that somehow made him more handsome and distinguished. His sharp eyes pierced her as he raked them over her person. Although she recognized his attractiveness, he gave her an uneasy feeling. She wanted to flee the room and his gaze. She set her jaw and kept her hands folded firmly in her lap as she felt Lucas shift closer to her. She dared not betray her unease any further to him, for she feared he would cut the interview short if he knew she was uncomfortable.

"You have come about the girl," Rathburn murmured without any preamble, sliding into the lush, velvet-cushioned chair behind his ornate desk. "I knew she would cause us trouble eventually."

Gemma felt herself tense, like a mouse stalked by a cat. She knew she could not show her reactions, as Rathburn was watching them both, a thinly veiled, predatory hunger on his face. She sensed instantly that he was about to attempt to manipulate them. Uncle Artie had taught her about venomous snakes; Rathburn fell into that category. The only way to operate when facing one down was to show no fear. And then cut off its head.

"Indeed," Lucas said, and Gemma knew from his neutral tone he had read Rathburn's conniving countenance at least as quickly as she had.

A stout woman entered the room with the tea service, and the air stilled as they waited in silence for the housekeeper to leave.

"You look like him," Rathburn said once they were alone again. "Your father."

"I've been told."

"Yes. Well. I suppose you've received letters as well?" Rathburn reached smoothly into his drawer and tossed a bundle of envelopes onto the desk. His willingness to share information with them, having just met, seemed too good to be true and put her on edge, but she had to restrain herself from snatching up the notes. Lucas didn't even glance at them.

"I have, yes. Although it looks like he has devoted more time to you. I have only received a handful," Lucas said, not taking his eyes off Rathburn. The tension between the two men was suffocating to her. She felt as though they were two beasts about to leap at each other's throats. Had Lucas neglected to fill her in on anything? Thinking back on their conversations, she was certain he had not indicated he'd had close contact with the man. Perhaps it was just a gut reaction, she thought. Rathburn certainly had not put her at ease, either.

"The ramblings of a madman, I assure you," the man drawled, flicking a dismissive finger at the letters. Lucas finally reached forward for the bundle, untying the red ribbon with a distinct lack of urgency.

Rathburn lounged in his chair, watching Lucas. An aura of power and arrogance cloaked his every gesture. She could see why Rose had kept his company for so long. They both had a steel edge to their beautiful smiles.

Lucas flipped through a few before handing them to her. She recognized the handwriting and paper immediately as she began reading them. The first few began with vague threats and promises of revenge that escalated in the later notes.

"I know what you did to her, you will pay. You will pay for the life you took. *Inveniam viam aut faciam*," she murmured as she read one of the earlier letters. "What does he mean, 'the life you took'?"

Rathburn's eyes tightened briefly at the corners before his face relaxed into a careless expression. "Like I said, ramblings. I've never so much as hit a man outside the boxing ring, let alone taken a life. It is some madman's vengeance fantasy gone wrong."

"None of these contain blackmail threats," Lucas finally said, looking up at Rathburn. For the first time since they'd been shown into the study, Rathburn looked off guard. He stood and turned toward the window again, as if restless. Gemma guessed he was instead masking his surprise.

"No, that does not seem to be the goal, does it? I believe the intent is clear: the man wants my life, not my money," Rathburn said without looking at them, his hands clasped behind his back.

"You do not seem overly concerned with the threats," Lucas commented.

Rathburn turned toward them, one sardonic eyebrow raised. "No," he said simply. "So, you are being extorted, then."

"Yes," he answered. "The methods are different, but I believe we're dealing with the same person. Here is a sample of his work he's sent to me." Lucas tossed a letter toward Rathburn. "Do you know who it is?"

There was the question, Gemma thought. Rathburn had been acting peculiar throughout the interview, in a way she could not understand. She had a sense that he was only giving them information in small snippets. Things he felt comfortable divulging, but nothing more.

He stared down at Lucas's letter for a long, quiet moment before answering. "Not who. But why."

...

The tension that had been building within him erupted with the simple sentence. Rathburn had been toying with them the entire time. Lucas had recognized him as a master manipulator the moment they'd entered the room. The man must have written the script to this little melodrama in advance; the only time he'd been thrown even slightly was over the blackmail. Lucas wondered how long Rose had waited after they'd left before she sent a message to her former paramour.

"Do go on," Lucas said, letting his words drip with ennui. He knew from years of experience that the more interested in the information one appeared, the more difficult it would be to extract.

"I did not show you all the letters," Rathburn began.

"Of course not," Lucas said. He'd been surprised with the amount they had been able to read. Lucas guessed the ones that Rathburn had kept were even more damning. "There was a girl."

Rathburn tipped his head in acknowledgment of the point. "There's always a girl," he agreed with a world-weary smile. "We were boys back then. Your father, me, a couple of others." He settled back into his chair, steepling his fingers against his chest as he eyed them both. "We thought the world was ours: money, power, whores. All harmless fun."

Gemma shifted in her seat. Lucas didn't acknowledge the movement, but he wanted to pull her away from the story he saw coming. The ugliness of it.

"You started a club," he prompted Rathburn instead.

Rathburn's smile grew nostalgic. "The Kingsmen. So young, you understand."

"Was 'We shall either find a way or make one' the motto of this club?" Lucas asked.

Rathburn's lips curved up in a cat-like smile. "So young. And yes, that little boast was your father's, actually. We carried it over from university days. We even had rings made up for ourselves. We thought we were so clever." Rathburn shook his head. "If only we had been."

Lucas' stomach clenched. He'd maintained the hope that his father had not actually been involved deeply in whatever tragedy had set this all in motion. That did not seem to be shaping up to be the case.

"What happened?" Gemma's voice rang out clear in the air beside him.

"Ah, a little fun gone wrong, of course," Rathburn said, swinging his gaze to Gemma. Lucas did not like the sharp gleam in his eyes when he looked at her.

"The girl?" Lucas asked when Rathburn fell silent again. He was enjoying toying with them, dropping tidbits of information for them to clutch at, but not enough to hold on to. Lucas was losing patience.

"Yes, the girl. Her. She's the reason for all this…" Rathburn trailed off and waved a hand toward the letters and then to them. "She was just some whore we had some fun with. It was a house party we attended as the Kingsmen. I do not even remember which one anymore. I barely remember the girl except she turned up on my doorstep a few months later claiming rape and pregnancy from me. As if she could pin that on any of us. Foolish girl." He told the story as if they would find it absurd. Perhaps many in society would. Lucas did not.

"Why did she think she could, then?" Lucas asked with great restraint. Tolerating the man's presence while not planting a fist in his face was proving to be difficult. "If she was a whore, why would she think she could make any of you own a bastard?"

"I have no notion, nor do I care to delve into a whore's thinking," Rathburn said. "But I turned her out immediately."

"But how do you know this matter revolves around her? Hers is a sad story, but it is a common plight faced by women, particularly those of no means," Gemma said. She was clearly trying to maintain her composure, but Lucas could sense the anger bubbling away just beneath the surface. "An impoverished prostitute would hardly have the power or wealth to carry out such a revenge plot. And society cares very little for such women, unfortunately."

Rathburn shrugged. "I cannot comment on the reasons why a madman might champion such a stupid cause. I am sure the whore spun a pretty tale of horror to whoever is seeking vengeance." He twisted off the ring on his right middle finger and tossed it on the desk. "The letters, apart from some allusions to the night in question, mention our crest. Yet only a handful of people know about it."

Lucas didn't look at the ring, but Gemma picked it up. She traced the inside engraving even though she'd seen it before.

"Why would you show that to the woman?" Lucas asked. Rathburn was not telling them the whole story. He doubted, however, that the man would disclose anything further than what he had concocted for them.

Rathburn raised his eyebrows in a dismissive gesture. "She asked about us, I answered. Like I said, young and foolish. But certainly nothing that would warrant the terrorization we're now facing."

It was time to rattle the arrogant bastard.

"It's gone further than terrorization, Rathburn," Lucas said. "Dalton was killed last night in his own home."

"I had not heard," Rathburn said, looking remarkably

unperturbed. "We had grown apart, you understand."

"You had not talked to him about the letters?" Lucas pressed.

"No. I saw him in passing at my club, at most." His gaze flicked to the clock in the corner. "Now, you'll have to excuse me, I have an appointment."

Gemma carefully laid the ring back on his desk before they got to their feet. Rathburn walked them to the door but stopped them right before they left. "I do hope the madman is caught and brought to justice."

"Yes. I do hope justice is served," Gemma murmured before walking out without looking back.

Chapter Fourteen

"He is despicable," Gemma huffed as she clambered into the dark confines of Lucas's carriage. She wanted to put as much distance between herself and that wretch of a man as possible.

"He was certainly hiding something," Lucas said, settling himself into the velvet cushions.

"Something? Everything! He deceived us from the beginning and then continued along with the charade. As if we would believe his story." She shuddered, thinking about his smugness when he talked about the woman whose life he probably had been responsible for destroying. "There is much more to the story."

"Yes," Lucas said, looking out the window as their carriage eased into the streets, cutting through the fog of the day. "He gave us some information, but it was scripted, as you say."

"And he was far too eager to share it, at that," Gemma said, thinking of how willing Rathburn had been to hand over the letters. "You cannot remember your father mentioning the man at all?"

Lucas's fist clenched against his thigh, and she immediately regretted the question. *Stupid*.

But he answered anyway. "I confess I did not talk frequently with my father," he said. "I would not have thought to ask about youthful friendships he may have fostered. Ours were mostly conversations about how I was not fulfilling my responsibilities as heir."

Gemma made a low sound of distress. "How could he say that? You clearly value family responsibility over all else."

He turned from the windows and smiled at her, though she thought it might be directed at himself. "He wanted me to stop…traveling and marry to carry on the line. He worried our estate would otherwise go to a distant cousin."

"Maybe it wasn't just about that," she said, realizing just how complex their relationship must have been. "What if it was his way of keeping you safe? He was worried about you."

Lucas fell silent again. She wanted to wrap her arms around him and lay a comforting head on his chest, but she did not dare encourage him to think of her in that way. It would only make it worse when they called everything off.

He turned his thoughtful green eyes on her with a sharp intensity. "How was that man one of his closest confidantes? Rathburn is scum. How did my father not see that? How was he so blind? If nothing else in this world, I believed him to be intelligent. Harsh, but smart…" He trailed off and Gemma felt his pain as if it were her own. She tried to imagine learning similar information about her uncle, and what she would want to hear in the situation.

"While I do not believe youth excuses folly, I do believe we are not at our most perceptive at that age, and we are subject to outside influences," she began softly. "Your father may have gotten caught up in a silly club, but he also removed himself from his acquaintance with those men and lived a moral life after that. It's not always about the mistakes we make. Sometimes, it's what we do after that matters," she said, holding back the impulse to stroke his hair in reassurance.

He was quiet for a moment, and she worried she had overstepped. False engagement aside, at the end of the day, they were simply partners in an investigation. She did not have the right to pry into his life or emotions.

But a moment later, his arms shot out and he pulled her onto his lap. He crushed his lips against hers. This kiss was not gentle; it was an assault. His tongue slid inside her mouth and grappled with hers. His teeth nipped her lips. It awoke a need in her that she'd felt last night, and she clutched at his shoulders, wanting more. Just as she moved to straddle his legs and press her body more firmly against his, he softened the embrace, pulling back after one more affectionate brush of his lips. He rested his forehead against hers and took a deep breath. She gathered her own as she tried to steady her racing heart.

"I shall obtain a special license as soon as possible," he said. "It is no longer safe for you to live with Roz."

Gemma reared back in dismay. He caught her just before she disgraced herself by tumbling onto the floor of the carriage.

"I do not need or desire your protection," Gemma said, forcing herself to speak the words even as her heart screamed that they were lies. "We had an agreement."

"I do not understand why this is coming as such surprise to you," Lucas said, watching her with hooded eyes. "If you have not already noticed, we are affianced. Did you think we would escape from this unscathed?"

"I am supposed to break it off with you, my lord," she cried out. She should have known he would try to do the honorable thing in the end. Lucas was nothing if not honorable. "You promised."

"I promised no such thing," he assured her, retaining his grip on her. "But our reputations aside, you are an intelligent woman, my dear. You must realize there could be consequences from our actions last night."

Gemma's breath caught in her throat, and her hand went without thought to rest above her womb. She saw herself holding their child, and could not believe she had not considered that possibility. She pictured a little girl with raven hair and her blue eyes, or a boy with flame-red locks and green cat eyes. Their child. Lucas's child. Hers. She felt a pang.

"If there's a child, he or she will need a father," he pushed on over her silence. "They would need the protection of my name."

He had a point, and he knew that she knew it. She could not and would not deny her child respectability. But still something held her back.

It wasn't that she did not want to marry him. He had become home to her. But she wanted to be that for him. Wanted him to love her as fiercely as she did him. Wanted to be his true partner, his companion, his lover. She craved a relationship, not a caretaker. Not someone forced into it through his own ironclad sense of responsibility. And she could not bear the thought of forcing her child—their child— to become the same type of burden she had been.

She met his eyes. He'd been watching her. Her eyes roved over his face, down to where his hand held hers prisoner. The other was clenched on the soft velvet of the seat. He was nervous, tense and unsure about what she would say. He was trying not to show it, but she knew him better than that, she realized. For some reason it relaxed her.

"If there is to be a baby, we can make the decision when we know," she said. It was what she was willing to give for now.

"That's not good enough."

Convince me. Convince me you want this.

But he just stared at her, his aristocratic brows raised.

He was so used to ordering people around, he was wholly unfamiliar with someone saying no. Well, he was going to have to get used to it if he really did want to marry her.

"I don't see why not," she said, annoyed that even though she had logic on her side, she was the one stuck defending her position.

"People will talk," he gritted out. He was not pleased.

Tough. Neither am I.

"And then they'll move on to their next topic before the ink on the wedding certificate has dried. Marriage erases all sins, as well you know."

If his grimace was any indication, he wanted to argue. But he couldn't. She was right.

"It's a moot point," he said, and she braced herself. "I need you under my protection. It's not safe for you to be living with Roz. You're far too vulnerable there."

"Hire runners for me then," she countered. "You can have me watched every hour of the day if you'd like. There's no need to marry me for that."

"But then it wouldn't be me watching you." He forced the words out from his clenched jaw. She almost, almost, took slight pleasure in his annoyance.

"Does that matter?"

"Yes." His voice was unusually loud in the close confines. "Don't you realize that? Don't you realize that you matter? You are what's important. The only thing that's important."

Her breath caught, and her eyes shot to his. He hadn't meant to say that, she realized. His face gave him away. He wanted to take the words back.

Because they made him vulnerable.

And that meant they carried weight. The other things were still there. He felt responsible for her safety. But maybe that was because he cared about her. He wanted to give her protection if she was with child. But maybe that was because he was concerned about her security and happiness and that of their possible child.

Maybe she was reading too much into it. But his ragged breathing, and the shuttered look in his eye did more than all of his well-thought out arguments could have. It made her think maybe they actually had a chance.

Am I brave enough to risk it?

She didn't know. Walking out of his life without at least trying though, was something she wasn't willing to do. Not after he'd told her she was important to him.

The words slipped from her lips and sealed her fate. "All right."

· · ·

There was still a slight buzz in her ears as she walked into Roz's house a few moments later. Lucas was on her heels, even though she had been hoping to shake him at the carriage. She desperately needed a few seconds to herself to regain her composure.

It was immediately clear that she would not be granted that blessed privacy any time soon, however. Mrs. Bird, her aunt's housekeeper and Bird's long-suffering wife, was in the hallway, waiting for them.

"A Mrs. Williams is here to see you," she intoned. "Not in there," she continued as Gemma nodded and headed toward the drawing room.

She paused mid-step and turned back to Mrs. Bird.

"In the kitchens," Mrs. Bird answered the unasked question.

Gemma exchanged a glance with Lucas, whose face was still inscrutable, as it had been since she'd agreed to marry him. He lifted an eyebrow now, though. "Do you know a Mrs. Williams? And why is she in the kitchens"

"I do not, and I have not a clue. Mrs. Bird?" Gemma could not quite follow the conversation, and for that she blamed her unsettled state. It was not every day that a woman agreed to marry the man she loved. If only he loved her, too, and didn't just see her as a responsibility.

"She is the housekeeper," Mrs. Bird said, a nudge in her voice. She glanced at Lucas, before turning her attention back to Gemma. "The one you asked about."

"Oh!" Gemma exclaimed as the mystery snapped into place. She stripped off her gloves and tossed them on the sideboard before hurrying toward the back of the residence. Lucas kept pace easily with his long legs. She burst into the kitchen, startling the pale, mousy woman who sat drinking tea at the thick wooden table in the center of the room.

"Mrs. Williams, how lovely to make your acquaintance," she said. "I am Gemma Lancaster and this is Lord Winchester. We appreciate you stopping by to answer a few questions."

The woman shrunk even further at the greeting. She darted her eyes to Mrs. Bird, who stood behind them at the threshold. Mrs. Bird nodded once, and the nervous woman seemed to relax.

"Mrs. Bird said ye were looking for information about Lord Dalton's death," she said. "I had nothin' to do with it, I swear it."

"We know you did not," Gemma reassured her. "We will not go to authorities nor inform anyone you were here."

Mrs. Williams eyed them warily. "Mrs. Bird mentioned a reward. Y'see, I haven't been able to work since we fled after his lordship's, er, demise. No character references."

"We shall take care of that and offer you compensation for the information you are able to provide," Gemma said. She was not surprised the woman was seeking a bribe; she would have been more suspicious had she not asked for anything. Gemma nodded to an amused-looking Lucas, who tossed several coins on the table in front of the housekeeper. "Could you tell us about the night Lord Dalton was shot?"

Mrs. Williams scooped up the gold, running her fingers over the coins before slipping them in a pocket. "It was me night off. I was supposed to visit me sister, but she came down with a fever and told me not to come. I didn't inform his lordship because he would have acted as if it was not me night off, even though it was me night off, y'see. I retired early, but I heard him movin' about above me for a good time after that. I should have stayed in me rooms, that night."

Gemma held her breath when Mrs. Williams paused, but did not want to interrupt her with questions.

"But me joints were paining me, and I needed me tonic. I was quiet as could be," the housekeeper continued. "I made it to the kitchens to grab the bottle when I heard his lordship's voice. He let out a yell, and for a moment I thought he'd seen me. But then I heard him ask someone, 'What are you doing here?' The answer was too low for me to hear."

"Where were they in the house?" Gemma asked.

"In the hallway by the entrance," Mrs. Williams responded. So not the study, Gemma thought, before waving her on to continue. "They were havin' a conversation and I wanted to try to get back to my rooms, so I snuck by to the little servant's door that led up that way. But I didn't dare open it, for it makes a nasty creakin'. I only saw the back of the man talkin' to his lordship."

"Can you describe him?" Lucas asked.

"Just that he had yellow hair and was dressed in expensive clothes. It was dark, y'see," she said with a shrug.

"Did you hear anything else they discussed?"

"Only his lordship," the housekeeper answered. "He said it was not his fault, and he was not to blame for something. I did not hear what it was, though. The next thing you know I heard the shot."

"What did you do, then?" Gemma asked.

"What do you think I did, now?" she responded, with a look that suggested Gemma was a bit of a dolt for asking the question. "I ran as quiet as could be to me rooms, pushed my wardrobe in front of me door, and curled under me bed until dawn. I've been hidin' at my sister's ever since, until Mrs. Bird came round saying you two were payin' for information."

"Did you notice anything missing the next morning before you left for good?" Lucas asked.

"We're not thieves, y'hear," Mrs. Williams said emphatically. She waited for both of them to nod before continuing. "But no character references, you understand. And we hadn't received our quarterly wages yet, neither. The butler found his lordship the next morning. He came down to my rooms, told me I had to leave. But we were owed."

"Of course, Mrs. Williams. Please continue." Lucas was clearly trying to tamp down his impatience.

"The only thing missin' was his lordship's treasured pocket watch," she said finally. "It was one of his most prized possessions. He would not even let me touch it to clean it. It was very, er, ancient, as you might say."

"Thank you, Mrs. Williams, you have been very helpful," Lucas said. He gestured to Gemma with a tilt of his head.

She smiled her thanks at both housekeepers and assured Mrs. Williams she would help her find work. She followed Lucas out of the kitchen, and both remained silent until they were ensconced once again in the sanctuary of the study.

"It was the same blond man from Vauxhall, do you think?" she asked. "And the man from the jewelry store?"

"I think that hair color is one of the easiest physical attributes someone can alter, and it is one of the most easily remembered by witnesses," Lucas repeated. "You'll notice it keeps cropping up throughout this investigation. Do you think a villain who has been smart enough to elude capture thus far would be so obvious as to have his hair color remarked on time and time again?"

"A wig? Dye, perhaps?" She pondered the idea, turning it over in her mind. In each interview they'd conducted, and from her own experience, the one thing everyone seemed to recall was the color of the man's hair. Lucas had a fair point.

"Not necessarily. He did not expect to be seen at Dalton's, so he may not have taken the precaution. Or, whoever it is, he may believe himself safe enough from discovery to not go to the lengths that would take. However, it does seem to be a possibility. Either way, I do not think we have broken the case open tonight," Lucas said, looking as if it pained him to be the voice of reason.

"The pocket watch is an odd turn of events, though," she mused. She agreed with him that they could not place much faith in the description of his hair, but they did not seem to be able to turn a corner in this case without stumbling over a watch.

"In both cases, it seems an afterthought to the crime, and not the motivation," Lucas said. "He could not help himself."

"Nigel's watch was acquired by Uncle Artie on a trip to Italy. It was said to be one of the original pocket watches created," Gemma remembered. "It would be worth thousands, but to someone who appreciates history, it would be priceless."

"We do have the list Beatrice and Harrington compiled," Lucas reminded her. "Perhaps we should give that another thorough look. It could tell us something more than we realized at first glance."

They both fell quiet, deep in thought, until Gemma broke the silence. "Shall I pour you a drink?"

Lucas glanced at the decanter then back at her, studying her face. He shook his head. "I shall take my leave, my dear. It has been a long day, and we have a wedding to prepare."

"And a murderer to catch," she said, and wished she felt less trepidation about the former than the latter.

Chapter Fifteen

As a rat skittered across his freshly polished boots, Lucas thought about how thankful he was that he had not mentioned his destination to Gemma. She would have wanted to accompany him, and though he had been unusually accommodating to her wishes, he had to draw a line somewhere.

Instead, he'd brought George Harrington. They'd split up with plans to search for their target. Word was that he preferred a few of the seedier taverns on the docks. Lucas had been to two already without any success. George had taken the other half of the list.

There was a possibility that Gemma would be angry with him once he told her what he'd done. No, not a possibility. A certainty. But he wouldn't think about that now. There was no way he'd let her within ten meters of the filth—both the rubbish and human kind—that was the mainstay of the London docks. He could handle her anger. What he couldn't handle was her being hurt in any way.

He heard the birds cawing from the docks not far from

where the dirty little pub stood, beckoning sailors and workers to spend their meager earnings on a tankard instead of heading home to their families. Two burly men pushed past him, their shoulders knocking into his, catapulting him forward a few steps.

"Git out the way, ya bloody gent," one spat back at him, as the dockman pushed through the pub's door. Lucas braced himself for the putrid smell of stale alcohol and smoke, and followed behind them.

He lingered in the doorway, letting his eyes adjust to the darkened interior. The men had settled themselves at a table, and one had already pulled a scantily clad barmaid onto his lap. The other was eyeing a prostitute who was clearly trolling for customers.

A man, who barely resembled a human being, was huddled in the farthest corner of the pub, almost disappearing into the shadows. His skin was thick and drooping under the weight of poor living and age. Bloodshot eyes peered at Lucas from the dark, and a nervous tongue darted over cracked lips. His body was lost under a mountain of loose, grubby clothes. Even his gloves were unraveling from his hands.

It could be him. He fit the general description Lucas had been given.

"Carsons?" he asked, keeping his voice low. He didn't want to give away his purpose to the room at large if this wasn't his man.

The man's darting eyes roved over Lucas.

"Aye," the man finally croaked before downing a swig of his ale.

Satisfaction burned in his stomach, and he swung the chair out to sit down across from the ball of rags.

"You were Lord Rathburn's valet for a time?"

"Rathburn." The man said the name like a curse. He even sucked up a wad of saliva and spat on the floor. "That's what

I think of Rathburn."

"Yes, I was told you were not on good terms," Lucas murmured. "The world of servants is a small one, is it not?"

"Whaddya want with Rathburn?" Carsons asked, slamming an empty tankard down on the scarred table. He eyed Lucas meaningfully then looked back at the glass. Lucas smiled and signaled for the server.

"I would like some information regarding the time you were employed with him," Lucas said after Carsons was settled once more. "It was for three years?"

Carsons went to spit on the floor again, but swallowed it after Lucas raised a single brow at the action. He settled back into his chair instead. "That's right. Son of a whore turned me out without a reference. Without reason. Never been good since then. Never."

"You performed all the normal duties, I suppose," Lucas prompted.

Carsons's gaze shifted to the side. "Could say that."

"Could say that?" Lucas pounced. "Or would say that?"

Lucas chose that moment to slip his hand in his pocket and jingle the small bag of coins he had there. Carsons's entire body tensed at the sound, and a greedy look came into his eyes. Still he didn't say anything. It must be bad. This man had not an ounce of loyalty toward Rathburn, and yet he was resisting an obvious and seductive payday.

"Were there any unusual requests he made of you?" Lucas tried.

Again with the shifting eyes. They darted around the room, before landing on the drink in front of him. He took a loud gulp.

"I promise, it will be worth your while," Lucas assured him.

Carsons nodded without looking up, clearly having a conversation with himself. He seemed to reach a decision, for he leaned forward, crooking one dirt-encrusted finger at Lucas to come closer. He obliged.

"He had…particular interests with the ladies. A few had to be disappeared, if you know what I mean."

Lucas felt his stomach clench. "How is that?"

If it was possible, Carsons moved even closer, so that his rotting breath was hot against Lucas's face. He resisted the urge to pull away. "He liked to make them hurt. Lots of blood. All the servants knew, but none of them had to drag the girls down to the Thames, if you follow the story."

Lucas fought his revulsion. He had more questions to ask after all. "Did he ever mention the Kingsmen?"

"That bloody secret club?" Carson asked, sitting back and relaxing. "Aye, he mentioned it. Couldna stop talkin' about that club. He'd go into rages about the girl, too."

"The girl?"

"Not like the rest, that one," Carsons said. "She was the one who done it, who ruined it all, he'd say. She was the one who caused the rages."

"Ruined it all?" Lucas asked.

"He had these big investment schemes mapped out with his Kingsmen partners," Carsons said, clearly derisive of the plans. "They were going to be richer than gods, as if they weren't already, you follow?"

"And the girl ruined it all?" Everything in him told him that he was close to an answer. He just needed to drag the information out of this wretched excuse for a human.

Carsons bent in close again. "Ya know, I think he killed her. It was real bad there for a while. With the other girls. A couple a month, and then it stopped. No more trips to the Thames for Carsons."

"But you were not called upon to handle that particular situation," Lucas clarified.

"No. But I knew. Who did he think cleaned up his shirts?

Ordered the water for him to wash the blood off his hands?" Carsons coughed, flecks of brownish spittle flying from his mouth. "He stopped with the rages after that night," Carsons continued and took a loud gulp of ale. "And there was a boy around that time."

Lucas opted for silence and waited for Carsons to fill it. "Aye, there was a boy," Carsons said again, nodding and eyeing Lucas. "Heard tell the lordship set his man of affairs to watching out for the boy, just at that time. We all thought it peculiar. Why would he set watch on some boy in an orphanage in the Lake District?"

"You are certain it was the Lake District?"

"Aye, heard tell," Carsons confirmed. "But then I was turned out. For nothing! For nothing!"

"Indeed," Lucas said, pushing up and away from the table. He was eager to be on his way, and not just because of the information he had received.

"Oy!" Carsons yelled. "Where's the blunt?"

"Never fear, my man," he reassured him, reaching into his coat pocket for the coins he kept there. He pressed the bag into Carsons's filthy hand. "If you think of anything else, please send round for me."

Carson licked his lips as he palmed the bag, weighing the fullness in his hand. "Aye, will do."

Satisfied with the transaction, Lucas made for the door. He stepped out into the air and was almost surprised at the daylight. The pub had been so dark and dingy it had felt like it would be the middle of the night. He took a deep breath and let the air refresh him as his mind worked furiously over the information Carsons had given him.

He and Harrington had agreed to meet back at Lucas's house when they were finished. As he climbed into his carriage, all Lucas could think was how much he wanted to tell Gemma all he had found out. It was an unusual feeling, that—having someone he wanted to tell about his day. Something told him that he could get used to it.

...

Beatrice read the same page in her book for the third time and knew it was hopeless. There was no way she was going to make it through poor Mr. Shakespeare's lovely drama, as compelling as it was.

She set it down on the small table beside her and let her thoughts drift as they wished.

Lucas had left a few hours earlier, and he'd been so vague about his plans she was sure he was up to something. She wondered if it had something to do with Gemma.

She couldn't help but hope the two would work through the problem. The more she saw the two of them together, the more she found it a pity their engagement was purely fictional. Lucas needed a strong, intelligent partner. He would never be satisfied with a young chit right out of the schoolroom. He would end up dictating to her instead of talking, directing instead of discussing. He would be bored senseless within a day of the marriage. Gemma would thrive under the stability Lucas could provide. He would challenge her and make her angry, but then be there to kiss the temper out of her. It was so clear to Beatrice. But then, she was perhaps not in the clearest frame of mind regarding love these days. Her thoughts drifted unbidden to the kiss she had shared with George Harrington, and she touched her lips at the memory

She wondered where he was just then. Did it have something to do with Lucas's mysterious errand? She had clenched her jaw at that. She expected to be left out of Lucas's interviews, but she had been quite helpful when George had taken her along. Until someone had tried to run her over and they'd ended up in that alleyway, pressed against each other...

At that moment, the door opened to admit the man himself into Lucas's study. His eyes roved over her, then around the room checking for other occupants. When he found none, he returned his gaze to her person. Only then did she realize his arm was bloody.

She gasped and leaped to her feet, rushing over to him. "Please do not concern yourself, it is nothing," he said before she could utter anything. "A mere scratch."

Panic receded into anger at his words. "Oh, yes, I can see that you are in perfectly fine health, sir," she said, her voice icy. But her hands were gentle when they directed him onto the chaise near the fireplace. She sat beside him, her knees brushing his, and bent over his arm to study the mess he had made of it. She pulled the cloth from his torn coat away from the wound. Some of the pieces were matted to the skin with blood, but he didn't even flinch when she tugged at them. Once she could see it more clearly, she relaxed and summoned the butler to bring her warm water and bandages.

She turned back to him to find his eyes unnervingly close to hers. Their faces were separated by only a wisp of air. She cleared her throat, but couldn't seem to find her voice.

"See," he murmured, not retreating. "A mere scratch."

She pulled away to look at it once more. "Not quite a scratch, sir, but it does not seem to require me to fetch my sewing kit."

His eyes crinkled in humor that did not reach his lips. "Thank heavens for that."

The butler reentered the room with her supplies before she could work up a proper retort. She pursed her lips as she surveyed him. "You need a drink," she said. She walked over to the crystal decanter without awaiting a reply. She splashed some liquid into a glass, then splashed a bit more. She took a sip of it herself before turning back to him. He raised his eyebrows in amusement, but he took the drink without comment. "Fortification," she muttered.

"Indeed," he said, swallowing a healthy dose.

"The coat has to go," she said, sitting beside him once more and picking up the scissors.

He closed his eyes as if in pain at the thought. "Just promise to make it quick."

She laughed at the absurdity. As if this man would care a whit about his clothes. She went to work cutting away the material, washing the wound, and wrapping clean white bandages around his arm. He did not make a sound through the whole ordeal.

She, on the other hand, could not seem to keep her mews of distresses under control. She was even perspiring at the end of it. When she finally finished and sat back, she looked up and found herself under his studious gaze once more. He had been watching her the whole time. His lips curled up in that half smile, and he offered her the brandy again.

"More fortification?" he asked.

She took the glass without shame and sipped, letting the fire burn to her belly. It settled her again, and she set the drink on the table.

He looked down at his arm, then back at her. "Thank you," he said, his voice devoid of his usual irony.

"You're welcome," she managed to get out, moved by the emotion she saw in his eyes. She looked away. "Now. How did this happen?"

"Ah, a few men wanted to relieve me of a few coins," he said, as if it was nothing more dramatic than a walk in the park.

"In broad daylight? Where were you?" She was appalled.

"Ah…" He didn't meet her eyes and he shifted on the seat.

"I knew it." She poked a finger at his arm, and he winced. She was immediately contrite. "Oh, I'm so sorry. But how dare you work on the investigation without me?"

He knew he was caught. "I was with your brother."

Her eyes narrowed. "Lucas."

He smirked at her annoyance, clearly relieved to at least split the blame.

"Let us pretend I don't want to brain both of you for keeping me—and I can only assume Gemma as well—out of these plans, and you'll tell me if you found anything out."

He grimaced at that. "Well, I only have this to show for my day," he said with a gesture to his injury. Any lingering irritation fled at that. She looked down at the bandage.

"You could have been killed," she whispered. She didn't want to picture it. Thugs lurking in dark alleyways, waiting for unsuspecting victims. She was only thankful that he was sitting in front of her, mostly whole. If she had simply heard the tale from her brother, she would not have been able to stop herself from rushing to find if he was well. Even now, she wanted to touch him to make sure his solidness was still there.

He studied her for a long time. "Would you have cared?"

She jumped to her feet. "Of course I would have cared, you stupid, stupid man," she said, incensed.

Quick as lightning, he grabbed her hand and pulled her down next to him once more. "Why would you have cared?" he asked, forcing the point. His eyes were intense on hers. Her stomach dipped as her anger and fear faded and she realized what she'd said. What she'd given away. Her palms went clammy, and she tried to tug her hand out of his. He squeezed it tighter, keeping her trapped where she was. He was not going to let her ignore it, or pretend it hadn't happened.

"Why would you have cared?" he asked again, his voice like velvet.

There was no answer she could give him that would make sense. Why did she care? Why did seeing him hurt affect her? She had nothing she could say. She simply lifted one shoulder in a helpless shrug.

They sat in tense silence until his eyes dropped to her mouth. His lips followed suit.

The world stilled around her at the first touch. It was gentle, undemanding. Just a press.

"Beatrice," he whispered, and the warmth tickled her skin. Her lips parted on a sigh, and he pushed inside. And then it was no longer gentle. It was a fierce siege on her mouth, but she returned the passion with equal fervor. She wound her fingers up around the nape of his neck, making sure she didn't bump his injury. She tugged him closer. Ever closer. One of his hands cupped her cheek while the other dug into the soft flesh at her hips.

It was only when she let out a little whimper that he pulled back. Their broken and ragged breathing filled the quiet space between them.

She tried to regain control of herself, as her thoughts bumped and cascaded into each other, a wild riot in her mind. Was she just a wanton when it came to men? This was different though than it had been with Ralph. It felt different. Yes, there had been passion. But there hadn't been that underlying tenderness she felt when George held her in his arms. She hadn't noticed the lack of it at the time, but the difference was stark. Ralph had charmed her. Had offered her a glimpse of something she'd never experienced before. But it hadn't been like this.

This. This was not sordid. This was love.

Despair followed quickly on the heels of euphoria. It might be love, but it could not be. She had ruined all her chances at happiness with one foolish decision. She would pay for it the rest of her life. She just hoped eventually those around her would stop having to pay for it, too. She dropped her eyes, not wanting him to see the tears in them. She had to hold herself together long enough to get out of the room.

But again, he did not let her escape. She had no fear of him physically—she knew he would never hurt her—but he would not let her run away from this.

He tucked a finger under her chin, forcing her to tilt her face up and meet his eyes.

"What is this?" he asked, catching a tear with this thumb as it escaped to roll down one of her cheeks.

She took a breath. There was no turning back now. But just as she was about to respond, the door slammed open, and Lucas swept into the room.

He halted when he saw them seated on the chaise. "Harrington! What happened to your arm?"

Beatrice knew she had to flee. She leaped for the door. She brushed past Lucas, her head down, hiding the evidence of her tears. He exclaimed something, but she didn't stop to answer. She didn't stop until she reached her room. She threw herself on her bed, her heart in her throat. She touched shaking fingers to her lips again, and let herself dream that love was possible.

Chapter Sixteen

The bride wore her favorite blue dress to her wedding. It was to be a small affair in the early morning light. Gemma had her maid dress her hair simply, slicked back into a silky chignon with a few curls escaping to frame her face. She stood in front of the glass, bent slightly at the waist, peering critically at herself. She stuck out her tongue at the reflection, wishing a more classically beautiful one stared back at her.

Uncle Artie had not put a premium on telling her she was beautiful. Any praise had been limited to whatever he'd been teaching her. There was a confidence in that. She trusted that she was reasonably intelligent and could hold her own with a blade. But no one had told her she was pretty. Not that she would expect her crusty old uncle to have lavished her with compliments on her looks. But it had made her doubt that there was anything there to compliment.

When Lucas had started paying attention to her, part of her always wondered why such a handsome gentleman would cast his gaze her way. Slowly he'd built her confidence up, though. Without her even realizing it. Now, there was warmth there. He made her feel pretty. Desirable, even.

It made her wonder what Uncle Artie would have thought of Lucas. Though, she guessed they would get on famously once they started comparing all the places they'd traveled to. Artie would be enamored from the first story.

Nigel would have been harder to impress. Protective to a fault, that one had been. He would interrogate Lucas on how he would be able to take care of Gemma, even though it was well known he was wealthy beyond any concern. Lucas's straightforward and honest answers would have relaxed her cousin, though. They both would have liked him, she decided in the end.

Her heart ached at the memory of them, wishing they were there. She sniffled a bit into a hankie and allowed herself a moment of grief before she gathered herself. It wouldn't do to have her look like she'd had a good cry right before walking down the aisle. Lucas deserved better than that.

Nerves fluttered like butterflies in the pit of her belly.

Will this be the biggest mistake of my life?

Part of her wished she had never met him, that she still had her simple life in the country. There had been no fear or uncertainty there. But there had also not been this love and friendship and excitement, either. Were the highs worth the lows? To have the full range of life's emotions? Or was it better to sail along through life, happy and content, a burden to no one?

She pressed a flat hand to her stomach, closed her eyes, and let herself picture her groom, all brooding and mysterious. But she had been allowed to see the warmth underneath that hard exterior. He had let her in. And it hadn't been easy for him, either. She wrapped that knowledge around her shoulders like a cloak, to protect her against her own insecurities that battered against her, wanting to chill her bones.

Now was not the time to think about what would happen

when the case ended. Or the time to wonder if all of it would wither into resentment and disappointment once he realized they were tied for life.

No, now was the time to be happy. She was marrying the love of her life. All she could do was move forward. And hope.

She took a deep breath, smoothing a gloved hand over a slight wrinkle in the blue muslin, and then turned for the door.

...

The little church was bathed in light. It streamed in through the rose and yellow and green stained glass windows throwing a riot of colors onto the simple floors all around Lucas. Missing was that weighty hush that usually made him tug at his cravat and check his pocket watch wondering if imminent escape was possible.

He had no desire to escape, now though. There was no place he'd rather be. No one for whom he'd rather be waiting.

The rush meant it was a simple affair—close family and friends only. They were scattered and mingled in the first few pews as they all waited for the bride.

If he was honest with himself, he had been expecting nerves. A tinge of panic. Nothing that would make him change his mind, of course, but maybe a passing thought to wild oats unsown, or the fact that his life was no longer just about him. It would never be again.

But he'd never been surer of anything.

He'd heard other men bemoan their wives. Turn to mistresses and brothels to overcome their boredom within their own marriage. They were the ones who slapped newly engaged young bucks on their shoulders and told them to run when they could.

He couldn't imagine ever being bored of Gemma. She

was an endless treasure to explore. He wanted to learn and memorize every expression, every smile, every laugh, every frown. To savor every part of her and let it become a familiar taste against his tongue. To know her secrets, know why she smiled and laughed and frowned. It would take more than the lifetime they would have together to accomplish that. No, he wouldn't be bored.

The only doubts that shadowed the day came from her reluctance. He'd had to all but beg her to agree to marry him. He'd been so scared she would say no, that she would reject him outright. When she'd finally agreed, something had loosened in his chest and he'd been able to breathe again. But he couldn't forget the uncertainty that had lingered in the corners of her lips and the fear that had lurked in her eyes.

He knew she was independent. Was she thinking of the freedom she was giving up by tying herself to him? Marriage did not exactly favor the woman if she had enough resources to survive without it. But surely she knew marriage to him would be different. He had no desire to stifle her or dampen her spirit, even if that were possible. It was what gave him life—to see her shine.

Everything would be easier once they caught their villain. Then there wouldn't be anything between them. And he would be able to concentrate on making sure she was the happiest of married ladies. He bit back a grin as one idea of how to accomplish that flitted across his mind.

He was quickly pulled back to reality, though, by a commotion in the back.

This is it.

Everything went quiet when he saw her. The low hum of appreciation as the guests shifted in their seats, the noise from the streets, the clergyman clearing his throat beside Lucas. It all went quiet.

There was only her. She was all he could see.

The ceremony was a blur until his vows. He knew he'd said all the right things in the right places, but his mind was still trying to figure out how he'd ever managed to convince her to take a chance on him in the first place.

But now she was looking at him. Everyone was looking at him. He cleared his throat and repeated the words the priest gave him. Her small hands were cradled in his, and his thumb found the impossibly soft spot right beneath hers.

"To love and to cherish," he promised, his eyes on hers, his fingers pressing against hers. He hoped she understood. These weren't just empty words. "To love and to cherish," he said again, interrupting the clergyman. A few nervous titters erupted from the crowd, but he didn't take his eyes off Gemma. She searched his face. For a moment, he wasn't sure if she got it. Then a slow smile crept in. She tucked her fingers into his palms, and he relaxed.

He lifted a brow to the clergyman as if asking him what the hold up was. Gemma stifled a giggle at the man's affronted expression as he carried on with the ceremony.

The light caught on her ring as he slid it onto her finger. It looked so right there, and he couldn't help but linger over the smooth metal. She was his. He was hers. He swallowed hard against the tight ball of emotion that lodged right beneath his breastbone. A romantic would say it was in the region of his heart.

He cleared his throat and leaned down. "Something tells me we're going to have to work really hard on that 'obey' part."

She pulled back slightly, eyes wide. Then she tipped her head back, laughing. It sounded like delicate chimes.

He couldn't resist. Lips met smiling lips. And he did not give even a little damn that his guests must think him a fool in love.

...

Following the ceremony, Roz hosted a breakfast for the couple. They gathered in Lucas's house, which was now Gemma's house. She was a countess. It would take a while to get used to the position. She knew she was capable of running a household; she had been Uncle Artie's hostess as soon as she had made her debut. But was she capable of the rest of the social responsibilities that came with the title? She thought of her promise to herself to not let her insecurities creep in. And then thought of the way Lucas had watched her during the ceremony. He certainly thought she was fit to be his countess.

A nudge at her elbow brought her back to the present, and she turned to find Beatrice with a cup of tea.

"I am so glad we are sisters now, Gemma," her new sister-in-law said, with her usual bright smile. "But you look troubled. You can tell me what is wrong."

Gemma laughed off the concern. "What could be wrong? It's my wedding day, the happiest day of my life."

Beatrice studied her. "Forgive me for prying, but you don't look like a woman on the happiest day of her life."

Gemma grimaced. She had always been an expert at hiding her emotions, but she was raw from the past few hours. Her practiced facade seemed to have been stripped. "Oh, please believe me, I am overjoyed to be married to your brother. I care for him deeply."

Beatrice's entire face brightened, looking like the sun on a beautiful summer day. "He cares deeply for you." She paused. "But you are still worried."

"It's not that simple," Gemma admitted.

"It is. You love each other. Anyone can see that," Beatrice said, and Gemma wished she could believe her. There had been that moment in the church. The one in which he'd seemed to pour his soul into his vows of love. But mayhap she had just wanted to see that.

"It all just happened so fast," was all she said. It was the easiest way to put her doubts into words that made any sense. "I don't want him to regret it."

Beatrice tilted her head as she considered Gemma's words. "My brother doesn't make quick decisions. You must know that about him. He's so rational and logical. Almost to a fault."

It was true—Gemma did know that about him. That didn't reassure her. He was also fiercely protective, with a strong sense of responsibility.

"I was actually growing worried for him before he met you, you know," Beatrice continued. "I didn't know if was capable of letting his guard down enough to find someone to love, and be loved in return. I thought he was going to become a grumpy old curmudgeon, if I may tell you the truth."

Gemma laughed to cover her racing heart. "I don't think it would have come to that."

Beatrice reached out to squeeze her arm. "Lucky for us we don't have to find that out."

Instead of feeling comforted by the exchange, she simply felt more confused. It would be much easier if Lucas would just tell her how he felt about her. But she didn't know if she was strong enough to hear that he simply cared about her wellbeing. Her mind flicked back to his warm, steady fingers pressing into hers.

Maybe he had meant it.

The intensity with which she wanted that to be true scared her. So she changed the topic.

"You and Mr. Harrington have worked quite well together," she said. She bit back a grin as a telltale blush stained her sister-in-law's cheeks.

Beatrice cleared her throat and cast a furtive glance back toward the gentleman in question, who was standing next to the pianoforte. Lucas had asked him to join them for the celebration, and after only a slight hesitation, the man had agreed to come. Gemma was glad of it, and wondered when he and Beatrice would realize they were meant for each other.

"He is so kind and intelligent," Beatrice gushed. "I like him ever so much, but…"

"But?" Gemma asked.

She bit her lip. "I have not told him about…" Beatrice finally confessed, her eyes dismayed.

Gemma was relieved to be able to comfort someone else, and for the first time all day take her mind off her own troubles. She took Beatrice's hand and squeezed it. "Oh, my dear. If you are meant to be, he will not care a whit about something that happened in the past. I am sure he will actually be furious at the man for how he treated you, but nothing more. He seems like a very level-headed gentleman."

"Do you really think so?" Beatrice asked.

"I do," she answered. "It may be hard to tell him, but I believe it will be worth it."

"Oh, thank you, Gemma," Beatrice said, throwing her arms around her. "I may never gather the courage to do so, but I will have your words in my head if I do."

Gemma actually laughed at the show of gratitude. "You are stronger than you think, Beatrice."

"And so are you," Beatrice whispered in her ear. "Don't give up on him. Or yourself."

Gemma was left standing alone with those cryptic words repeating in her head while Beatrice took herself off to chat with an acquaintance. Gemma noticed her deliberately not noticing Mr. Harrington, who was deliberately not noticing her in return.

"Do not fret, dear heart," Roz said, sweeping in and replacing Beatrice at her arm.

Gemma laughed, turning her attention away from the

young pair. "Am I so obvious? You are the second person to comfort me."

"Worry lines," Roz said, tapping a finger to Gemma's forehead. "They betray you. But the more pressing question is, why?" Roz waved a hand as Gemma began to speak. "Oh, never mind. I know why. You think because of your…unusual upbringing that you will never be a suitable match for a man like him. You think that he was forced into this because of circumstances."

"Well, it is true," Gemma cried. Why did no one else see the problem?

"It is not," Roz said. "I know your past has made you worry about many things. But you are an absolute catch, dear heart. If he's not in love with you yet, well, make it happen."

If only it were that easy, Gemma thought, sipping tea that had gone lukewarm.

...

"You have been avoiding me." A low voice near Beatrice's ear rousted her from her daydreaming. She whirled toward it. Her plate, filled with soft pink angel cakes, nearly collided with a solid male chest.

George Harrington smiled and removed the plate from her hand so that she did not disgrace herself further. She did not resist. He looked quite handsome. The most handsome she had ever seen him — not that that mattered to her. He was dressed in a fine dark blue coat with buff breeches. His hair was tousled so a lock fell across his brow and into his light hazel eyes. He was not a tall man, but he was solidly built. She remembered his muscle under her hands as she had tended to his wound. Yes, he was solid, she thought, flushing at the memory and cursing the ivory complexion that revealed her every thought in her cheeks.

She watched as he set the plate on the mantle of the fireplace, where she had been hiding within the warm safety of several female relatives. They had all somehow disappeared without her realizing it. That's what she got for daydreaming.

"You are right, sir. I have been," she admitted. There was no point in hiding the fact, she decided. She had gone quite out of her way not to spend any time with the man in the past week. The wedding planning—done mostly with Roz, as Gemma had seemed determinedly unenthusiastic about it—had taken up much of her days. But she would have made herself busy in other ways if it hadn't.

His eyebrows shot up at her honesty, and he rocked onto the heels of his boots. "Walk with me?" he asked and proffered his uninjured arm.

She hesitated, but then let him lead her out through the French doors into the enclosed gardens. The air was crisp and filled with the scent of lilacs, her favorite flower. She nodded to another couple before ducking under a particularly aggressive lemon tree. Her hand curled slightly into his arm, her fingertips digging into the expensive fabric. She wanted to remember every detail of the moment.

"Well, my lady," he said, seating her at a small stone bench tucked into a secluded corner behind the rose bushes. He propped a polished boot next to her hip and leaned on his leg. She stared at a small yellow flower erupting out of a crack in the path. "Will you at least inform me why I am being avoided?"

She breathed deeply. This was really it, she thought. This was the turning point in her life. She would tell him, she decided. There was nothing to be gained from deception, save her pride. She tried to think of where to start.

"Lucas brought you here to investigate a murder," she finally said. He did not react to what must have seemed like a change of subject to him. She bit her lip and gathered her courage. "But it was not just that."

"Yes, I know," George responded, with a casual ease.

"What do you mean, you know?" she asked, thrown off her planned speech and, truthfully, a little peeved about it. She'd spent many a night the past week rehearsing in her head exactly what she'd tell him if this moment came.

He had the audacity to look slightly annoyed himself. "Winchester would not have brought me in on an investigation if it had merely involved the murder of a stranger's cousin," he said, as if he were talking to a not particularly bright child. "It would have had to involve someone under his wing. And that would leave you, my de — my lady."

"Well. Hrmph," she muttered, the wind taken out of her sails. If she had not been caught up in her own emotions, she might have guessed he would figure it out. He was nothing if not intelligent.

"I do not know exactly what it entails, nor do I care," he said after she was silent for a minute. "I presumed it was blackmail of some kind."

"It seems you have it all figured out, sir," she said, mortified and relieved all at once. She could take the easy route and not tell him all the details, she thought. But he deserved to know. And then he would turn from her in disgust.

He smiled, a bit more fully than usual. "Not quite. Enough to know that exactly what happened is unimportant. Enough to know you need to be protected. That is all," he said. He was reassuring her, she thought. He was so kind. She twisted her hands in her lap. "That is all I need to know."

"I met him at my coming-out ball," she said, staring at the ground again. The murmur of voices and music spilled from the house a little distance away. The air was heavy and perfumed by the roses, and the sun was warm on her face. But none of that registered with her. Her life had narrowed down to just him, and the story she had to tell. "He was not the most handsome man there, but there was something about him."

"Please, you do not have to tell me this," George cut in. "It does not matter."

She turned to him, blinking back the tears that threatened to spill out. "I have to tell you," she said. "Do you understand? I have to tell you."

He gazed back at her for a long moment. Then nodded. "I do. Go on."

"Lucas was an overprotective brother," she said. "He kept me quite sheltered in the country after our parents died. He loved me, you see, but he did not really know what to do with me. But for my coming-out ball, that would all change. I was so excited. I had made my bow to the queen. I had bought so many pretty dresses. Everyone kept saying I would be the match of the season, that the beaux would flock to me. I am ashamed to admit, I let it turn my head."

"You were young," he commented.

"It was only a year ago," she said, with a slight smile. "Not so young, unless I am young now."

"You have lived since then," he said.

She tilted her head in consideration. "You are right. I have." She paused then returned to her tale. "I will spare you all the details, but it is fair to say I was led on a merry chase, as they say, but the end was not the altar. It was disgrace, if anyone ever found out. I let myself be charmed by a snake and then was surprised when I was bitten. Thankfully, he actually knew how to maintain some discretion, and with Lucas's help, we managed to squash any rumors of it. He soon left for India, though not because of me, I assure you. But it is true. It was not just that I stepped out into the air too long with him, and that ruined my reputation. I am no longer… innocent."

The last part was the hardest to get out, because she knew it sealed her fate with the man she loved. But once she admitted it, defeat and relief both surged through her. He would turn from her now in judgment of her sins. The kindness in his eyes, the softness there, would shift now to disgust, she was sure. But at least she'd shared her secret. There would be no more deception, she thought.

"I would gladly hunt him down and kill the man," George finally said, his fists clenched. But he did not move away. Quite the opposite. He sat on the hard stone beside her, taking her chin in his hand. "I will kill him."

She let out a gurgle of laughter that was right on the edge of tears. "That is quite unnecessary, sir. I have long since recovered emotionally from the experience. And I have a guess that Lucas has not made his life easy since. He might not have been able to call him out without plunging me into scandal, but there are other ways to ruin a life."

"I would still enjoy the pleasure of making the… gentleman pay," George said, letting his hand drop from her. She missed the warmth immediately. "But you have not answered my question, my lady."

Her eyes flew to his. Was he going to make her spell it out? "Mr. Harrington, please do not think me a woman of loose morals because of my past behavior. I do not frequently kiss gentlemen just to kiss them."

He smiled fully this time, a smile that turned the corners of his lips up and crinkled the delicate skin around his eyes, and her heart turned over in her chest. "What other reason would there be?" he asked, his voice innocent and curious. She swatted at his uninjured shoulder.

"You tease me," she accused. "But I was worried you would think…" She trailed off, unable to finish her thought without coming off as arrogant or unladylike.

"That I would think of courting you?" he suggested. "And is that your only concern about such a match? How I would feel about your past?"

"Of course," she said, confused by his meaning.

"Ah, Beatrice," her name sounded like a caress on his lips. He closed his eyes, turning his face to the sun and taking a deep breath. "How foolish we both are."

"What on earth do you mean?" she asked, confused.

He looked back at her, their eyes locking. He shifted and took her hands in his own, bringing one up to his lips. He turned it so he could lay his lips against her palm. Electricity shot from her heart to her womb when his tongue darted out to briefly touch the delicate skin. He dropped their hands to her lap but did not release them.

"I am the fourth son of a gentleman," he said, finally.

"Yes, I know," she said, the vague feeling of annoyance returning. She was not a simpleton, no matter what anyone else might think.

He smiled, but the gesture had returned to the crooked half smile and did not light up his eyes. "I have no land. I have a small house here in London, but I prefer working in the country on your brother's estates. I have no further ambitions other than to be a man of affairs. I have no great wealth to offer, nor any position."

"You have so much to offer," she said and squeezed his hand in reassurance. She would not have guessed he had thought thusly. He always appeared confident and in control of all situations.

"I love you, Beatrice," he said, his eyes warm on hers. "I love your light. I love your intelligence. I love the way you prickle when I tease you. I love that you bring sunshine and happiness wherever you go, even though your life has known stormy weather. I love your strength for experiencing that and coming out the other side a better, more mature person. I love that you aren't afraid to say what you think, and that you feel deeply. I love you, Beatrice."

She did not even try to stop the tears that flooded her

eyes. Could these words be true? She had spent the past year convinced that any words of love were lies, that she would never know the truth of a man's passion. And yet, he, George, would not lie to her. She knew this of him.

"I do not expect you to return the sentiment, my love," he said as she gulped and tried to staunch the river running down her face. "But I would like the opportunity to try. If my station is not something to turn you away."

She laughed and hiccupped and knew she was a general mess. "You silly man," she finally managed. "I love you more than life. I would take an eternity living in a hovel with you over one in a palace without you."

He leaned forward and captured her lips with his. "Well, we certainly will not live in a hovel."

"A shack?" she teased when he released her mouth. "A hut? A shed?"

"Minx," he said, his teeth sinking into her lower lip.

Chapter Seventeen

It was his wedding night. Lucas rolled the tumbler of amber liquid between his long fingers. He and Gemma were married, and she was stuck with him now. He supposed he should feel guilty for rushing her into the union. It had been a faster timeline than he'd originally anticipated. But he was a man who seized opportunity when it presented itself.

She had doubts, though, and that ate at him. During the reception, she'd smiled and mingled and been a beautiful hostess. In the quiet moments, though, shadows slipped into her eyes.

He'd wanted to shake her and then kiss her and then get her to tell him that she was happy they were married. But he'd done none of that. They'd had a perfectly pleasant day, but that guard that he couldn't quite figure out how to dismantle was a wall between them. If he didn't figure out how to tear it down, he worried they'd be doomed.

He shook off the dark thought and glanced at the clock on the mantle of the study. He had wanted to give her some time to adjust to her new bedroom before going to her. Her things had been efficiently packed up and moved over during their wedding breakfast. Their rooms were adjoined, as was proper for an earl and a countess, but he had no intention of sleeping in separate beds, that night or ever. He swallowed his scotch, enjoying the slight burn that did nothing to dampen his anticipation for the night to come.

He did not want to think about the blackmail on the night of his wedding, but his thoughts turned toward the case.

With all of the wedding preparations taking nearly a week, he had been forced to pay the latest demand to buy them time, and that had not sat well with him. It would be worth it in the end when they finally caught the bastard, but Lucas had struggled against his pride as he left the money at the specified location.

Rathburn's story, and then Carsons's information, had shed light on the tragedy motivating the villain, but Lucas had not yet formulated a plan for how to proceed after learning what they had. And they had not made progress in the past week. Harrington had been busy learning the background of the men who appeared on all three lists: the guest lists for the house party and his own, and the list of antique watch collectors. It might be a stretch, he thought, but something in their histories might spark an idea.

He gazed into the fire, emptying his mind so he could see more clearly any patterns that were emerging. There was something there, flying away at the edges every time he went to reach for it. He would look at all the information again in the morning. Perhaps that would illuminate the idea he could not quite form.

But it was his wedding night, and he had not had much access to Gemma all week. There had been a few furtive kisses stolen at what all turned out to be inopportune moments for anything further. He'd been left in some inconvenient discomfort several times when Roz had burst into the library with wedding questions and plans.

He finished his drink and rose to his feet. He forced himself to take the stairs slowly, amused at his own schoolboy eagerness. The special license had taken a few days to acquire, and then Gemma's aunt had insisted on planning a wedding brunch as well.

But now they would have hours to satiate themselves with each other, and they were assured not to be interrupted. Because she was his wife. For now. For however long. For all time.

Gemma was his wife.

...

Gemma was being absurd. It wasn't as if she were an innocent any longer. But knowing it didn't stop her from being nervous.

There was something special, different, about it being her wedding night, though. It heightened all her emotions—ones that were already fragile from the day.

She was married. The enormity of it washed over her even as she sat still beneath the careful ministrations of her maid. Lucas was her family now. For the first time since her parents died, she had a family.

She immediately felt blasphemous toward Uncle Artie and Nigel at the thought. But she knew, although they had loved her dearly and she them, that it was not the same. She was now directly responsible for someone's happiness and he for hers. She remembered what he'd whispered to her that first night in the carriage.

We are in this together now, my dear.

Her maid finished weaving the white ribbon through her hair, and Roz's words from earlier rang in her head.

If he's not in love with you yet, well, make it happen.

It was not like her to be so passive when it came to

something she wanted. She had come to London to hunt a murderer, for goodness sake. Why was she sitting back, letting fear take control? Fear of rejection. Fear of being vulnerable. Why, when it came to one of the most important things in her life, was she not fighting?

Because it would hurt so much if I lost the battle.

But she was already losing by not trying. She was worth loving. If Lucas didn't see that, well, he was a fool. And he was no fool.

At the realization, the vise that had been wrapped around her rib cage all day long loosened.

She smiled and dismissed the maid. Should she arrange herself somehow on the bed? Or was that too forward? Should she sit demurely sewing in the chair by the fire?

Before she could decide, she heard a soft knock on the door that connected her bedroom to Lucas's.

She curbed the urge to run to him when he entered. It was hard, though, because he was just so handsome, and she was just so happy with her newfound mission in life. He'd skipped his usual unrelenting formal black for a loose white shirt and grey trousers. His feet were bare, and for some reason that put her more completely at ease than any words would have. A giggle burbled up, and she clasped a hand over her mouth to try to contain the mirth.

"Not exactly what you want from your wife on your wedding night," Lucas murmured.

She glanced up at him as he stalked toward her. The laughter died in her throat at the look of burning desire on his face. She leaped toward him, and he caught her against his chest. Their mouths found each other and hungrily feasted. He slid his hands down her back and under her backside, hoisting her up so that he held her off the ground as if she weighed as much as a feather. She wrapped her legs around his waist, pressing against him right where the storm was building. A quick turn brought her back up flat against the wall.

He used one hand to encircle her wrists so that he could hold her arms above her head. She felt powerless and cherished when faced with such raw strength and control. He took advantage of her position by nibbling on the sensitive skin of her neck, his tongue soothing the nips from his teeth. She could do nothing but throw her head back and push herself closer to his hardness as he worshiped her skin. Desire pulsed through her.

When she could not take the gentle torment any longer, she pulled her arms out of his grasp and brought his face to hers for a deep kiss of tongues battling and warring for mutual pleasure. He growled deep in his throat, and an answering awareness tugged at her breasts and womb.

He shifted back and laughed, glancing around the room. "Shall we try to make it to a bed this time, my dear?"

"A bed? How novel," she quipped back, enjoying their banter in the midst of such a passionate interlude. "I suppose we should try it at least once."

He laughed, a low rumble against her ear as he bit the lobe and slid his tongue along the rim.

The spark the slick caress sent along her nerve endings surprised her. Would it feel that way for him? Did she have enough courage to try? There was something about tonight that made her think she could be brave enough to do anything. She mimicked his sensual ministrations, and his groan told her everything she needed to know.

Suddenly, he turned, still holding her in his strong arms, and in three strides was across the room, tumbling her onto the bed. The soft, silken bedding was cool against her heated skin, and she held up her hand for him to join her.

"You are so unbelievably beautiful," he said as he stripped out of his shirt, revealing the contours of his thickly muscled chest. The sight of him above her, his arousal obvious in his skintight breeches, flooded her with longing. She wanted her hands on him. Immediately. Wanted his body pressed to hers. It was an ache that thrummed in time with her frantic pulse.

Together, they rid her of her nightgown until she was bare beneath his gaze.

He didn't touch her at first.

With someone else, she might have felt self-conscious, or at least the need to cover herself from hungry eyes. But with him—well, with him she felt powerful. Seductive. Safe.

He devoured her with his eyes, just as she was doing to him. At last, he brought a reverent hand to her breast, grazing the delicate pink nipple that had risen to insistent attention. The tension within her built as he cupped her, nuzzled at her. When he sucked her into his mouth, she couldn't bite back her mewl of desire.

A thought crept in as he pulled back, kissing the underside of her breast and then each rib down to her belly. She caught his chin in her hand forcing his gaze up to hers.

She almost lost her nerve under his heated eyes.

Tonight she was brave enough to do anything.

She took a deep breath and blurted it out before her courage could desert her. "Can I—Can I try doing that to you?"

Mortification threatened when he squeezed his eyes shut tight. But it was chased away when he looked at her again and all she could see was fire.

He cleared his throat. "You don't have to, love."

"I want to try it," she said, and he groaned, shifting up so that he could slant his mouth over hers.

"God, give me strength," he murmured against her lips. Then he moved so that he was lying back against the pillows and she was straddling his hips. His fingers traced their way over the vertebrae of her spine, and she shivered against him.

Be brave.

Taking her lesson from what she had liked, she bent, finding his neck with her open mouth. She licked at the skin there, and the stubble was rough against her tongue, in a good way. She let her teeth sink into the sinew of his shoulder for a moment before shifting down. His skin burned beneath her hands.

She had never felt more powerful than when he moaned as her teeth grazed over his nipple. It gave her courage. It made her burn. Something about bringing him pleasure like this only served to heighten her own.

She lingered there before moving down. The muscles of his stomach were taut, and she spread her fingers over them, marveling in the way they bunched beneath her hand.

But she had more interesting things to see. She'd shifted so that she was between his strong, lean thighs.

Gemma found him watching her, with a slight smile on his lips. Breathing deep, she reached out a shaking hand and caught him in her fingers. Heated silk, was all she could foolishly think. Her hand tightened reflexively around him when he shifted, and he groaned in response.

"Ah, love."

"Did I hurt you?" she dropped her fingers immediately, horrified at the possibility.

He laughed, a low rumble that edged on the side of desperate. "Not how you think."

He brought her hand back to him, and guided her into a light stroke. It wasn't enough, though.

His eyes had drifted closed so he didn't realize her intent until her mouth covered him. He cried out and his hips rocked up, and she took him deeper. It was pure instinct that had her pull at him with her lips as he rested heavy against her tongue. He was pure tension beneath her hands, and she once again reveled in the way he responded to her. Just as she knew he must when she cried out for him.

She tried licking along the underside of him, and it seemed to snap his control. Slipping his hands beneath her, he hauled her up so that she was once again astride his hips. He was hard against her bottom.

She smiled down at him, and he laughed up at her.

"You are trying to kill me, aren't you?"

"Well, it's either that or obey you, and we both know where I stand on that particular vow," she replied.

"We shall see what we can do about that, wife," he murmured, and her pulse skittered. Wife. She liked the way that sounded.

There wasn't time to linger over the pleasure it gave her, though, because his fingers had found her and were busy building that delicious tension she'd experienced the night in the library.

She was whimpering within moments, and he smirked at her, clearly pleased. She rocked her hips back against him, and the smile died from his lips, quickly becoming a groan. The result prompted her to try it again. The movement, combined with his fingers, was too much for her. Her head fell back, her curls cascading down her back. He took advantage of her position, one of his hands finding her breast. When he pinched her nipple, she lost all coherent thought.

"All right, love, all right," he soothed when she cried out The tips of his fingers slid back down to her hips. "Just…"

He lifted her slightly so that she was positioned above him. It was a tortuous descent for both of them. He was sweating by the time she was filled to the hilt, their hips all but fused to each other.

Air. She needed air. She couldn't quite get enough to properly fill her lungs.

Moving didn't help. He was guiding her, helping her find a smooth rocking rhythm that set her blood on fire.

"So beautiful." His voice was dazed, and she wondered

what she looked like to him. Riding him as she was, her hair wild and loose around her shoulders, her skin flushed in the firelight. She didn't care if she looked like a wanton. What did propriety matter when he gazed at her like that?

It only took her a few moments before she was able to set the pace. And then his hands were everywhere, stoking that fire that had been building all night.

She was on the edge of a cliff and kept toeing closer. This time when she slid down along his length, she stayed there and rocked her hips. He must have sensed she was there, ready to fall into the abyss.

"Let go, love." His voice was rough. She found his eyes just as his fingers pressed against her and she obeyed him.

The moment she did, he followed her off the precipice.

Only the sound of ragged breathing filled the room. She didn't think she could say anything even if she wanted to. Though, she didn't want to. She didn't want to do anything to disturb the bliss.

"I believe I have lost the ability to speak, my dear," he murmured against the top of her head, echoing her own thoughts.

She laughed, pulling back to peer up at him in amusement. "And yet you disprove your claim with the same breath you use to speak it."

"Ah, you and your logic." He smiled down at her, and it lit up his eyes and made her feel precious. "Those are the only words I can utter. You have left me quite useless otherwise."

"Whatever shall I do with myself if you cannot keep me entertained with conversation, my lord?" she flirted. It was an enjoyable feeling, that. Flirting with one's lover.

With one's husband.

"Mmmm." His voice rumbled in his chest, tickling her cheek. His heart beat a slow, reassuring tempo against her ear. "I believe I could come up with one or two suggestions of what you could do with your mouth instead of conversing."

She blushed but refused to back down from the challenge. "But, my lord, I thought I had rendered you quite speechless."

"My suggestions don't necessarily necessitate words, my dear," he said, lifting her chin and pulling her mouth to his. The kiss was lazy, as they were both spent and physically exhausted. This wasn't about lust. This wasn't about the all-consuming desire that flared between them. It was more than that.

He pulled back, kissing her forehead, and shifting so that she was curled into his arms at his side.

"You will be the death of me, woman," he said. "But, oh, what a sweet death it will be." The warmth of his body lulled her just as much as the fingers that were rubbing a circle between her shoulder blades. Her cheek was against his heart. She wanted to live in the crook of his arm forever.

He poked her when she giggled at that thought, but she didn't tell him what she was laughing at.

It seemed like she would get her wish, at least for the night, as his breathing evened out. She knew most married couples had separate rooms, but she would have been devastated had he pulled away and gone off to his own. It also seemed they would not put on their nightclothes again, but lay entangled together without a stitch on. She would have predicted she'd be embarrassed by such a notion, but she felt not one whit of discomfort. He was her husband. She had nothing to hide from him, nor he from her.

They stayed that way for a long time, both lightly caressing and soothing the other. She felt sleep pulling at her relentlessly.

"Gemma?" he asked just as she was about to drift off into oblivion.

"Mmmm," she managed to say, her satiated body wanting to sink into the warmth of him and the bedding. She did not think she would be able to open her eyes if she tried.

"Why did you marry me?"

Because I love you. She thought the words as sleep claimed her.

. . .

Lucas stilled. The words were uttered so softly he almost missed them, but they burned their way onto his soul.

He pulled her closer against him, and she nestled into the nook of his arm. He stared into the dark night for a long time before sleep finally washed over him.

When he woke in the morning, she was gone.

Chapter Eighteen

The storefront was rotting, the window dusty. The place had the feel of a tired old man on the doorstep of death. None of the passersby paid it attention, other than to take a few steps away on the sidewalk as their eyes slid from the perfume shop on one side to the milliner's on the other, both of which were old but well-kept and somewhat respectable.

Gemma glanced at the address and compared it to the one she'd written down earlier, before dawn when she'd been unable to fall back asleep. Lucas would probably be unhappy with her if he knew where she was, but she had not wanted to wake him. If she was being honest with herself, she was terrified to face him. The memory of his question haunted her and had caused the jolt that had woken her hours later. Had she actually uttered the words aloud, or did she imagine that? She was being cowardly, but she couldn't quite bring herself to deal with him in the light of day yet. So she had fled.

On a productive errand, she told herself.

Something had been nagging at the back of her mind for a few days: the locations of the blackmail payments. Out of the ones they knew about, many were in open, public spots, such as the park. Or at large, public gatherings, such as the house party. But one of the earlier ones that Lucas had told her about, and which matched one of Perry's locations, which she'd written down following their foray into his apartments, was different. She hadn't recognized the address other than to realize that it was in a more disreputable part of town than the other respectable spots.

She'd arrived by hackney, and she told the driver to wait for her.

The air was crisp as it blew from the Thames, and she pulled her light shawl tighter against her shoulders. The hairs on the back of her neck prickled. It was a warning sign. Uncle Artie had told her to always heed it, never to discount it as foolish. It had saved his life more times than he could count, he told her.

But she'd come this far. Though it was still early, the bookshop door swung open when she tested it. She stepped out of the light and into the dark, musty store. She coughed as a plume of dust hit her.

An elderly man crouched behind a desk in the front of the shop looked up over thick spectacles. His hair was a wild riot of white poking straight into the air over large, dangling ears. He was clearly in the middle of a book, his finger holding his place.

"'Ello?" he croaked at her with a voice unused to talking. She wondered how he kept the shop running, even as dismal as it was. It would still take energy and money to keep it open. She smoothed a nervous hand over her stomach before walking closer to him.

"Could you tell me about this shop, sir?" She had decided to go with general curiosity. Pretending to look for one thing in particular could limit her options depending on how he answered. "I was walking by and wanted to see what it was."

He peered at her skeptically for a minute, and she did not blame him. Anyone who passed by, especially a well-dressed countess, would not actually come into a place like his.

He shrugged, though, and said, "Rare books. Very rare." His eyes traced over her expensive clothing, sizing up his potential profits. "Museum upstairs."

She paused. "A museum?"

He nodded his head toward the back of the shop. "Buy yer ticket here. Staircase in the back. Bring the key back when you finish."

"What is the museum for?" she asked, but she was already pulling out the price of admission. She dropped it in his wrinkled, papery hand as he heaved an annoyed sigh.

"Intrigue. Scandal. Murder," he said, dropping her coins into the till and pushing a pamphlet in her direction. "Been about thirty or so years now, not many go up there any longer. A few blokes recently. You'll see that happen." He gave her a look. "Scandals come back in style and the fancy folk like yerself want a little thrill." He handed her a heavy brass key and motioned her away.

Gemma weaved her way through tall, creaking bookshelves toward what she hoped was the back door to the store. The shop was a labyrinth of heavy leather tomes, but she found her way eventually. The key was in the lock, so she let herself out into the alley.

The stench of it hit her first, and she grabbed for a handkerchief. It was a horrid mix of death, rot, and human excrement and she hurried up the rickety wooden staircase to the rooms at the top.

She fumbled with the key for a moment before getting the heavy door to creak open. She pushed it mostly closed behind her and for the first time glanced at the pamphlet the shopkeeper had pushed into her hands. The front cover showed a woman clearly in distress, a hand up over her head as she cringed away from a hulking shadow of a man. A child hid in the corner of the page, hands over his ears, curled into a ball. "A murder most foul: The tale of the shopkeeper's assistant and the gentleman," was printed across the top in dark black bold letters.

She opened the pages and continued to read the sad tale. The victim had been a widow with a young boy. She had been employed by the shopkeeper for several years after she'd shown up, newly pregnant and having just buried her husband. She had been quiet and kept to herself mostly, but the shopkeeper told investigators she'd had a lover in the few months leading up to her death. She got greedy and expected the gentleman to take up with her, he'd said, but he'd warned her that the man would never marry her. He was a lord. The shopkeeper had not known who it was, but the widow had let that slip a time or two. There was even a hint of blackmail in the story.

Gemma knew not to take the pamphlet for truth. These were common at attractions in London to drum up intrigue and ticket prices. But she could not help but think of Rathburn's story, and how it could match the basic premise of the one she was reading. It said the assistant was a widow, but if she'd been pregnant and unmarried, there was no better way to survive than to pretend respectability. She remembered she had cursed herself for not coming up with the same solution when Lucas had proposed. She kept reading.

One night the shopkeeper had heard screams from the widow's rooms. He'd raced from the bed, he claimed, but had not made it in time. He arrived to find the widow sprawled out on the mattress, her throat cut and blood seeping from the wound. He'd found the boy in a closet, shaking and mute.

What had made the story notable with the press—and why there was still a museum dedicated to the gruesome crime—was that police had found a symbol scrawled on the wall in blood. It was about the same time women had been turning up with the same symbol carved into their skin. Some were alive and had been sussed out by the police after the shopkeeper's murder, and some were found washed up on the banks of the Thames, according to the pamphlet. The police surmised it might be the work of a madman loose on the streets of London, but none of the girls who were still alive could remember enough details about the man to help with the search. Or they chose not to remember. She could easily imagine how the tale would have sent all of London into horrified delight at the time, latching onto any murder as if it were the latest gossip from the ballrooms. Especially since the women showing up dead were only prostitutes.

She stopped reading and glanced toward the mostly empty walls. Her stomach chilled at the sight of the faded dark brown symbol that still clung in traces to the wilting yellow paper. It was not the blood that disturbed her, though. It was that she recognized the symbol.

"I shall find a way or make one." A deep voice resonated in the quiet rooms. She tried to spin toward the door but a man's arm pressed around her neck, and she felt a cloth pushed up against her face. She smelled the sickly sweet chloroform even as she kicked out at her attacker. It was no use, though. With her last conscious thought, she dropped her handkerchief on the floor, hoping against hope Lucas would find it and know she'd been there.

...

Lucas wasn't annoyed. He'd started out disappointed. Disappointed that his wife wasn't in his arms when he had awoken. He'd shifted to "irritated" when he'd discovered she'd left the house completely without telling anyone where she was going. But as the hours passed by without word from her, he moved swiftly away from irritated to something that chilled him to the core.

No, he wasn't annoyed. He was near panic. It was a new feeling, and he did not like the cold ball of ice that sat heavily in his stomach.

He sat behind his desk, where she had clearly been before she left, studying the papers that were sprawled there along with a quick note to him saying she'd be back shortly. Why had she not waited for him?

Lucas ran a hand over his face. He looked back at the pile in front of him: the drop-off locations, the note she'd received at Vauxhall Gardens, and the guest lists for the house party where her cousin was murdered and the one where his sister's diary was stolen. The list of known watch collectors.

On top of the pile was a piece of paper with notes his wife had jotted down in a map-like pattern. Arrows connected "historic relics" to "pocket watch" and "blond." "Timing?" stood out by itself and was underlined several times. As was "baby?" He had been trying to decipher it for the past hour. She must have seen something he was clearly missing. He was struggling to think straight with the panic that continued to claw at his stomach.

He pushed to his feet and slammed his fist onto the papers. He wanted to crumple them and toss them into the fire in frustration, but he knew that would be the epitome of foolish, irrational action. So he paced to the window instead, trying to control his emotions. He could not lose her now. Not now. He had just found her.

A knock sounded on the door of the study. He wanted to lash out at whoever dared interrupt him in the moment, but he tempered his voice. "Enter," he hissed through clenched teeth.

Lucas spared no time on niceties when he saw who it was. "Harrington, what do you have?"

His man of affairs did not even flinch at the abruptness of the question or the tone in which it was asked. He simply pulled a sheet of paper from his pocket and turned it over to Lucas.

"I have been compiling all the information I could find on the men whose names appeared on all of our lists, and who fit some of the other descriptors we have narrowed down thus far," Harrington said, without any preamble. Good man, Lucas thought. He stared at the letters scrawled on the page but could barely concentrate enough to process them. Focus, he told himself. It would do her no good if he fell apart. Harrington continued as Lucas read on, "I talked to a few other men of affairs, secretaries, and valets. The ones for whom I could not find more than a few tidbits are underlined there."

Lucas's eyes traced over the names he had studied so many times. He went back to his desk and placed the new list on top of the other documents. Focus, he told himself once more. His finger paused on one of the names on the sheet Harrington had just given him. His instincts buzzed at him, a feeling he knew well not to ignore. "Lake District?" he asked looking up at Harrington.

"Yes, I noticed that, too. The man in the pub did say that's where the boy was sent," Harrington said, his eyes steady. "Sometimes when people create identities, one or two truths slip in. Or it could be a coincidence."

Finally, the pieces clicked into place. He followed one of the arrows on his wife's map to the list of drop-off sites. It seemed their murderer had a weakness for his past. It would lead to his downfall.

He started for the door, brushing past Harrington without a word.

His wife was the most brilliant and most foolish woman he'd ever met, and he was going to throttle her as soon as he knew she was safe.

• • •

Lucas's first stop proved to be fruitless, but his second was successful. The old shopkeeper directed him to the rooms upstairs, where he'd sent a lady a few hours earlier. When Lucas inquired as to why it hadn't seemed odd that the lady hadn't returned through the shop, the old man shrugged a heavy shoulder and returned to reading.

Lucas tore through the shop and up the old stairs. The door was ajar, and he nudged it open with his boot. He stepped into the darkened room that smelled of must and neglect. His heart froze when he saw the handkerchief on the floor. A few strides and he was kneeling by the delicate white lace; he picked it up and touched it to his nose. Gemma.

He pushed aside the panic that threatened to suffocate him with every gasping breath he took, and surveyed the room. It was small, with few furnishings to clutter the place. There was a bronze plaque on one wall proclaiming that a body had been found in said location. There was a knife in a glass case on the bedside table, with another plaque reading that it could have been one such weapon that had killed Claire St. James. He ignored the bloodstained walls and opened the only other door in the residence. The pamphlet the old man had pushed into his reluctant hands had said the boy was found in the closet. There was nothing in it, even for display purposes. But the boy had been found there, presumably after having witnessed his mother's murder. Why had he not been killed as well? Unless he'd been in the closet the entire time the murderer was in the apartment, and the killer never knew he was there.

Lucas dropped to the floor and began feeling for loose boards. If the boy had been sent to the closet whenever Claire's lover visited, surely he would have made a space of his own in the small enclosure. He found the right board toward the back wall, pushed down, and then pulled up. The wood came away in his hands, revealing a dark recess beneath. Lucas plunged his hand in and came back out with an old wooden box, big enough to hold some toys and keepsakes.

He stepped out of the closet and dumped the contents of the box onto the floor in the main room. Paper and some children's trinkets scattered. But several small leather-bound books also thudded heavily onto the wood. He thumbed through the first one, recognizing the name of one of society's darlings for the season. He tossed it aside and picked up the next one. His sister's. He recognized the handwriting immediately and pocketed the small, damning diary that had started the mess in the first place. There were two others, one that looked barely used, and another whose pages were yellowing from the years. He ignored the new one and went for the older one.

He read through it, pausing only a moment when he saw his father's name. By the time he finished, he knew one thing: he had to find Gemma. Fast.

...

The carriage rumbled to a stop with a jolt that threw Gemma against the door. She willed herself to remain limp even as pain radiated from the impact at her shoulder. She had roused a few minutes earlier but had made sure not to alert her kidnapper to the fact. Gemma did not have any idea how long she'd been unconscious, but she still heard the sounds of city life outside the conveyance. She prayed they were in London, because if not she had no hope that Lucas would be able to track her in time. She mustn't think that way, though, she told herself. Now was not the time for fear or despair, now was the time for action.

She assessed the situation as best she could with her eyes closed. They had been stopped for a few moments, but her attacker had not spoken. She tried to keep her breathing even, as if she were still under the influence of the drug, but tested moving her limbs. Her legs were free but her wrists were tied behind her back. The rope was not so tight as to cut off circulation, something for which she was immensely thankful, even if her shoulders throbbed from both the awkward position and from her earlier encounter with the door. She was lying on the floor of the carriage, without much room to maneuver even if she somehow escaped her bonds.

The silence in the cab was deafening. She could hear the blood pounding in her own ears and willed herself not to open her eyes to relieve the claustrophobic panic. But the wait seemed endless. Finally, she sensed her captor shift against the seats. He was preparing to exit. Light hit her face for a brief moment as she felt him step over her and heard him leap to the gravel below. Pebbles crunched beneath boots. They were in an alleyway. She wondered if she should scream on the chance a passerby would hear, but if no one was about, she didn't want to lose the advantage she currently had. She waited until the door closed again before opening her eyes and snapping into action.

She had to get to her knife.

She arched her back—careful not to rock the carriage—until her hands met her feet. She groped under her dress for a moment and had to bite back a cry of despair when she found the holster empty. He'd found her blade.

Blackness threatened at the corners of her vision. She blinked it away. She had never fainted in her life, and she refused to start now.

Breathe in. Breathe out.

When she felt in control of herself once more, she was

able to think again.

So you don't have your knife, girl. Improvise.

It was almost as if Uncle Artie was in the carriage with her.

There was slack in the rope, just a bit. Enough to give her hope, though. She sat up, bringing her legs underneath her, and let her eyes adjust to the darkness. Then she scooted her hips back until she was in the corner of the carriage.

Find something sharp. Anything will do.

Her fingers fumbled along the floor, clumsy and groping. But then she felt it. A jagged little piece of metal. She nearly cried out. It wasn't sharp enough to cut through the thick rope, but it didn't need to be. Maneuvering so that her restraints were poised above its tip, she let it dig into the tightly wound thread. She bore down with the entirety of her desperation.

Once she'd pierced the rope, she began flexing her hands. Her skin burned from the roughness, but it didn't matter. She kept shifting, working her wrists against the knot. She wouldn't pull at either end. That would only tighten it. But between the leverage from the sharp piece of metal and her movements, she felt the rope give. A little.

She didn't know how much time she had so she kept at it for another moment until she felt the rope shift once more. Yanking it up from where it was caught proved excruciating to her shoulders, but she bit back the yelp of pain. If the ride to wherever her captor was taking her was long enough, she might stand a chance.

She made sure she was in the same position as he'd left her, and then she went back to feigning unconsciousness even as her heart thudded painfully against her chest.

It was still some time before the carriage door swung open once more. "Help me, you great oaf," her assailant said, his voice muffled and strained. She heard the driver lumber down from the perch, the carriage swaying from the movement. A moment later, a body was tossed onto the seat above. She hoped fervently that the person was alive and that he would not roll onto her during whatever journey their captor had planned. That would be far more than uncomfortable. He vaulted back into the cab after giving a terse order to the driver to continue on to their destination.

She stilled completely as ice washed through her veins.

She finally recognized his voice.

...

Lucas pounded on the door to Rathburn's residence with barely controlled fury. He ignored the curious and scandalized gazes of those passing on the street. He had one goal.

A few minutes passed before the harried-looking butler opened the door.

"Rathburn," Lucas growled out.

"His lordship is…not…home," the butler stuttered. Lucas studied him closer. The man looked nothing like the unflappable servant who had answered the door when he and Gemma had visited. He looked on the verge of losing his composure completely. His face was ashen, and his hair was sticking out as if he'd been running worried hands through it. His eyes darted from the street, back to Lucas, and back again. Lucas could almost see the waves of desperation rolling off him.

"What happened?" Lucas asked.

"His lordship is not home," the man repeated, moving to swing the door closed. Lucas put a hand out against the wood and stepped into the foyer.

"Tell me," Lucas said simply. His tone left no room for disobedience.

The butler crumpled before him, his face breaking for a second from the mask all servants employed. "His lordship has disappeared," he finally said.

"What do you mean disappeared?" Lucas asked. "When did this happen?"

"He was in his study earlier. He ordered tea, but when the maid brought it in only a few minutes later, he was gone. No servant saw him leave, and I would have noticed him exiting the front door. We cannot summon the police on his lordship, but we are distraught." The butler's words tumbled out at a frantic pace.

"Show me," he said.

The butler led the way back to the study.

Lucas scanned the room. Nothing looked disturbed. He went over to the large window. It overlooked the small garden in the back of the house. A fence closed off the space from the alleyway behind it. He knelt on the floor under the window. Gravel and a small bit of dirt had found its way onto Rathburn's opulent carpet.

The villain had kidnapped Rathburn in broad daylight. Even on a quiet street, that was taking unnecessary risks. He must have been desperate, Lucas thought. Perhaps Gemma had surprised him with her visit to what he thought was his secret location. Or he'd been following her since she left the house, waiting for an opportunity to seize her.

No matter what happened, the villain had escalated his plans in a wild manner. Where did he take them? Was he in London? He wouldn't go to his apartments; even if he was confident no one would figure out his identity, they were in too crowded and respectable a neighborhood for him to get away with carting two resistant people in from a carriage. And when Lucas had stopped by it earlier, the residence had been empty and shuttered.

Lucas pulled out the old diary once more and flipped through it, his eyes scanning for any potential locations. He paused.

There. It made sense.

He reached in his coat for several of the papers that had scattered across the floor of the museum. He found the one he was looking for: a deed to a castle not far from London. Lucas vaguely remembered the old earl who had lived there had died a few years back and the property had gone to a distant relative, or so the *ton* believed.

If he was wrong, it could cost Gemma her life.

He started for the door.

Chapter Nineteen

"Wake up, dearest Gemma," Collin Peterson's voice reverberated through the small drawing room. Gemma had managed to feign sleep through the journey, which had felt like an eternity but had, in reality, likely been less than an hour.

She'd started out the morning with the feeling the locations were important, but she would never have guessed that the meek and mild Mr. Collin Peterson had anything to do with her current predicament. She thought about his eagerness when chatting with her about travel journals and ancient civilizations. She pictured the way his puppy-dog face lit up when he talked with her. He'd seemed like a different man than the one who leaned over her now, his non-descript brown eyes roving over her face.

Blind panic nipped at the edges of her sanity when she met his empty, soulless gaze. But she knew if she gave in to it, if she let it wash over her, pull her under into the waves, all would be lost.

His breath was hot on her face, as he studied her. Then

he reached out one long finger to touch the soft skin at the corner of her eye. It trailed along her cheekbone then down her jaw before coming to a rest at the seam of her lips.

She swallowed hard against the bile that burned in her throat.

Without pausing to think, she bared her teeth and snapped at his finger. The move surprised him into pulling his hand back out of her reach.

"Ah, ah, my dear." It wasn't the anger she had expected to see there on his face. It was amusement. He almost seemed pleased. "So much fire."

His eyes drifted to her hair, but he stilled his hand before it reached for the strands. The thought of him burying his fingers in her curls brought the nausea back.

Anchor yourself. Think of Lucas.

She gripped the thought of him tight against her like a talisman.

"Why don't you come closer? I can show you just how fiery I can be?" It wasn't quite bravery. It was more bravado. And her voice might have quivered when she'd said it. But she'd take it.

Lucas. Lucas. Lucas.

He would want her to fight. The slack. She had worked at it in the carriage when she could. But the movements had been frustratingly limited. Now, though, Peterson was distracted enough not to notice her fingers plucking at the rope.

Just a little bit more.

"Oh, we'll be close soon enough," he purred at her, his voice sliding over the fine hairs at the nape of her neck like a palpable thing. Revulsion threatened.

Anchor yourself. Lucas.

She needed him distracted. Her eyes had been locked on him, but she let them flicker over the room now. They caught on Rathburn, who was sprawled, unconscious, on the sofa.

Peterson followed her gaze.

"Ah, yes. We wouldn't want him to miss out on the fun, for he is the guest of honor at this little party." Her stomach dropped at the malicious glee in Peterson's voice. He went to work on Rathburn, lifting him off the sofa with a disconcerting ease.

Evil is strong.

Peterson proceeded to secure him to another chair in the room, close enough for Gemma to hear Rathburn's slow and steady breathing. Peterson stepped back to admire his work then pulled over a side table with a knife and a pistol lying on it. She shivered at the sight then flinched as Peterson slapped Rathburn across the face at full strength. She was thankful she had not received such an awakening.

Rathburn came to with a gulp of air that was half scream, half gasp.

"Hello, Father," Peterson said genteelly, as if they'd run into each other at a ball. "So lovely to see you looking well."

Rathburn reeled back. He looked over at her with bleary, confused eyes, but he dismissed her quickly, turning back to Peterson.

He then spit at Peterson's feet. "You are not my son, you bastard spawn of a whore."

Gemma thought perhaps Rathburn should have kept his mouth shut in his circumstance, but was relieved over the opportunity to continue to work on her bindings.

Peterson was *tsking* at Rathburn as he went to examine his weapons on the table. He stroked the pistol with a lover's touch before moving on to the blade.

"You mean the whore you murdered?" he asked calmly as he plucked up the knife and moved closer to his prey. "The one you carved into bits as I watched? The one of many, it seems, dear Father."

He pushed the tip of the steel delicately into Rathburn's throat, drawing a drop of blood before retreating. She saw Rathburn swallow convulsively.

"You are a madman. You have no idea what you are talking about," Rathburn croaked. She wondered if it was wise to call the man holding the knife at his throat a madman, but she put that thought aside as she began tugging her wrists apart.

"Ah, so now I am the madman?" Peterson purred the question before slashing the sharp knife across one of Rathburn's taut forearms. The man let out an unholy scream that turned her stomach. She wondered if she was about to see someone tortured. She didn't know if she could handle it without stepping in to intervene, even if Rathburn deserved his fate. "I am not the one who sliced up women for pleasure, am I, Father? I am not the one who left them for dead."

Rathburn's jaw clenched, but he said nothing. Peterson leaned in, his mouth almost against Rathburn's ear. "I know about you," he sang softly, tauntingly.

"You know nothing," Rathburn spat, jerking his head away from his tormentor.

Peterson laughed. "Ah. What do I know? What do I know?" he said, as if in contemplation. He twirled the knife carelessly. "I know that you liked to cut up whores to watch them bleed. I know that you did not care if they lived or died." He took the blade to Rathburn's hand, drawing a thin line of blood from the skin. "Do you like to watch yourself bleed, dear Father? I know I like to watch you bleed. I know you used to rut at my mother like a wild animal. I know I watched from the closet while she told you she'd sent me away on some errand. I know you took a knife to her and made her bleed like your whores. But you made a mistake, because she was *not* one of your whores, Father."

Peterson's arm arched again in a violent slash that belied

his calm voice. Blood seeped out of the wide cut across Rathburn's face.

Rathburn let out a grunt but said nothing.

"I was disappointed there were only two of you left alive," Peterson said, grazing the tip of the blade against Rathburn's temple. "Of course, you were the worst of them. The others only watched, but they still deserved punishment. I had to make do with toying with their spawn, which was much less satisfying. I am so glad, though, that it was not you who had gone to be judged by your maker. Eternal damnation is nothing compared to what you will face from me." He flipped the blade and brought it down directly through Rathburn's uninjured hand. Rathburn screamed and fainted. Gemma felt her stomach heave as she heard the knife strike the wood beneath.

"Collin!" she said finally, unable to bear the torture any longer. She had to distract him or he would end up killing Rathburn right in front of her.

Her wrists were raw, but she was almost out of her bindings. It had loosened up enough for her to get her fingers around the rope. When the moment was right she would be able to slip free of the restraints. But for now, the madman with a deadly knife had turned his full attention on her.

The eeriest thing was not the weapon, though. It was his eyes. She expected them to be wild and darting. They were calm and focused, instead. She wondered if she had just made a fatal mistake.

"Was it you? Did you kill my cousin?" She had to know. If nothing else, she wanted to die knowing.

"Ah. That was unfortunate," he said, looking regretful for the first time. "I was saddened that I had to take that step. He seemed to be a reasonable gentleman. But he was lurking in the library while I collected the funds necessary for me to continue with my revenge. I could not let him leave and ruin everything. Everything I had worked so hard for." He shook his head. "I wish it had not come to that. I do not enjoy taking lives for no purpose."

It was what she had been suspecting for some time. She felt something give, deep in her heart. She could mourn Nigel now, but move on from the obsession of his death. It was a tragic end to a beautiful life, a light extinguished too soon.

She nodded as if she agreed that it was the only logical path he could have taken. "Did you take his pocket watch?"

"I am not a common thief," he said, but then he reached in his coat to withdraw the item in question. "But I had admired it earlier in the night, and he informed me it was an original. Sixteenth-century Italy. It would have been a shame beyond words for it to end up buried with him."

She felt the urge to lunge at him, but restrained herself. She decided in that moment, though, that not only would she survive this night, she would get the watch back from him.

"How do you know he's your father?" she asked, tamping down the rage in her voice. She hesitated to bring his attention back to Rathburn, but Peterson seemed to feel like talking, and she wanted to use it to her advantage. The longer he talked, the more time Lucas had to find her.

He glanced back at his victim, bound and bleeding in the chair, but returned his gaze to her. "He was the only one it could be," he answered cryptically.

"The only one out of whom?" she asked, though she knew the answer.

"The Kingsmen. Idiocy is what it was. The noblemen and their grand plans. He was particularly fond of all of trappings of it," he said, nodding toward Rathburn, then throwing her a conspiratorial smirk. "You may have noticed."

She gave him her best blank stare. As if she would ever let herself be pulled into agreeing with him on anything.

"Your husband's father was one of them as well, you

know," he continued. "Of course you know. I wish you had not been brought into this. How could I have predicted the two of you would come together?" He said this last part more to himself, disbelief coloring his voice. "All my planning…" He trailed off before turning sharply toward her. "It does not matter. You will be mine."

"I am married to him now," she reminded him. She thought perhaps it was foolish to enrage him further, but she felt the need to say it.

Lucas. Lucas. Lucas.

"Not for long, my love. Don't you see?" He swept a hand toward Rathburn. "Winchester goes mad with rage after he discovers his bride with Rathburn at their secret rendezvous. He kills Rathburn, of course, but you escape. Knowing he cannot go on without you, he ends his own life. I just have to get him out here… But that shall not be difficult, my pet. Not with you here."

Gemma's stomach clenched, and she wondered if she would actually vomit at the sheer horror his gleeful words provoked. She must change the subject if she wanted to maintain her composure. She reassured herself that at least he did not seem to harbor plans to murder her at the moment.

"How could only Rathburn have been your father?" she asked, in an attempt to turn his thoughts from Lucas's death and onto what had happened in the past.

He turned contemplative. "My mother was a nobleman's daughter," he said. "The daughter of an earl. The earl who owned this castle." He swept an arm out to encompass the room. "My mother kept a journal. I was too young when she died. She did not tell me the tale herself, but she recorded what happened."

"Of course," she murmured, not sure what she was agreeing to, but sensing she should say something so that he would continue.

"My grandfather threw a house party one week toward the end of the season, and the Kingsmen were invited. Foolishly." He shook his head in derision of the past decision. "They had been making their way through society that year, carousing and whoring but never quite far enough so as not to be invited to respectable gatherings."

She glanced at Rathburn, who was bleeding profusely from his face and hand. He remained unconscious. That was probably for the best, given the pain he must be in.

"My mother immediately developed a *tendre* for him," he continued with a dismissive nod toward Rathburn, not even looking at him. "And he seduced her. He played on her naïveté as a girl who had not been exposed to the rogues of the town. Grandfather was not a young man even when he had her. He was not able to protect her from this one's charms. The week of the party, she met with Rathburn secretly many times. He told her about the Kingsmen and how they would take on the world. And she fell in love with him.

"On the last night of the party, he made plans to meet up with her in the gazebo out toward the edge of the property. She showed up expecting a marriage proposal. He brought his friends. They raped her and beat her and left her unconscious," he said. "Grandfather found her the next morning and cast her out. She went to London and worked in a milliner's shop for a few months before discovering she was increasing. She tried to get help from the men who left her in her condition but all turned her away without so much as talking to her. She was an earl's daughter."

His voice had been steadily rising, and he yelled the last part, enraged. His breathing was ragged, and she knew she had to calm him down. Rathburn's eyes had opened, but he remained silent, and his breathing was shallow.

"Why was this not a scandal?" she asked. "An earl's daughter, left pregnant and abandoned? The scandal would have lasted for years."

"Grandfather told everyone she died—a fall from horseback. He buried an empty coffin and mourned for her. He would rather have a dead daughter than one who had a child out of wedlock. He blamed her, you see. He said she brought it upon herself for flirting with Rathburn in the first place. He was a harsh man," he said. His eyes turned nostalgic. "But he died painfully."

She didn't want to think through the implications of that. "If they all raped her, how do you know Rathburn is your father?" She was careful not to be accusatory in her tone, even though her heart hurt for Lucas.

Peterson's eyes slid to the side, and she knew there was more to the story. "The three of them only watched the debauchery."

"This was all in her journal?" she asked.

"Yes. I managed to hide her diary before I was shipped off to the orphanage," he said. "They drank and whored with her, laughing at her before three of them left. And then Rathburn remained." He swung back to the bound man, advancing on him. "And then you raped her again and beat her unconscious, leaving her for dead, did you not?"

"Lies," Rathburn hissed. "Lying whore."

Peterson lunged, and Gemma knew it was her moment. She took off running, pulling at the rope as she went, not glancing back as she heard an anguished scream erupt from Rathburn.

"No!" she heard Peterson yell, but she kept running. She was in a long hallway lined with pictures of past earls. She wasted precious seconds ridding herself of the remnants of the rope that had bound her. There might have been pain, but pain meant she was alive.

She could not operate on pure panic, so she forced herself to focus and think. She'd managed to sneak a look as she was being carried in and knew if she went out the front door she had a wide expanse of open lawn to cover before she could reach the security of the forest. He would be able to overtake her quickly if she attempted to flee that way. She paused at the foot of a wide staircase until she heard a gunshot from behind her.

Rathburn.

She pushed the thought of him away. Distraction would be fatal.

Her skirts tangled around her ankles as she flew up the stairs.

"Whore," she heard Peterson scream in rage from the hallway. "I wanted him to suffer."

She reached the second floor but kept going, hoping to buy time if he assumed she would duck into a bedroom there. She found the next flight of stairs and took them as fast as possible. They led into a huge attic room outfitted as a torture chamber. Chains hung from the wall, and an ominous looking table bearing cruel instruments stood in the middle of the room. A large four-post bed was pushed up against the window, and there were pieces of rope tied to each corner. A heavy wardrobe seemed like her best option. But first a weapon.

She went straight for the table that held an assortment of sharp objects, plucked one off at random, and then scrambled into the wardrobe. She heard Peterson below. His voice had calmed but was still loud enough to carry. He was working his way through the second floor bedrooms that were close to the stairs.

She tried to slow her erratic breathing and fumbled for her knife. He would find her and she had to be ready. But it would be on her terms.

He was playing with her now. "Gemma," he all but sang out. "You cannot hide from me, my pet. You are my destiny."

His footsteps were heavy on the stairs, slow and tortuous. He was in no rush to end it. She was trapped and he knew it, and he was getting a thrill from hunting her like an animal. But he wasn't taking into account that when animals were trapped, they didn't give in, didn't give up. They fought. They bared teeth and lunged and found a strength they didn't even know they had.

She gripped the hilt of the blade tighter.

"Come out, pet. I will not hurt you," Peterson said when he reached the top of the stairs. "I know you are here. I will find you. If you come out now, it will be better for you, I promise."

As if she would ever surrender to him. The promise was a lie, anyway. There was a sick anticipation in his voice that slid down her spine and curled itself into her belly.

No. Fighting was the only option.

"The first moment I saw you, I knew we would be together, darling," he said, and she tried to track his voice around the large room. He was headed toward the bed, she guessed. "I just needed you to stay out of my way until I took my revenge. I tried to warn you. I did. But you would not leave it alone."

There was a moment of silence where she pictured him kneeling by the bed. She knew the wardrobe would be his next choice. Her heartbeat thrummed in her ears, so loud she could swear he could hear it. She sipped in air trying to calm it.

Footsteps started over the creaky wooden floor.

"Your cousin cried like a baby, you know," he said, getting closer. "He begged me like a coward not to kill him. A sniveling, whining…"

She seized the moment right before he opened the doors to her hiding place. She burst out of the wardrobe and caught the look of shock on his face before she landed on top of him. The knife she'd grabbed sunk into his shoulder, and he staggered under her weight but didn't go down. She dropped to the floor before he could grab her and swept an expert foot behind his ankles. He had not regained his balance and the extra movement sent him to the floor. The pistol skittered out of his reach and she took off running once more toward the stairs. He scrambled to his feet after her, not even bothering to pull the blade from his arm. She gauged the distance between them, then stopped short of the long, stone staircase. She spun in a quick movement when he thought she would continue to run. He teetered at the edge for a long, fraught second before his momentum carried him down the stairs. The fatal crack of head against stone came moments later.

She walked to the top of the stairs, and saw his body crumpled in a small pool of blood at the bottom. The fierce relief that rushed through her at the gruesome sight almost brought her to her knees, but she couldn't give in to it. She wasn't safe yet.

Far beneath her, the main door slammed open, and she heard footsteps thundering across the great hall.

Move.

But she couldn't. She was too numb to even search for another weapon or try to hide. The person was getting closer, and once more she willed herself to act. Her legs finally listened to her, and she shifted back, thinking to hide in the wardrobe once more. But just then, the person came charging around the corner. She was still vulnerable, open to attack. Her mind froze.

Then she realized who it was, and she sank to the ground in absolute relief.

Lucas. Lucas.

He took in the scene in a glance, barely acknowledging the man at his feet. He stepped over the body, rushing up toward Gemma.

He knelt and gathered her in his arms, murmuring her

name over and over again. She let herself sink into oblivion with one thought: Lucas was here now; she was safe.

· · ·

Lucas held Gemma for a long time, and her heartbeat against his became his whole world. The sound of her breathing. Her warmth.

Her head nestled underneath his chin, and he buried his face in her hair.

She was alive. Alive.

It was a mantra. The only thought he could hold on to.

In his mad rush to the castle, he hadn't let himself think about what would happen if he arrived too late. But the fear had been there — in the ice that froze his blood, in the vise that squeezed the air from his body.

To never see her smile again. To never feel her beneath him. To never hear her laugh as she teased him. It was a grim, unbearable future. And in those dark moments, he could only believe she was alive. He wouldn't have been able to function otherwise.

But now, holding her, actually feeling her body against his, running his hands over her unharmed skin, brought every desperate thought crashing into him. He'd almost lost her.

Tears threatened, but he squeezed them back and breathed in her sweet scent. Her own sobs had quieted to jagged little hiccups, but he didn't relax his hold. If he gripped her a bit too tightly, held her a bit to close, well, she didn't seem to mind. And he couldn't seem to give even a centimeter. Now that he had her safe in his arms, he didn't ever want to let her go.

He knew he should start moving and get her away from the scene. Her reputation would be in tatters if anyone ever realized what had happened here. But he took another moment, his lips finding her damp cheeks. He kissed her there. Then at the corners of her eyes. Her forehead. The tip of her nose. Soothing her, yes, but also reassuring himself.

He finally laid his lips against hers.

She was alive.

In that moment, something shifted deep in his soul. It was almost an audible click. An unlocking of something he hadn't realized was locked up. And what rushed into the spaces was warm and light and chased away any darkness that lingered there.

It was Gemma. It was always Gemma.

Chapter Twenty

Several days later, Lucas, Gemma, Beatrice, Harrington, and Roz sat around their breakfast table. Lucas had assured Roz of Gemma's health and wellbeing, but they could only hold her at bay so long. And if any of the others found it odd that Harrington, who was technically an employee of the family, was seated at the table as well, it was not mentioned.

Gemma recounted the story as her aunt and sister-in-law drank tea and her husband read over the post. Harrington simply watched her, neglecting the sausage in front of him.

"Fascinating," Roz murmured as Gemma detailed the sad tale that had brought Peterson to his maddened state.

"And do not forget, he witnessed his mother's gruesome murder before being shipped off to a dreadful orphanage," Gemma reminded her.

Lucas glanced up at that and raised an eyebrow at her. "Never say you are feeling sorry for the man. He would have killed you."

"Well, yes, that is true," she conceded. "It just isn't as black and white as one would expect. Rathburn was a terrible man as well."

"You are a heroine," Beatrice breathed, watching Gemma with wide eyes.

"Never say so," Gemma protested. "I was terrified for my life the entire time. And my actions resulted in a man's death."

"That you were scared makes it all the more impressive, to be sure," Beatrice said, undeterred. "The press has gone wild with the story."

"They could not get a story right if it were written down for them," Gemma said. She had seen the papers. They all declared Lord Winchester's gallantry in saving his wife from ruin and torture at Peterson's hands. Certainly none had said anything about the truth. "The truth is not quite so glamorous, I promise you." Even days later she woke up screaming with nightmares. Lucas was always there to soothe away the terror, but she knew she would be facing them for some time. She still saw Peterson's face right before his fall when she closed her eyes.

"Well, I am just thankful you were able to escape unscathed," Beatrice said. "Lucas, how on earth did you figure out it was the timid Mr. Peterson who was the villain?"

He seemed to contemplate the question for a moment. "Harrington here helped with the final pieces," he said with a nod at the man, who had not said much since she'd started the story. "He tracked down the old valet who gave us the tip about the boy in the orphanage in the Lake District. After that it was just a matter of connecting that to Peterson's backstory of being from that area."

"I wanted to return to the original premise that we were encountering many of the same people throughout the case," Harrington said. "I compiled a brief biography on each of the men who showed up on several of our lists."

Beatrice beamed at him. "So clever, sir," she said, and Gemma smiled and wondered what Lucas thought of that match. Gemma thought they would suit quite well. Beatrice's sunny enthusiasm and Mr. Harrington's calm demeanor would complement each other. She watched as he smiled at her sister-in-law, his eyes gentle. It seemed it was a mutual affection brewing.

"And Gemma, were you ever so shocked when it turned out to be Mr. Peterson was the killer?" Beatrice had turned back to her, eyes wide.

"I was," Gemma assured her. "I focused on that payment location because it was one used early in the case and the only place he used twice. He seemed to get sloppy when it came to the past. But you can tell, he learned quickly to direct his victims to more neutral locations."

"So you deduced that there was something particular about that address," Roz filled in.

"Yes," Gemma said, turning toward her aunt. "But I had no idea who the killer would turn out to be until I recognized his voice on the way to the castle. It makes sense though, if you think about it. The one thing anyone would tell you about Peterson is that he is nondescript. He is the type of gentleman to skate by on guest lists because he can entertain matrons and wallflowers. You remember that all our witnesses could remember about him was blond hair?"

"It was a running theme," Beatrice said.

"It was really quite ingenious," Gemma mused. "And did not take much effort on his part, either."

"You are brilliant, Gemma," Beatrice said.

"You are all brilliant," Roz corrected. "And justice has been served in all cases. I never liked Rathburn from the moment I met him. How he avoided a hint of scandal with all of this in his past is a mystery the *ton* should feel ashamed of missing."

"That is only one of the things I have been wondering about this case," Gemma said, thoughtful. "An earl's daughter was violated and left pregnant by a lord of the realm and then murdered years later by the same man. I wonder why the servants did not gossip."

"Perhaps the grandfather colluded with a doctor to tell the servants she died from her trauma. She was obviously bruised—to say she fell from a horse and broke her neck probably seemed logical. There would have been no reason not to believe him," Lucas said.

"I do remember the tale now," Roz said. "It was all very tragic. She was his only child. But there was never a whisper of anything scandalous."

"That may be true, but why did she let the man responsible for her fate back into her life?" Gemma asked.

"I was curious as to that, as well," Beatrice chimed in. "He destroyed all that she was, and then she welcomed him back. She ultimately paid the price with her life."

"Women take drastic measures when their children are involved, though," Roz said.

"I might be able to help here," Lucas said, walking from the room to return a moment later with the old diary in hand. Gemma had not looked through it, as she hadn't wanted to violate the dead woman's privacy. She let Lucas read it and tell her anything relevant. "It does seem he lied to us, and he was actually paying Claire a small stipend every month since she'd come to the city. She was dismissed from the milliner's shop when was found to be pregnant out of wedlock. After Rathburn turned her away the first time, she started sending him letters. Telling him that she'd have her father force a marriage, or ruin Rathburn's fortune. I am guessing she was bluffing, but he doesn't seem to have been willing to take that bet. He was still young, remember.

"He left her mostly alone for a few years after Collin was born," he continued. "Then he began coming around, asking for favors in return for his 'investment.' His word."

"He was despicable," Gemma interjected.

"Indubitably," Roz confirmed with gusto.

Lucas raised an eyebrow at both of them and continued. "She didn't want him to have any interaction with Collin, so she always had him hide in the closet whenever Rathburn came around. She knew he was capable of evil from what he did to her, but she couldn't lose her source of support. The assistant's position did not pay enough to feed and clothe her and her son. Without Rathburn she might have lost Collin to an orphanage. He was very young then."

"Does she say what set him off in the end?" Roz asked.

"She seemed to have been trying to break free," Lucas said. "She knew about the women, she told him. Only a few actually died from their wounds, but that was enough. Society was abuzz about a potential madman roaming the streets, and here he was in her rooms. She was terrified to do it, she writes, but she was terrified not to. If she could blackmail him for enough money to leave the country, she would be free. If she did not, she was certain she would wind up dead anyway. She had to at least try, she writes. For Collin."

"How tragic," Gemma said on a sigh. Poor Claire, she thought. Her life had been one disaster after another. "It is interesting to me that no one ever noticed that Peterson came from nothing. I was always informed that he came from a small holding in the north. Not rich as Croesus, but not a church mouse, either. How he managed to infiltrate the *ton* will be a lingering mystery we may not solve."

"Well, you know better than most that the *ton* is easy to fool," Roz said with a meaningful look. "It often sees what it wants to. And when he turned up claiming a distant relation to a marquis in the borderlands, I think the mamas were simply thrilled to have a well-mannered gentleman to dance with their wallflowers. But this scandal will live on for years, Gemma. Society thrives on tearing imposters and frauds down to size."

"Indeed," Gemma said. "I believe I am quite over living amongst them."

Roz threw her a sharp look before her glance slid to Lucas. She stood then, without much to do. "I need to make my rounds. I am in high demand now, you know," she said with some irony.

Gemma stood and hugged her aunt. "Thank you for checking in on me, and for helping me with the case. You were invaluable to the investigation."

Roz patted her back. "Of course, dear, of course. And now you can move on past your beloved cousin's death. It is a tragedy, but now you have answers, and the villain who was responsible has paid with his life."

Roz bumped Beatrice's shoulder with her hip and then sailed out of the room to deliver every juicy tidbit to the waiting wolves.

Beatrice tracked Roz out of the room and then put down her teacup with deliberate nonchalance. "Mr. Harrington, I believe I require a bit of fresh air after all this talk," she said turning to the man in question.

He smiled and pushed back from the table. "It is getting quite a bit stuffy in here, is it not? Nothing like a brisk walk in the park to start the day." He held out an arm to her, and she laid a hand on it, smiling up into his eyes. Gemma's heart melted a bit.

He escorted her to the door, but just before walking out, Beatrice turned and rushed back to Lucas to wrap her arms around his shoulders from behind his chair. His face looked pained. "Thank you again for finding my diary. You have saved me my happiness once more."

"You have already thanked me," Lucas said gruffly, but reached up to squeeze her hand.

"I just want tell you both, Mr. Harrington knows the

full truth of it all," she said. Gemma glanced approvingly at Harrington, who looked amused by the entire scene. "And he loves me anyway. No, this isn't the time for that," she said when Lucas started to speak. "We shall talk about settlements and such later." With that proclamation, she turned back to her beau and they breezed out the door. Together.

Gemma glanced at Lucas, a smile tugging at the corners of her lips. It died as she met his watchful gaze. He seemed so serious.

"Would you join me in the study?" he asked, rising from his place at the table. The familiar clutch of panic began in her belly as he formally offered her his arm. She rested a trembling hand on his sleeve, and they walked across the hallway in silence, although she was certain he could hear the frantic thumping of her heart. Now that the case was over, was there anything left to keep them together?

He deposited her at one of her favorite chairs in the study and went to stand by the window. He clasped his hands behind his back, the light casting him in shadow. She knew the stance and location were deliberate, to put him at an advantage with the speaker. She'd witnessed him do it many times. She wondered why he felt the need to do so with her.

"I do not wear my father's ring," he said. Gemma nodded. She had noticed, but had not wanted to ask. "The ring. It is odd that it became a central piece of the investigation. My mother hated it, and though I did not know why at the time, I now suspect it was because it was associated with those men. She met him when they were both young, and I believe she linked it with his wild days. I began to resent it as well."

He paused, rolling his shoulders. "My parents did not have a happy marriage. It was not an unusual one, and he was not cruel, but they were both unhappy their whole lives because of it. My father took many mistresses, as is common, and my mother dosed herself with laudanum so she would not have to face the cruel negligence."

Oh, Lucas.

Gemma wanted to go to him and slide her arms around his waist and rest her face on his broad back. She wanted to hug the sadness out of him. But instead, she sat as if paralyzed and said nothing, her only movement the throbbing of the blood in her temples.

"When he gave me the ring, he told me it was my responsibility to find a suitable wife so the earldom would have an heir. I was to give the ring to my son, as a representation of that duty. I promised myself that day I would not end up like them, and locked the ring away."

Her heart sank. Was he telling her that he had married her because of a sense of duty? After all they had been through?

She ached for the little boy he had been, trapped with two miserable, battling adults. That was no way to grow up.

But she ached for herself as well. They weren't his parents. He had the chance to have something different. Why couldn't he see that? Why couldn't he realize that what they had between them was rare and precious and not something that would break easily.

She wanted to rail at him, shake him, make him see sense. But something held her back, and she realized maybe she wasn't as brave or sure of herself as she wished she were.

They remained in silence for a few moments.

"Do you regret now being stuck with me, Gemma?" he finally asked. His voice was quiet and devoid of emotion.

"How could you ask that?" she said.

"You married me under intense circumstances. One could even say I persuaded you into the union over your protests. It seems perfectly reasonable that you would feel trapped in this marriage now that the excitement and danger have passed. You did not wish to marry in the first place, and now we are wed for life," he said.

She gaped at him, stunned. It wasn't as if she hadn't been obvious in her utter devotion to him. But then she thought back. Had she let him know how she'd felt? She realized she'd been so worried about pressuring him that she'd kept her feelings hidden, locking them away so they wouldn't be a burden to him.

Or maybe you were scared to be vulnerable.

She studied his face and was amazed to see anxiety there. He honestly didn't know how she felt. Now was not the time for fear. She nibbled her lip, trying to find the right words.

"When I went to live with Uncle Artie, it was the first time I could remember actually feeling as if I were part of a family," she began hesitantly. He gazed down into her eyes. She could not read the expression in his. "I am sure my parents loved me, but I was so young when they died I do not have memories of it. I only have memories of being unwanted by those around me. Uncle Artie convinced me I was loved, but I never stopped feeling like a responsibility to him. He had to give up so many of his desires to care for me. I was not hesitant about marrying you, my lord. I did not want to be just another burden to you, though. I did not want it to be that way for us. I could not stand to live that way when I…"

She trailed off, meeting his eyes. The hope she saw there gave her the last bit of courage needed to push her over the edge. "I could not stand to live that way when I love you so dearly."

In that moment, all of her fears evaporated into wisps of smoke. Lucas, who had been tense and withdrawn, immediately came to life. Surprise, relief, joy all chased each other across his face, and she felt like she'd just handed him the most precious gift in the world.

Why had she waited so long to tell him? She laughed because she couldn't contain the emotions that scraped at the back of her throat. It was either that or give in to foolish, happy tears, and then she'd be an absolute mess.

He crossed the room in three strides, and her laughter died on her lips as he crushed his mouth to hers.

When he finally pulled back, he stroked a thumb over her cheekbone. "You could never be a burden to me, Gemma. I love you. I love you more than I have loved anything in my life."

He took her hand and placed it on his chest over his heart, before covering it with his own. The beat was strong and steady. "I feel you here. Your heart in my heart."

Her breath hitched. "Lucas."

"When you were missing..." His voice was thick with emotion, and he had to pause to clear his throat. "When I didn't know if you were safe or not, I was in hell. I thought I would go mad with worry. Because if you had died that night, a part of me would never have recovered."

She swiped at the dampness on her cheeks. "You saved me that night."

He shook his head. "I didn't get to you in time."

She placed a trembling finger against his lips, silencing his protests. "You don't understand. You saved me. I was so scared. So scared. And I wanted to give in to it. But then I thought of you. All I thought of was you. You would want me to fight. So I did. It was that simple."

He closed his eyes. When he opened them again, she knew she wasn't the only one fighting back the tears. "My brave Gemma."

"I knew that if I didn't fight I wouldn't get the chance to tell you how much I loved you," she admitted.

"You will get the chance to tell me every day of the rest of our lives," he promised. "And I will never let you forget how much I love you. You will grow tired of me telling you."

"Oh, that could never happen," she said.

"Every minute of the day?"

"Is that even possible?" she asked, teasing.

"In this moment, my dear, I feel like anything is possible," he answered, and she giggled.

"Well, that might be a bit much," she conceded.

He nodded as if seriously considering her point. "All right, I'll keep it to once every hour. But no less. Does that seem reasonable?"

"Perfectly." She couldn't stop smiling. This was why she loved Lucas so. It wasn't just the strength of his character, or his intelligence, or his kindness. It was these moments where they could laugh with each other over absurdities—and then want to kiss each other as if the world were ending in the next moment.

"Oh, before I forget," he pulled back, gently disentangling himself from her. "I have something for you."

He walked to his desk, opening the top drawer. He pulled out a blue velvet box. He hesitated, seeming almost unsure, before returning to her. He handed it to her without saying anything.

She was curious at his nervousness. She pried open the box and gasped.

"Nigel's watch," she said, touching a reverent fingertip to the delicate gold. She met his guarded eyes, and she realized he was not sure how she would react to the gift. "I could not have asked for a better wedding present."

He smiled and caught her lips in a quick kiss. "Good."

"But I have nothing for you," she said, appalled.

He smiled, pulling her against his chest, where she settled in against the beat of his heart. She felt his lips against her hair, and she sighed in contentment. She was home.

"All I need is you, Gemma," he said. "All I need is you."

Acknowledgments

A heaping of thank yous to the ladies who read this first: Dana Underwood, Marissa Carl-Acosta and Julie Reis. Your encouragement, support and friendship while I was writing and editing this book has been too precious to put into words. But I will always carry it in my heart.

I'd also like to thank Katherine Kline for being a cheerleader, a rock, a sympathetic ear, and a constant and joyous co-celebrator.

For my writing group loves, Katie Smith and Abby McIntyre, I would like to say a huge thank you for helping me hone the craft over wine, laughter and tater tots.

To my amazing editor Candace Havens, I cannot say thank you enough. Not only for seeing the potential in this, but for helping me sharpen it into what I wanted it to be. You challenged me and pushed me to be the best writer I could be, and for that I am forever grateful.

Finally, to my parents, thank you for everything you are and everything you have done for me. You taught me the beauty of kindness, the importance of words, and how to have fortitude in the face of challenges. And of course, how to be embrace the Labuskes mantra: "If you're confident, dude. Go for it."

About the Author

Brianna Labuskes is a D.C. journalist who has had a lifelong love affair with romance novels. An absolute sap for a happily ever after, she will never pass up the chance to read about soulmates stumbling toward each other through every obstacle a devious writer can place in their path. Spunky heroines who save the day — as their heroes watch on in awe — are a particular favorite, and that's what you'll see in her books. When she isn't writing, you can find Brianna playing with her two adorably precious nieces, having way too much fun editing health care policy news or searching endlessly for the best brunch in the city. Follow her @brilabuskes to find out if she's ever successful at it.

Discover more historical romance...

ONE LAST KISS
an It's in His Kiss novel by Ally Broadfield

Captain Mikhail Abromovich would rather single-handedly face the entire French army than follow orders to deceive Princess Anna Tarasova, the woman of his heart, by feigning a courtship to hide his covert activities.

VISCOUNTESS OF VICE
a *Regency Reformers* novel by Jenny Holiday

Lady Catharine wants a little excitement. Bored of playing the role of the ton's favorite slightly scandalous widow, she jumps at the chance to go undercover as a courtesan. Social reformer James Burnham is conducting a study of vice in England's capital. Catharine is the last sort of woman James should want, but want her he does. When Catharine and James are forced to band together, they'll be drawn into a web of secrets and lies that endangers their lives—and their hearts.

WHEN A LADY DECEIVES
a *Her Majesty's Most Secret Service* novel by Tara Kingston

In Victorian London, reporter Jennie Quinn goes undercover seeking justice for a murdered informant, only to be drawn into a criminal's seductive game. Matthew Colton is a dangerous man with secrets of his own, but the mystery in his eyes and the temptation of his touch prove too powerful to resist. Forging an undeniable passion, Jennie and Matthew must risk everything to destroy the web of treachery that threatens their love—and their lives.

TANGLED HEARTS
a *Highland Hearts* novel by Heather McCollum

Growing up on a pirate ship, every day was full of adventure for Pandora Wyatt. It was also the perfect place for her to use her magic without persecution. But after her surrogate father is imprisoned in the Tower of London, Pandora leaves the safety of the vessel to rescue him before he's executed. She expects her mission to be difficult, but what she doesn't expect is to have her life saved by the sexiest man she's ever met.

CPSIA information can be obtained
at www.ICGtesting.com
Printed in the USA
BVHW031758200621
610086BV00011B/61